Out of Her

Element

Also by E.A. West

NOVELS
Redeeming Honor
Crash Course

NOVELLAS
Running from Christmas
Christmas Harmony
Bogota Blessings
Breath of Christmas
Finding the Way Back

SHORT STORIES
Escaping the Past
The Key to Charlotte
Healing in Haven Falls
Dreams Do Come True

SHORT STORIES INCLUDED IN:
Second Chances: A Love Anthology

DEVOTIONS INCLUDED IN:
I Thirst: A 40-Day Journey Through Psalms
Red: A Weekly Devotional

Out of Her Element

E.A. WEST

Cover designed by Rebecacovers

Publishing History
First Edition, 2018

Paperback ISBN 978-0-9720919-6-1

To everyone who has started over

One

The three dogs crowded around Mira Hassan, and she fed each of them another bite of venison jerky. Like most hunting dogs she'd met, they were food-motivated, which made befriending them easy. A little jerky, some sweet talking, and a few scratches here and there had enabled her to come and go from the shed without fear.

She gave one last pat to the long-legged mutt with a big head and floppy ears. She had no idea what his name was, but he was a sweetheart and had become her best friend in the last few days.

"Don't bark at me when I come back."

The accent in her whispered words had made her something of an outcast in the area. Who knew a Palestinian accent flavored with a West Virginian drawl could make people so suspicious?

Then again, she *was* half Palestinian and had spent more of her life in the Middle East than in the United States. Suspicion due to fear of terrorism was pretty common in her life.

The mutt licked her hand once and sprawled on the

thick layer of straw covering the floor. Mira pulled her scarf up around her face and stepped out of the shed. The icy dawn air stung her eyes, and she huddled a little deeper in her coat. One of these days, she would have a warm house to live in again.

Her gaze went to the two-story cabin she'd lived near for the last seven and a half years, ever since she came to the United States as a thirteen-year-old orphan. The windows were still dark, offering a small measure of security as she crossed the clearing.

When she reached the woods, she slipped between the trees and into relative safety. She paused and glanced over her shoulder in time to see a light come on in one of the downstairs windows.

Her heart skipped a beat. Had they seen her? Should she run?

She remained frozen to the spot, waiting for some sign that she'd been noticed. The back door stayed closed. No sirens approached from the tiny town of Selma.

She released the breath she'd been holding. Nothing indicated the men in the cabin had seen her. The light probably meant they had awakened and were starting their day.

Since feeding their dogs would be near the top of their list of morning chores, she continued deeper into the woods. No sense in hanging around and letting them find her when all she wanted was to get away undetected.

The silence of the forest surrounded her, bringing a measure of peace. Despite the circumstances that had forced her to live in the woods full-time, she still loved the natural beauty. Being in nature had calmed her for as long as she could remember. Even as a small child wandering through her mother's garden, the simple act of being outside in the open air had lifted her spirits.

Now, as she approached the first of her snare traps, she was even more grateful for the bounty of the forest. Starvation was one thing she didn't have to worry about.

She collected the rabbit and reset the trap before moving on to the next. Normally she wouldn't worry about resetting the trap so quickly, but whatever she found this morning wasn't for her. She felt obligated to provide payment for her use of the shed as sleeping quarters. Since she had no job and no money, whatever she could trap would have to do.

She lucked into another rabbit in the second trap. The two large rodents would make a nice meal or two for the three men in the cabin. Surely that would be enough to make up for borrowing their shed since the weather turned frigid a few days earlier.

She reset the trap and circled back toward the cabin.

Mira scanned the area around the cabin, but no movement caught her eye. With any luck, they'd fed the dogs and were busy eating their own breakfast.

Moving as quietly as possible on the frozen ground, she crept to the small back porch and leaned down to lay the rabbits where the men were sure to spot them.

"Hey! What do you think you're doing?"

The shout scared her half to death. She jerked upright and whipped her head toward the shed. An angry man strode toward her.

Heart thundering in her chest, she whirled toward the woods as the back door flew open and another man appeared. She took off, away from the cabin, before he could say a word.

A handful of feet from the safety of the trees, someone tackled her. After a brief struggle, the man who had come out of the cabin hauled her to her feet and marched her back toward the building.

The angry man and the third man staying at the cabin, both of whom were older than the one holding her captive, turned from studying the two dead rabbits she'd left on the porch.

The man who'd shouted at her now seemed more confused than angry after seeing her offering. The third man's expression was impossible to read.

He looked familiar, but she couldn't quite place him. The adrenaline flooding her system made it impossible to think about much of anything other than finding a way to escape.

"Let's go inside and see if we can figure this out." He picked up the rabbits and carried them through the door.

She didn't have a choice but to follow since the guy who'd tackled her still held her arm in a tight grasp and propelled her forward. The other man entered last and closed the door. He studied her as he removed his coat, and she wanted to run.

What did these guys plan to do with her? Would they hurt someone who gave them food? She straightened her spine and met his gaze, determined to show no fear.

The familiar man laid the rabbits on the counter and faced her. "Did you leave those?"

She gave a quick nod, not ready to let them hear her accent. Once she was more sure of their character, then she would risk getting labeled a terrorist yet again.

"Why?" When she didn't answer, he motioned to the man holding her arm. He released her with obvious reluctance, and the familiar man spoke again. "What's your name?"

A modicum of trust was starting to form, but did she want to risk them hearing her last name? Too many people in the area had taken an instant dislike to her the moment they heard she was a Hassan.

"There's no need to be afraid. You obviously mean no harm. But I would like an explanation, young man."

She raised her eyebrows. He couldn't tell she was female? Yeah, she definitely had to say something. "I'm a girl."

"Speak up."

She must have spoken too softly. Looking him straight in the eye, she said in a clear voice, "I'm not a man."

She tugged her scarf down, revealing her face. Her long coppery hair with strawberry-blond highlights crackled with static as she pulled off her hat. Letting her hands fall to her sides, she gazed at the three men before her. She couldn't wait to see how long it took them to quit staring at her with wide eyes.

The man who'd yelled at her recovered first. "Is it safe to assume you own the knapsack and sleeping bag in the shed with the dogs?"

"Yes." She waved a hand at the rabbits on the

counter. "I brought those as payment for borrowing your shed."

"You've been *sleeping* with the dogs?"

"Yes." She lifted her chin, daring them to make a disparaging remark. It wasn't as if she wasn't used to it.

"Why?"

"Because it got too cold in the lean-to."

"What lean-to?" the younger man asked, his voice full of suspicion.

"The one I lived in until a few days ago when it got too cold."

The familiar man studied her. "Aren't you Harley and Marnie Davis's girl?"

Recognition slammed into her with the sound of her cousins' names. How could she have forgotten who he was for even a brief moment? After all, she was standing in his family's cabin. "Mr. Montaigne?"

"That's right. These are my good friends Richard Halliday and James Porter."

She silently appraised each of them. Richard was around Bill Montaigne's age, so somewhere in his fifties. James didn't look much past thirty. She returned her attention to Bill and steeled her emotions against the pain of what she had to tell him. "Harley and Marnie passed on early this year."

"Yes, I was sorry to hear about that." Sympathy filled Bill's voice. "Where have you been living since then?"

She shifted her gaze to the far wall, fighting the anger that always came when she remembered. "In April, when the weather got warm, Harley's kin made me leave the cabin. I've been living in the woods since then."

"You've been living alone in the woods for over seven months?"

She gave a small shrug. Keeping track of the time hadn't been one of her priorities, but that sounded right.

Richard cleared his throat. "Who exactly are you?"

"Mira Hassan. Harley and Marnie were some kind of cousins to my mother."

"Why don't we all sit down and have breakfast while we talk?" Bill said.

Richard's eyebrows rose, but he didn't argue. Mira wasn't about to pass up a free meal, especially since it meant spending more time protected from the elements. Bill set an extra place at the table, and James served the bacon and eggs keeping warm on the stove.

Now faced with the reality of eating with two strangers and a man she hadn't seen in a few years, Mira battled a sudden bout of nerves. She remained where James had left her while she dug deep for courage. Bill paused in pouring orange juice and sent her a smile.

"Why don't you take off your coat and join us?"

She studied him for a long moment, doubts hitting her as to the motive behind his breakfast invitation. Hunger won out over caution. "Okay."

She hung her coat on an empty peg by the back door and tried not to be ashamed of her current outfit. The men wore nice clothing that looked new. She'd gone for warmth over style. Not that she had a lot of choices, and she definitely didn't own anything as expensive as what these guys wore.

Still, the baggy sweater over a pair of battered

overalls and her sturdy, well-worn boots made it clear she came from a different world than the men. She had no chance of impressing anyone with sophisticated style. All she could do was show them respect and hope for the best.

She joined them at the table and waited until they started eating to pick up her own fork.

They were nearing the end of the meal when James spoke.

"How have you survived all these months?"

"I've been living off the land," Mira said with a shrug. "I had a big garden in a clearing over the summer, and I dried a lot of stuff. I killed a deer a couple of months ago and turned most of the meat into jerky. There's fish in the river, plenty of small animals, and edible plants. Whatever else I need I trade for at this little store about a mile from here."

"And you've been living in a lean-to."

"Right." She ate the last bite of her breakfast.

"Where did you learn how to do all of that?"

"My mom taught me a bit, but most of it I learned from Harley and Marnie."

Richard leaned forward, his expression curious. "Where are your parents?"

"Buried in a little town in the West Bank." She used years of practice to keep her emotions hidden. Showing any kind of vulnerability could lead to ridicule or worse.

"Do you mean the West Bank in Israel?"

"Palestine, actually, but yes."

The men fell silent, and James got up to clear the table. Had she made a mistake by telling the truth?

Richard studied her, making her even more nervous.

"How did you come to have the last name of Hassan?"

"My daddy was a Palestinian. My mama was a blonde from here in the US. She went to Israel to play the violin, fell in love, and married my dad."

Maybe if she told him a little more of the story, he would quit staring at her like she was some kind of alien.

"His family disowned him for marrying an American woman, so after my parents got killed I was sent to live with my mom's relatives. Harley and Marnie are the ones what took me in. The rest had disowned her for marrying a Palestinian man."

He tapped his chin. "Did you grow up speaking English?"

"No, until I was thirteen I only spoke Arabic and Hebrew. My mom had just started teaching me English when I came to live with Harley and Marnie. They helped me learn English as well as they knew it."

If she'd known she would end up living in the United States, she wouldn't have resisted her mother's efforts to teach her English for so long.

Bill leaned forward. "Where are you going to live now that it's too cold to live in the woods?"

Mira scrutinized him, searching for a motive. Did he actually care, or was he just making conversation? Not that it mattered either way. "I don't know. I'll probably see if I can sleep on the storeroom floor at my friends' store."

James set the last plate in the drainer on the counter and returned to his seat. "Why don't you get a job and rent a place?"

She gave an unladylike snort worthy of Harley's stubborn old draft horse. "Nobody 'round here's gonna hire *me*."

"Why not?" Richard asked. "From what you've said you're a hard worker, and you're obviously intelligent."

How could a guy that old be so naive? "There isn't anybody in these parts interested in hiring someone with the last name of Hassan, and especially not since the terrorist scares."

"Why not go to the city to find a position?" James asked.

"'Cause I'm not much good at anything I can get paid for. Besides, at least here I know I'm not gonna starve." She pushed back her chair and stood, tired of the interrogation. "Thank you for the breakfast. Now, I better go rescue my pack from your dogs and see if my friends will let me sleep in their storeroom tonight."

She headed for the door and pulled on her coat. As soon as she'd wrapped the scarf around her neck and settled the hat on her head, she reached for the doorknob.

"Mira, wait." Bill's voice stopped her before she could turn it.

She looked over her shoulder. Did he want her to do some chores to pay for her meal?

"After you get your pack, why don't you come on back in here? We're heading home right after lunch. You could stay and eat with us, and then we'll drop you off at your friends' store."

"I guess I could." As much as she wanted to get away, she couldn't deny the appeal of spending more time in the warm cabin.

"Great." He smiled and she went out the door wondering if she'd made the right choice.

Two

Mira sat in the thick straw covering the shed's floor, desperate for a chance to think. The big, gangly hound flopped across her lap, and she stroked his head.

Although she'd met Bill several times since she moved in with Harley and Marnie, she hadn't seen him or his family in the last few years. According to Marnie, their annual vacation to the cabin had fallen by the wayside as their busy lives got in the way.

Mira had missed seeing the Montaigne family every summer, but she'd adjusted and let them fade from memory. Now, however, she needed to remember as much as possible if she wanted to relax until Bill took her to Sally and Jack's store.

Bill owned a big company of some kind. Something to do with electronics, maybe? The industry didn't matter as much as his personality. He'd always been friendly toward everyone, even the most uneducated people in the area.

His wife, Della, was a small woman with a big heart. She had treated Mira kindly. Even when Mira first met the Montaignes and didn't know much English yet,

Della had been courteous.

They had a son, Josh, two or three years older than Mira. He had always been interested in the plants in the forest and their uses.

And then there was Tabby, the baby of the Montaigne family. She would be nineteen or twenty now, about a year younger than Mira. Tabby's interests had changed every time Mira saw her, but the younger girl remained consistent in her love of people.

Did they remember her? Bill had, but she didn't know how much he remembered of those vacations in years past. She'd spent more time with his kids than with him.

Thinking about Josh and Tabby now made her miss them with an intensity she hadn't felt in a while. They had been almost like siblings to her when they stayed in their cabin, and she missed their friendship.

Unable to find a reason to stall any longer, Mira gave the hound in her lap one last scratch. "Sorry, buddy. I have to grab my stuff and go back inside. Maybe I'll see you again later."

She gave him a gentle shove, and he rolled off her with a groan. Despite all three dogs begging for attention, or maybe jerky, she collected her pack and sleeping bag and returned to the cabin.

She stole a peek at the room while she set her things on the floor by the door and hung her coat on the empty peg. Richard still sat at the table, but James stood at the counter, knife in hand, with the rabbits in front of him. Bill was conspicuously absent.

The way Richard kept assessing her made her nervous, so she joined James.

"What are you making?"

"I was thinking about rabbit stew." He glanced at her. "If I put it on now, it should be perfect by lunch."

Maybe she could help him out to repay him for breakfast. "You want me to skin and cut up the rabbits for you?"

"If you'd like."

He handed her the knife and joined Richard at the table. Mira quickly skinned both rabbits and set the pelts aside. She could trade them at the store after she cured them, unless one of the men wanted to keep them.

Working with practiced fingers, she soon had one rabbit boned and cut into bite-sized pieces. Bill came into the kitchen as she started on the second.

"Hey, Mira, I have a proposition for you."

"What is it?" If he wanted to offer her a job, she would give it serious consideration.

"How would you like to come live with my wife and me?"

She almost cut herself. He wanted her to live with them?

Stilling her hands for a moment, she took a breath to compose herself. Her mind raced faster than her pulse. Moving into his house was a far cry from working for him.

She went back to work on the rabbit. "Is Mrs. Montaigne okay with this idea?"

"She's hoping you'll say yes. I just got off the phone with her, and she made me promise to call her back just as soon as I have your answer."

Mira finished butchering the rabbit while she

thought. Why did they want her to live with them? Did she even want to live there?

Unlike Sally and Jack at the store, the Montaignes could afford to take her in. They had more money than she could imagine, but they never acted like it when they came to their cabin. Would the same be true in their home?

Her thoughts whirled, giving her no answers. Finally, she faced Bill. "Why do y'all want me?"

"Why?" His eyebrows shot up toward his graying hair. "Because we care about you and hate to think of you sleeping in a storeroom."

His answer was too generic. She would give him one more chance to convince her that they truly cared and didn't have some self-serving reason to take her in.

"Mira, Della and I were good friends with Harley and Marnie," he said, moving closer. "If we had known sooner that you needed a place to stay, we would have been down here immediately to pick you up."

The sincerity in his voice and the compassion in his eyes softened her skepticism.

"I know that if the situation was reversed and something had happened to Della and me, Harley and Marnie would have taken in Josh and Tabby. We want to do the same for you, if you'll let us."

The mention of Harley and Marnie's kindness did in her last bit of resistance. At least with the Montaignes she wouldn't have to worry about freezing to death, and she knew they wouldn't let her starve. She dropped the chunks of rabbit meat into the pot James had placed nearby.

"Okay. I'll go with you." She washed her hands and

placed the pot on the stove. "I have to go collect my traps and provisions."

"Why don't you take James along with you? He can help you carry whatever you have."

Take James?

Mira cast a doubtful glance at the man who had tackled her. Even though he'd been kind since then, she wasn't sure she trusted him alone in the woods. However, she couldn't risk offending Bill by refusing to take him along. She needed somewhere warm to stay through the winter.

"I guess that would be okay."

James added the rest of the stew ingredients to the pot, and then he and Mira bundled up and headed outside. According to the thermometer on one of the porch posts, the air temperature had warmed to just above twenty degrees.

They didn't speak as they walked through the woods. The quiet soothed Mira's nerves, giving her the strength she needed to carry through with collecting her possessions in preparation for leaving.

They arrived in a clearing, and Mira walked to a stick curving down into the tall yellow grass. She held it down as she released the trigger stick held in place by two more pounded into the ground. She'd learned the hard way how much it hurt to accidentally set off a spring snare trap in her face.

After removing the wires from the trigger stick and the tall one she'd used for the spring, she pulled up the remaining sticks and tossed them all aside. She placed the wire in her pocket and crossed the meadow to repeat the process with another spring snare trap.

As they headed into the trees again, she noticed that James seemed almost as comfortable in their current surroundings as she was. Did he spend a lot of time in the wilderness? She doubted he'd ever been forced to live in the woods, but maybe he liked camping.

She led him to another large clearing, this one containing the remnants of her garden. After dismantling another trap, she walked past the cultivated ground and stopped just inside the line of trees. A good-sized lean-to thatched with long meadow grass stood against the hillside, sheltered from the wind by the ground's slope and several berry bushes that had long since quit producing fruit for the year.

"Welcome to my home," Mira said as she crawled into the sturdy structure.

Few belongings sat inside. She'd never had much, but getting kicked out of her home had forced her to whittle her possessions down even further. She emerged carrying a thick, hollow walking stick containing one of her most prized possessions; a small bundle of pelts; and two deerskin bags.

Close by, a large black trash bag dangled at the end of a rope draped over a tree branch and tied to the trunk. She set the items from the lean-to on the ground and tried to untie the rope. It was no use. The sudden weather change and the snow had frozen the knot.

She retrieved the hunting knife from her coat pocket and cut the rope with the sharp blade. After lowering the bag to the ground, she pulled out deerskin bags of varying sizes. James watched her with a curious gaze, and she waved a hand at the growing pile on the ground.

"My provisions."

He ran an appraising gaze over her food supply. "That doesn't look like it would have lasted through the winter."

"It wouldn't." She folded the trash bag and shoved it in her pocket. "This would have lasted for a week or two. My friends are holding the rest of my provisions until I need them."

They divided up the bags to carry back. James carried the bundle of furs, and Mira picked up her walking stick. As they hiked through yet another section of forest on their way back to the cabin, James indicated the food pouches he carried.

"This stuff doesn't weigh much at all."

"That's because it's all dried." She dismantled another snare, tossing the sticks aside and pocketing the wires as they started off again. "Drying the food not only makes it lighter, but it keeps longer and takes up less room."

"What kind of things do you have in these bags?"

"Meat, vegetables, fruits, nuts. There's also herbs of all kinds in one of them."

"Herbs? Do you cook with them?"

"Some of them. Others are for healing, some for teas."

The conversation reminded her of Josh. Did he still live with Bill and Della? He was old enough to have his own place, assuming he'd been able to get a job. So many people around Selma had struggled with finding jobs. Then again, it was such a small town in a rural area that employment opportunities were rare.

"It sounds like you know a lot about living off the land."

"I guess so." She'd never given it much thought. "Harley and Marnie did a good job of teaching me."

"Why didn't you live with your friends?"

His sudden change of topic threw her off for a second, but then her thoughts shifted to the kind family who had apologized profusely for their inability to take her in. "There was no room. They had some kinfolk what fell on hard times and needed a place to stay."

"That's too bad," James said, his tone sympathetic.

They fell silent for the rest of the hike back to the cabin. When they arrived, they left most of her possessions on the back porch. She carried the walking stick inside.

Now that she had the option to take it somewhere warm, she couldn't bear to leave it in the cold a moment longer. The contents were irreplaceable, and she didn't want to risk damage from the winter weather if she could avoid it.

Richard and Bill looked up from their seats at the table.

"Did you get everything?" Bill asked.

"Everything that's here."

The men exchanged puzzled glances.

"I left most of my food stores with my friends," Mira said. "They're also keeping some things safe for me."

"If you give me directions when we head out of here," Bill said, "we can stop and pick up your things."

"Okay."

She removed her coat as James checked on the rabbit stew. Richard got up and poured two cups of coffee, handing one to Mira and the other to James. They joined Bill at the table, and Mira listened to the men discuss the preparations for leaving.

Her time in the only home she'd known in the United States grew shorter with each passing moment—a thought that would cause anxiety if she allowed it, but she didn't have that luxury. She had to go with Bill. If she stayed there, freezing to death was a very real possibility.

After a while, James set aside his empty cup and stood. "I'd better go pack up."

Richard rose as well. "I need to tie out the dogs and clean the shed."

"I'll be out to help you in a few minutes," Bill said.

"Don't wait too long or you'll miss all the fun." Richard chuckled as he pulled on his coat.

After his friends left the kitchen, Bill focused on Mira. "Della asked me to have you call her."

Nerves attacked like a swarm of butterflies. "I guess I can call her if you have a phone I can borrow."

"Sure." He did something with his cell phone and handed it to her. "It's already set to dial my home number. Just press the green button."

"Okay." Mira studied the phone for a moment. She'd never held one before.

She looked up at him again. Did he have any idea how little exposure she'd had to modern technology since moving in with Harley and Marnie?

"You go ahead and call Della." He stood and offered an encouraging smile. "I'm going to help Richard with the dogs."

She watched him leave and turned her attention to the phone. A green square with the silhouette of a telephone receiver sat in the center at the bottom of the screen. She pressed it and raised the device to her ear.

"Hello," a woman answered. "Montaigne residence."

"Can I speak with Mrs. Montaigne, please?" Nerves thickened her accent. Would the woman understand her, or would she have to try again?

"And whom shall I say is calling?"

"Miranda Hassan." Intimidated by the woman's formal tone, she gave her full name.

"One moment, please."

She took a deep breath while she waited for Bill's wife to take the call. Did she really want to do this? Did she have a choice?

"Hello, Mira!" Della's voice came over the line, full of friendliness and excitement. "I'm so glad you called."

"Hello, Mrs. Montaigne." A sudden attack of shyness hit.

"Please, call me Della. And call my husband Bill, if he hasn't told you already."

"Okay, Della." What should she say now? Ask the woman if she actually wanted her moving in?

"Bill tells me you've been living in the woods since April."

"Yes, ma'am, I have." Pride filled her, making it easier to converse. "And I've been surviving just fine."

"I'm glad, dear." The smile in Della's voice soothed a few of Mira's nerves. "Bill also told me you worked hard to prepare enough food for the winter."

"Yes, ma'am. Since you're taking me in, I'll give you what provisions I have to help out."

"You don't have to do that."

"I want to." How could she explain that she didn't want to burden them in any way without insulting their generosity? Giving them food was the only way she could prevent it.

Plus, Harley and Marnie and her parents before them had taught her to help out where she could. Giving the Montaignes her provisions was her only option at the moment since she didn't have any money to pay rent.

"Well, that's fine. You're so thoughtful."

Mira stayed quiet, not sure how to respond.

"Is there anything you need, dear?" Della asked. "Do you have enough clothes?"

"Yes, ma'am." Maybe a compliment would keep the conversation moving. "Although nothing so nice as I remember you wearing."

"Why, thank you! Is there anything you might need before tomorrow?"

"Just a shower." Honesty might be embarrassing, but she'd been taught from birth to always tell the truth. "I've been sleeping with dogs for the last couple of days, so I'm sure I don't smell very good."

"You can take as long a shower as you want when you get here."

"Thank you." Could she say anything that surprised this woman? "I have some rabbit pelts, if you want them. Two are fresh and still have to be scraped and cured, but the others are ready to use."

There was a pause on the other end of the line, and

then Della spoke with a cautious tone. "I appreciate the offer, but I wouldn't know what to do with them. Would your friends with the store like them?"

"Most likely. I've given them all of the others." How had the woman kept her composure so well? If she remembered right, Della had never been much of an outdoorswoman.

"Well, you have Bill take you there so you can drop them off."

"Yes, ma'am."

"I look forward to seeing you again," Della said, and Mira breathed a little easier now that the conversation seemed to be winding down. "I'll make sure there is a room prepared for you when you arrive."

"Thank you." Why were these people she only knew from the vacations they spent in Selma being so kind?

"I'll see you this evening, Mira."

"Okay." She waited for Della to hang up before pressing the red button and hoping it disconnected the call.

Even though their generosity in taking her in filled her with gratitude, she wasn't sure how she would adapt to living with rich people. Without a doubt, they were used to an easier life than the one she'd led so far. Would they expect her to live the same easy life?

Although not having to worry about going without sounded wonderful, she had a hard time imagining herself doing anything other than working hard every single day.

Three

Mira pushed her arms into her coat sleeves and tugged the zipper up. James came downstairs carrying a duffel bag. He set it beside her stuff and pulled on his coat.

"Why don't you go ahead and bring your things out? We'll pack them into Bill's truck."

She slung her pack over her shoulder, picked up her sleeping bag, grabbed her walking stick, and followed him outside.

The dogs were tied to the tailgate of a newer pickup truck with a cap. Their gazes locked on Mira, and they began to whine and wag from the tips of their noses to the tips of their tails.

Nothing like a happy dog to make a girl feel loved, even if it was only because she'd been bribing them.

She set her things on the porch and retrieved a deerskin pouch from her coat pocket. Smiling, she joined the dogs and pulled several small pieces of jerky from the pouch.

"I know what you guys want," she told the excited canines crowding around her.

They devoured the treats she offered. After

rturning the pouch to her coat pocket, she knelt and petted the dogs while they licked her and tried to get the jerky out of her pocket.

Mira laughed as she shoved away a cold wet nose. "Yeah, it's good, isn't it?"

She scratched behind a few more ears and stood. The three men stared at her while the dogs continued to act as if she were a long lost friend. Were they angry that she'd fed their dogs without permission? She knew some people could be picky about their dogs' diets.

Bill shook his head and smiled. "I wondered why the dogs didn't bark when you were staying in the shed. Usually old Dan is loud enough to wake the dead when confronted by a stranger."

"I guess it's true that bribery gets you everywhere." Richard chuckled.

Mira grinned, thankful they didn't mind her giving their dogs treats. "I don't know about that, but jerky's great for getting a dog to like you."

"What kind of jerky is that?" James asked. "The dogs are crazy about it."

She moved away from the animals in question and retrieved the pouch. "Deer jerky. Want some?"

The men exchanged glances and shrugged.

"Sure, why not?" James said and pulled a small piece from the soft leather pouch.

The other two followed suit, and Mira pulled out a slightly larger piece. She enjoyed the impressed expressions on the men's faces as they tasted the smoky flavor of the jerky she'd made.

"This is really good," James said.

"Thank you." A smile spread across her face despite

her best efforts to keep her emotions hidden. Compliments weren't common for her in this part of the world, especially not in the last several months.

Richard lifted an eyebrow. "Dare I ask how you killed the deer?"

"Sure." She walked over to the porch and picked up her walking stick.

"You beat it with a stick?"

She smothered a laugh and shook her head as she twisted the top of the stick and removed it to reveal a smaller stick with a piece of antler on the end.

"I used this," she said, pulling out an unstrung bow about five feet long.

She strung the bow and retrieved a small drawstring pouch from one of the deerskin bags on the porch. As she removed a small metal arrowhead from the pouch, Bill spoke.

"You're a bowhunter?"

"I guess so." She held up the arrowhead. "This is what actually killed the deer."

Richard turned from studying the hollow, thin-walled walking stick. "This is ingenious. Did you make it?"

"No, Harley made it and the bow for me."

"He must have been a talented man."

"He was." A pang of sadness hit, and she ran her fingers across the silky wood of the bow.

She unstrung it and returned it to its case. Now was not the time to think of the cousins who had treated her as their own child. She could do that later, when she was alone. Too bad the sense of loss often hit at inopportune times and wasn't so easily shaken.

Richard went back to cleaning the shed, and James went with him. Bill joined Mira as she returned the arrowhead to the bag she had retrieved it from.

"Did you talk to Della?" he asked.

"Yes, sir." She pulled the cell phone from her pocket and handed it to him. "She says I'm supposed to call you Bill."

"That's right." He studied her small pile of belongings. "Let's load this in the truck."

"Okay." She pushed back the lingering grief and focused on gathering her meager possessions.

They carried everything to the other vehicle parked beside the cabin, a newer SUV. Bill opened the back, and they packed everything in beside a large cage. Mira studied the cage. Was it for one or more of the dogs?

Bill tapped it with a smile. "This is where Dan rides."

She handed him the last bag and looked toward the dogs. "Which one is Dan?"

"That large, long-legged mutt with hound ears."

"He curled up against me at night to keep me warm." Her heart lifted. Maybe she could spend time with him while she was at the Montaignes' house.

"Dan's a big softy." Bill closed the hatch as Richard and James came around the side of the shed. "I do believe it's time for lunch."

Mira followed as he led the way into the cabin. They gathered around the table to enjoy the thick stew that had been filling the cabin with a delicious aroma for the last couple of hours.

Hope and doubts whirled through Mira's mind in a

tornado of thoughts that distracted her from the conversation. Was she making a mistake by going with Bill? How much better would her life be living in the Montaigne house? Did she have the strength to carry through with the plan?

As soon as she finished eating, she pushed back her chair and stood. She needed time alone to reconsider her decision to live with Bill and Della.

"I'm going outside."

Before the men could object, she put on her coat and went out the door. The dogs rose expectantly the moment she stepped onto the porch.

"Sorry, I don't have anything for you," she said as she joined them and sat on the frozen ground.

Dan padded over and sat beside her. When he leaned against her shoulder as if giving her a hug, tears flooded her eyes, and she wrapped her arms around the big dog.

"Am I doing the right thing?" She spoke softly in Arabic. Even though she knew the dog didn't understand a word she said, it helped to think he was listening to her thoughts. "I can't stay here. It's too cold to live outside, and I have nowhere else to live. Harley and Marnie always told me I could trust the Montaignes, that they're good people, but I barely know them."

Dan licked her nose, and she gave him a bit of a smile as she dried her eyes.

"Yeah, they've always been nice enough, and Bill and Della both seem concerned about me, but living with them? I don't even know *where* they live."

She sighed and shifted so that only one arm draped

across her canine companion.

"What am I thinking, going to live with near strangers? I know it's better than being homeless and risking freezing to death, but still. I must be crazy. I mean, what do I really know about these people?"

Dan whimpered and licked her again. Mira gave the dog another small smile.

"I know that Bill likes dogs and you're a sweetie. Della doesn't seem to mind people what don't know English very well. I don't know much about Josh, but Tabby and I always got along pretty well."

Tears stung her eyes as the truth came to the surface.

"I guess the main thing is that I know nothing about their way of life. I'm about to leave everything familiar behind for who knows what. I don't know if I want to do that again. It was hard enough when I first came to America."

The door of the cabin opened, and she glanced over her shoulder to see James standing in the open doorway.

"What do you want me to do with these rabbit skins?"

Mira stood, patted Dan one last time, and walked toward the cabin. "I'll take care of them."

Someone had cleaned up the kitchen. The only things left on the counter were the two rabbit skins. Mira reached into her coat pocket and pulled out the black plastic bag that had kept her provisions dry.

Under the watchful gazes of the men, she wrapped the skins in it and did her best to ensure the fur would stay clean during the short trip to her friends' store.

Once the plastic-wrapped bundle was ready, she turned to James.

"What did you do with the brains?"

The men's eyes widened. Why were they so shocked? They were all hunters and had surely cured hides before.

James glanced at the bag of trash waiting to be tied and hauled to the nearest dumpster.

"I assume they were in the skulls when I threw them away. Why?"

"You need the brains to cure the hide." Okay, so maybe they didn't tan the hides of anything they killed. She walked over to the trashcan and peered in. Sure enough, two rabbit skulls sat on top. "Do you have something I can wrap these in?"

Bill reached into a drawer and pulled out a plastic bag. Mira retrieved the skulls from the trash, relieved to find the brains intact. She placed them in the plastic bag and set it with the well-wrapped skins. Then she washed her hands while James scrubbed the counter.

Richard glanced at the plastic-shrouded bundles and grimaced. "That's disgusting."

"It's perfectly natural," Mira said. "As Harley always told me, 'Every animal has enough brains to tan its own hide.'"

Bill stared at her. "Are you bringing that stuff with you?"

She grinned at his worried tone. Apparently, he wasn't as much of a country boy as she'd thought. "No, Della said I could give the hides to my friends."

"Are they going to want those?" Richard pointed toward the bundles on the counter.

"Sure. They know how to tan a hide, same as me."

"Okay, I think we're ready to go," James said, tying the trash bag closed.

Mira collected the rabbit hides and skulls while the men pulled on their coats. They headed outside, and Bill locked up as Richard and James untied the dogs and loaded them into their cages. Dan was the only dog that went into the SUV. Bill and Mira climbed into the SUV, and James and Richard got into the pickup.

Following her directions, Bill soon pulled into the parking lot of a small general store. She hopped out and retrieved the pelts, both cured and uncured, from the back of the vehicle before heading inside.

The older woman behind the counter offered a friendly smile.

"Hey, Mira!" Sally Miller said. "I was wondering how you were surviving this cold snap."

"I'm surviving." She held up the pelts. "I brought you some furs, although two of them still need to be cured."

"That's fine. My oldest boys get a kick out of tanning hides. Do you need to borrow the washing machine or the shower today?"

"No." She hesitated, knowing this was her last chance to stay in West Virginia. But, it wasn't fair to put her welfare on Sally's family. Not when she'd already been offered a place to live. "Actually, I came to pick up my stuff. The Montaignes are giving me a place to stay."

"The Montaignes?" Sally's eyes widened. "Aren't they those rich folk what own the cabin down the road from your old place?"

"That's them. When they heard about my situation, they asked me to come live with them. They were good friends of Harley and Marnie."

"That's right." Sally nodded. "Well, it's good you have a place to live. You want some help carrying your stuff?"

"No, I'm just taking my clothes and books. You and your family can have the food." Sally's family needed her provisions more than the Montaignes. As her friend had pointed out, the Montaignes were rich. Sally's family was just as poor as everyone else around Selma.

"Thank you." Appreciation shone bright in her eyes. "I'll go get your bag."

She disappeared into the back room and returned a moment later carrying a large canvas duffel. Mira accepted it and a hug.

"You be sure to let me know how you're doing from time to time," Sally said, handing her a slip of paper with her name, address, and phone number.

"I will." She shoved the paper in her coat pocket. "Give everyone a hug for me."

"Okay, Mira. You take care now."

"You, too."

She stowed her duffel in the back seat of the SUV and climbed in beside Bill. He faced her as she fastened her seatbelt.

"Ready to go?"

She scanned the familiar scenery and sighed. She would miss this place, tiny and not always friendly to her as it was. "I guess."

Bill pulled onto the empty road with James and

Richard following. "I think you're going to like your new home. We have about ten acres of woods and fifteen acres of pastures and meadows."

"What about crops?"

"We don't grow any. We do have several horses, though."

"Do you have cows, sheep, or hogs?"

"No, the only livestock we have are the horses."

"Y'all don't even have any goats or chickens?" The idea of so much land and no crops or farm animals amazed her. What kind of life did these people live?

"No, just the horses and Dan. We also have a cat named Frank. He lives in the house with us. Frank is a purebred Ragamuffin and very friendly."

She loved cats, but she'd never owned a purebred anything. "What does a Ragamuffin look like?"

"Well, it has long hair and is kind of fluffy-looking. Its face looks like a kitten's. Frank is a blue mink Ragamuffin, which means he's a gray color."

"So, Frank's a friendly, fluffy, gray cat?"

Bill laughed. "That about describes him, except you forgot to say huge. He weighs eighteen pounds."

"That's almost twice as big as my last cat. She only weighed ten pounds."

Mira stared out the window, watching the forest and farmland pass by. Even the familiar things in the Montaignes' lives were unfamiliar. Who ever heard of a cat that big? And a purebred cat to boot. Every cat she'd ever met was much smaller and of the stray or barn cat variety.

After a couple of hours of driving down back roads and state highways, they got on the interstate heading west. Mira finally worked up the courage to ask the question that had been plaguing her for most of the trip.

"Where is your house?"

"It's just outside Dayton."

"Where's that?" She'd never heard of it.

Bill glanced at her. "It's in southwestern Ohio, about forty miles north of Cincinnati."

She wasn't sure where Cincinnati was, but at least she'd heard of it. After the surprised look he gave her when she asked about Dayton, she didn't want to make it any more obvious her geography skills stunk.

"It takes about seven hours to get there from the cabin." He must have figured out she didn't have a good grasp on where places were in the United States.

Seven hours from all that was familiar? Mira's heart threatened to beat right out of her chest. "That's a long way. Harley took me to Ohio once to see about some hogs, but that was only three hours away."

"Ohio is a big state. We should get home around eight or eight-thirty. We'll stop somewhere later and get some dinner."

She faced the window and tried not to worry about what she would find at the Montaigne estate.

Four

Darkness fell shortly before they reached Columbus. Mira stared at the huge buildings and bright lights passing by her window, overwhelmed by the size of the city.

"There are so many buildings and cars." Would Dayton be similar?

"It's quite different from what you're used to, isn't it?" Bill said.

"Yeah." The glow from the dashboard lights illuminated his sympathetic expression. "It kind of reminds me of Tel Aviv."

"Did you live there before you came to the United States?"

"No, I was born and raised in a tiny village in the West Bank."

"What was it like there?"

"It was quiet, like the area around your cabin." Memories of her childhood home warmed her heart. "I knew everyone in the village, and they knew me. It was like having a big family."

"That sounds nice."

"It was. My father worked on a farm, and my mother taught at the school. I was always bringing home stray cats and dogs and trying to convince my parents to let me keep them."

"Did you succeed?"

"Sometimes, but they wouldn't let me have more than two cats and one dog at a time. The cats could live in the house, but the dogs had to live outside. My dad's upbringing taught him dogs were unclean, but I saw him outside playing with my dogs almost every day." She missed those happier times with an ache so intense it took all of her strength to keep her eyes dry.

"What happened to your parents?"

She stared out the window, and the dark Ohio landscape faded as the scene from over seven years earlier filled her mind.

"We went to Jerusalem to visit some friends of my mother. They took us to a café, and we ate lunch at an outdoor table. There was an explosion. My father shielded me somehow so that I survived."

"Mira, I'm so sorry."

"I was in the hospital during the funerals, but a lady from the American embassy took me to see their graves. Then she brought me to this country, and Harley and Marnie came to the airport to pick me up. I only knew a few words of English, so it was hard for a while until I learned more. One thing that helped me was gardening. My mother grew a garden in Palestine, and finding out Marnie had a garden was comforting."

A memory popped up that made her laugh softly, and she turned to Bill.

"Would you believe some of the first words I

learned here were the names of plants?"

"Knowing Marnie, it doesn't surprise me. I'll bet Harley taught you the parts of a tractor."

"Actually, it was a harness." Mira remembered the incident with a smile. "He found out I like animals, so he taught me to hitch a horse to a wagon not long after I arrived."

"That sounds like Harley."

They rode in silence for a while as Mira remembered the past and hoped the future would be bright. She'd been through so much, lost everyone important to her. Living with the Montaignes had to work out. She was out of options.

They approached another large city, and Bill took an exit onto a state highway.

"Welcome to Dayton," he said as he navigated through the city.

Curiosity sent Mira's gaze to the passing buildings. Businesses and churches, apartment buildings and houses... It resembled every other American city she'd ever seen.

They left the city and passed farms interspersed with a few mansions.

"We'll be at the house in just a few minutes," Bill said, turning onto a well-maintained county road.

"Will Tabby and Josh be there?" What would they think when they found out she was homeless? Would they still be as friendly as their father, or would they show disdain?

"If they aren't there yet, they will be soon."

"Do they still live with you?"

"Only during holidays and school vacations. They

live on their respective college campuses the rest of the time."

She dug deep for courage. "Will they be upset that I'm going to be living in your house?"

"Of course not." He turned onto a paved driveway and drove between an open a pair of wrought iron gates in a red-brick wall. "You know Tabby always wanted to bring you with us when it was time to leave the cabin and come back here. Josh may have treated you like an annoying friend of his little sister most of the time, but he always wanted me to make sure you had everything you needed and that you were happy."

"Really?" Josh had cared that much about her? "I didn't know that."

Bill smiled as he parked near the front door of a brick mansion with white pillars supporting the porch roof. "He never wanted to admit that he viewed you as a little sister."

"Oh." She stared up at the huge house. It was the biggest one she'd ever seen, with two stories stretching out on both sides of the porch. "Is this where you live?"

"This is it." He opened his door as a man in his thirties came around the side of the house. "It appears Lucas already knows we're here."

Mira climbed out of the truck as the man reached them. He sent a curious glance her way and let Dan out. The dog jumped off the tailgate and licked him before ambling over to sit beside Mira.

"I see Dan has a new friend," he said with a smile.

"Lucas, this is Mira Hassan," Bill said. "She's going to be living here for a while."

"It's a pleasure to meet you, Miss Hassan." Lucas

held out his hand, which she shook uncertainly. "I'm Lucas Bower."

"Please, call me Mira." Never in her life had she been called Miss Hassan. No one had ever considered her important enough to deserve it.

"All right, but only if you call me Lucas."

His easy-going demeanor helped her relax. "Okay."

"Lucas is my right-hand man around here," Bill said. "He takes care of the horses and Dan, and makes sure the grounds and buildings are kept in top shape."

"What he's not telling you is that I have plenty of help with the work," Lucas told Mira with a wink and turned back to his boss. "Do you want me to carry the bags upstairs?"

"Some of it goes to the kitchen. You'll have to ask Mira which ones go where."

"All of the food is labeled," she said.

Lucas studied the deerskin bags, holding them so the dome light illuminated the markings. "I don't know what language these labels are in, but I can't read them."

"Sorry. I forgot that most people in this country can't read Arabic." Mira's face heated, and she checked the bag he held. "That has venison jerky in it."

His eyebrows rose. "You know Arabic?"

"Yes, my father taught me." She sorted the bags and picked up the non-food ones. "The rest of this goes to the kitchen."

He looked at the two deerskin bags in her hand and the pack on her shoulder. "Is that your only luggage?"

"No, I have a bag in the back seat."

"Why don't you let Lucas carry your things to your

room?" Bill said. "He can take the food to the kitchen later."

"Okay." She handed Lucas the deerskin bags and her pack. Then she pulled her walking stick bow case out of the SUV. "I'll carry this."

"That's fine."

She followed him through the front door and into the large, marble-floored foyer. Ahead and to the right, a sweeping staircase led to the second floor. An archway by the base of the stairs led to a living room decorated with cream-colored furniture, vases of fresh flowers, and a few sculptures and paintings. A door on the opposite side of the foyer opened onto a formal sitting room.

"Della?" Bill called. "We're here!"

A petite, brown-haired woman in her late forties appeared from somewhere behind the staircase. She gave Bill a quick kiss on the cheek.

"Welcome home, dear." Della Montaigne turned to Mira with a warm smile. "Mira! I'm so glad you came. Do make yourself at home."

"Thank you," she said as she stepped out of Lucas's way.

"Miss Della," he said, "where should I put Miss Mira's things?"

"I had Anita prepare the room next to Tabby."

"All right." He carried Mira's possessions up the wide staircase.

"Have the kids arrived yet?" Bill asked.

"Josh should arrive in the next hour or so," Della said.

"And Tabby?"

A squeal from the top of the stairs answered his question. A younger version of Della ran down the stairs and threw her arms around Mira.

"It's so cool that you're staying here for a while! We're going to have so much fun." Tabby stepped back and wrinkled her nose. "Phew! You smell like Dan."

"I guess you could say Dan and I have gotten pretty close in the last few days." Mira exchanged a glance with Bill.

"Mom told me you wanted a shower when you got here. I'll show you to your room in a minute." She rushed to Bill and gave him a hug that rivaled the one she had given Mira. "Hi, Daddy! I'm glad you're home."

"It's nice to see you, too, sweetheart." He kissed the top of her head. "How was the trip?"

"Not too bad once I got out of Alder Creek. I think everyone on campus left today to go home for Thanksgiving."

"I don't know, I think there are probably a few who have classes on Monday and Tuesday. Unless, of course, all of the other students are like you and managed to arrange their class schedules to give themselves a four-day weekend."

"*Daddy.*" Tabby rolled her eyes. She sent her parents a hopeful look worthy of Dan. "Can I take Mira upstairs now?"

"Go ahead," Della said with a fond smile. "I think you might explode if you have to wait any longer."

Tabby giggled and grabbed Mira's hand, pulling her toward the stairs. "Come on. You're going to love your room."

The open area at the top of the stairs held a

conversational grouping of comfortable furniture. A short hall straight ahead had one door on each side. Tabby pointed to the door on the other side of the open area.

"That's Josh's room." She led the way around the furniture to the door of a large room overlooking the stairs. "This is the game room. We watch movies, play games, and just hang out in here."

Mira peered in, impressed by what she saw. A pool table dominated one side of the room. Twin sofas and a couple of matching chairs separated it from a huge TV and other expensive-looking electronics.

Tabby led her down the hall running past the left side of the game room. They passed a small balcony, three guest rooms, and a linen closet. After rounding the corner, Tabby stopped in front of a door.

"This is your room."

"Where's your room?" Mira tried to sound interested, but all she wanted was a long hot shower.

Tabby led her to the only other door in the hallway. "Right here."

Mira took in the pink and white bedroom with a canopy bed and an abundance of stuffed animals. "It's pretty."

"Thanks." Tabby bounded back to the other room and opened the door. "I put a couple of stuffed animals in your room so it wouldn't look so sterile."

Mira walked into the large room and stared in awe.

Thick cream-colored carpet covered the floor. Shimmery sheer curtains shrouded windows framed by mauve damask drapes. Opposite the cherry dresser stood a queen-size bed covered in an elegant mauve-

and-cream spread. Matching cherry night tables topped with gleaming cherry-and-gold lamps flanked the bed. A polished cherry writing desk with a matching chair stood between the windows.

Amidst the frilly pillows decorating the bed sat an adorable stuffed walrus. A large stuffed rabbit occupied the cream-and-mauve armchair in the corner.

"If you don't like the stuffed animals, I can take them back to my room." Tabby's voice was more subdued than Mira had ever heard it.

"Oh, no, I love them!" They were a nice touch, but how could she explain her lack of enthusiasm? "It's just that I've never had a room this fancy before."

"Don't worry, you'll get used to it." Her bounce and sparkle came back full force as she crossed to a door by the dresser. "I bet you've never had your own bathroom, either."

Mira joined her. The colors of cream and mauve carried through the bathroom as well. The sink and bathtub were the same shade of cream as the walls, and cream and mauve tiles covered the floor. Mauve towels hung on a chrome rack, and decorative soaps in the same shade sat in a glass dish on the counter.

"No, I've never had a bathroom to myself before." She'd never even seen one this elegant. "I almost feel like a princess."

"You're pretty enough to be one."

"I don't know about that." Had Tabby had forgotten she smelled like a dog? "But I do need a shower."

"I put some of my favorite shampoo and conditioner in here for you. There's also the stuff Anita puts out for guests. There are a couple of different kinds of soap. I recommend the lavender stuff. It smells better."

"Okay, thanks." Mira smiled, relieved that she seemed to be taking the not-so-subtle hint.

"When you finish your shower, come to my room. I'll give you a tour of the rest of the house."

"All right."

Moments later, Mira stood in the shower, relishing the feel of the hot water rinsing away the grime of the last few days. The shampoo Tabby had left reminded her of a fresh mountain breeze, and she savored the scent as she washed her long hair. The lavender soap had a gentle lavender scent. The other soap smelled like an overstocked flower shop.

Clean and refreshed, she wrapped herself in a soft, fluffy bath towel. After dressing in her nicest pair of overalls and an emerald green long-sleeved knit shirt, she put her hair in a loose braid down her back. Then she headed to Tabby's room and knocked lightly on the open door.

Tabby looked up from her magazine and smiled. "Are you ready for your tour?"

"I guess so." How much of a tour did one need for a house?

Five

The front door opened as Mira and Tabby came downstairs. A tall young man stepped inside, and Mira slowed her steps. Could that be Josh? His hair was the same shade of brown she remembered, but the wire-rimmed glasses were new.

Tabby launched herself down the stairs and wrapped him in a hug.

"Hi, Josh! You'll never guess who's here."

He stepped back with an indulgent smile. "Why don't you tell me, Tabby?"

"Look on the stairs."

He turned his green eyes upward and studied Mira for a moment as though trying to place her. Then recognition flashed, and he smiled as she finished coming down the stairs.

"Mira, is that you?"

"Hey, Josh." She'd always thought he was kind of cute, but he'd become even more handsome with age.

"No one told me you were coming." He gave her a welcoming hug and stepped back. "So, how long are you going to be here?"

"I, um, don't know." Why did he have to ask such a difficult question before she had a chance to see if he was still the same accepting guy she remembered?

"What do you mean, you don't know?"

"Your parents invited me to live here."

"They did?"

"That is so cool!" Tabby clapped her hands together and bounced on the balls of her feet. "Mom just told me you were coming to visit for a while. She didn't tell me you were moving in."

Mira closed her eyes against the threatening tears. It had been so easy to talk about her situation back at the cabin in the familiar hills of West Virginia. Now, after seeing the Montaignes' opulent house, she was ashamed of her homelessness.

"Mira?" Josh said. "What's wrong?"

His face didn't hold contempt as she had feared, only concern. She opened her mouth to speak, but no words came.

He removed his coat and handed it to his sister. "Tabby, will you please toss that in my room while I talk to Mira?"

"Sure." She headed upstairs, glancing back a few times with a worried expression.

Josh lifted a hand toward the living room. "Why don't we sit down?"

They entered the spacious room and sat on one of the sofas.

Mira clasped her hands in her lap.

Josh waited.

She dug deep and found the courage to speak. "I've lived in the woods since April. Harley's kin forced me to leave the cabin after he and Marnie passed on. I had nowhere else to go. But the weather turned cold, and I couldn't stay in my lean-to anymore. Your father found me, and when he heard I was homeless, he said I could live here."

She dried her eyes with the cuff of her sleeve. A gentle touch on her shoulder drew her attention to Josh's compassionate gaze.

"I'm glad he found you. I just wish we had known sooner so you could have had a home sooner."

"Really?" A new wave of tears sprang to her eyes. "You're not mad or ashamed of me?"

"Of course not. It's not your fault that Harley's family treated you so poorly. Besides, you're my friend. Nothing's going to change that."

"Thank you." Relief flooded her at evidence he wouldn't judge her for circumstances beyond her control. "I'm glad to know you think of me as a friend."

Voices came from the foyer, and she turned toward the doorway as Bill and Della entered the room.

"Hi, Mom, Dad." Josh stood and stepped toward them. "Mira just told me what happened and that she's living here now."

"That's right." Della gave him a hug. "How long have you been here?"

"Long enough to talk to Mira for a few minutes." He leaned down to kiss his mother's cheek. "I would have been here earlier, but there was a traffic jam on the interstate."

"That's quite all right. I'm just glad you made it safely."

Mira rose and moved to a spot by one of the tall

French windows that lined the end of the room. She might be welcome in their home, but she was more aware than ever that she wasn't a part of the family.

Bill joined her. "Mira, Della and I need to talk to Josh and Tabby for a little while. There's a hall running behind the stairs that has a library at the end. There's also a music room on the right."

"Okay. Would you like me to go get Tabby? I think she's upstairs."

"If you'd like. Or we can send Josh to find her."

"No need. I want to get something from my pack, so I have to go up anyway."

"All right."

Mira went upstairs and knocked on Tabby's door.

"Come in!"

She opened the door. "Your parents want to talk to you. They're in the living room with Josh."

"Okay." Tabby gave her a worried look. "Are you all right?"

"Yeah, things have just been kind of hard lately." Mira shrugged as they stepped into the hall. "I'm sure your dad will tell you."

"Aren't you coming?" Tabby asked when Mira didn't follow her toward the stairs.

"No, I'm going to get something out of my pack and sit in the library."

After retrieving her journal and a pen, she went down to the library. She found a switch on the wall beside the door and flipped it, illuminating the large room with a soft golden glow.

Floor-to-ceiling bookcases lined the walls, and she skimmed her fingertips across the spines of the leather-bound books. Did anyone in the family read them? Would she ever be able to read them?

She sighed and headed for a padded window seat. At least she could enjoy being surrounded by more books than she'd seen in a long time.

Opening her journal to the first blank page, she made a note of the date and wrote down the events of the day. She had to pause more than once and wipe tears from her eyes as she documented her thoughts and feelings on her current situation.

As she wrote the last few sentences, Josh came in and sat next to her feet. She finished the entry, closed her journal, and capped her pen. Lifting her head, she found Josh watching her with the same compassionate gaze he'd had earlier.

"I'm sorry things got so bad for you. I wish I would have known last spring. Maybe I could have done something to help you."

"I appreciate it, but I did pretty well on my own." His concern warmed her heart, but she didn't want him to feel sorry for her. "I built a comfortable lean-to, had more than enough to eat, and you know how much I love to be outdoors."

"But to be alone for so long..."

"To be honest with you, I didn't notice most of the time." Could anything she said help him understand? "I mean, yeah, there were times it got lonely, but I visited my friends at the general store on a regular basis. During the summer, their oldest kids camped out with me several times, and there were a couple of other people I visited. The rest of the time, though, I was busy preparing for winter and making improvements to my living area."

"That doesn't sound too bad."

"It wasn't. Until it got cold, that is. But I stayed warm at night by sleeping in the shed at your family's cabin. All that straw was good insulation against the cold ground, and your dad's dog slept curled up against me so we both stayed warm."

"That's what Dad told me." He looked at the cloth-covered book on her lap. "Is that your journal?"

"Yeah." Mira ran her fingers across it. "I try to write in it every night."

"It looked like you were writing backwards when I came in."

"It seemed normal enough to me." She fought a smile as she handed him the journal. "Here, take a look."

He opened the cover. "It's blank."

She laughed at his puzzled expression. "No, it's not. You're looking at it backwards. Try opening the other side."

He did and flipped through the pages, his eyes wide. Mira watched him for a moment, but then a huge gray cat leaped into her lap, startling her. Josh looked up.

"That's Frank. I think the best way to describe him is a gentle giant."

She stroked the cat's thick, soft fur. His purr filled the room, and he flopped across her lap. "Is he always this friendly to strangers?"

"It depends on the stranger. A lot of times he'll greet newcomers and head for the nearest familiar person. He must like you."

"He's beautiful," she said, scratching the cat's throat.

Josh closed the journal and handed it to her. "I had no idea you could write in Hebrew and Arabic. Where did you learn them?"

"It's what I grew up hearing and seeing." She set the journal beside her. "Both Arabic and Hebrew feel much more natural than English."

"I remember wondering why you didn't talk much when I first met you, but I thought it was because you were shy."

"No, I just didn't know enough English to carry on a conversation."

"That explains a lot," Josh said as his sister walked into the room.

Tabby grinned and waved a hand toward the cat. "I see Frank found you."

Mira scratched behind the cat's ears, earning a contented sigh. "Yeah, he decided to come say hi."

"Do you want that tour of the house now?" Tabby asked.

"Sure." She studied the cat falling asleep on her lap. "Do you think Frank would like to come along?"

"Probably. He likes to be held. Of course, he tends to get heavy after a while."

"I don't mind." Mira scooped the fluffy feline into her arms and stood. "Lead the way."

They left the library with Josh turning out the lights. Tabby led them through the only door on the left side of the hall.

The large, airy music room had a polished wood floor and walls the color of eggshells. A piano stood near the large windows at the far end of the room.

Between the door and the piano, near the center of the room, sat several white upholstered chairs and a small matching sofa.

A bookcase filled with sheet music and other books stood to the left. Two music stands sat next to the bookcase, behind an acoustic guitar on a stand and a flute in its open case sitting on a delicate wooden table. On the right, in a big alcove behind the door, sat another music stand, this one holding music. A heavy wooden table stood against the wall with an open violin case sitting on it.

"This is a beautiful room." The violin drew Mira's gaze like a magnet. "Who plays these instruments?"

"I played the flute for a while, but I was never very good," Tabby said with a sheepish grin. "Josh is responsible for the guitar. We both play the piano and so does Daddy."

"What about the violin?" She cast another glance at the instrument.

"That's Mom's. You'll have to get her to play for you. She's really good."

They went back into the hall, and Tabby pointed out Bill's office across from the music room. Instead of turning left toward the front door when they reached the end of the hall, they turned right. Bill and Della's bedroom was to the right. A door leading outside was straight ahead. To the left stood a conservatory.

Tabby led the way into the plant-filled space and turned on the lights. Windows lined three sides of the room. Wicker furniture sat among the tables and stands holding plants, providing a garden getaway even in the middle of winter.

"I love all the plants," Mira said, gazing around the room. "I may have to spend a lot of time in here."

"You might have to fight Josh for it. He's always liked to come in here for hours on end when it's too cold to go outside."

"That's because I like taking care of the plants." Josh rolled his eyes. "Plus, there's nothing better than being surrounded by green growing things when there's a foot of snow on the ground."

"I know the feeling," Mira said. "Marnie and I always had plants growing in the kitchen because it had the best light."

"Well, the kitchen is next on the tour," Tabby said.

They left the conservatory, and she led them down yet another hallway. Tabby opened the first door on the right, and they entered a huge kitchen.

A wave of sadness hit as Mira took in the room. Marnie would have loved the granite countertops and ceramic tile floor, as well as the simple wooden table surrounded by six equally simple wooden chairs.

Mira's deerskin bags looked out of place on the island in the middle of the kitchen. How had Bill thought she could fit in somewhere so fancy?

"Oh! These bags are *so* cool!" Tabby rushed over to examine them.

"Are they yours?" Josh glanced at Mira as he joined his sister.

"Yes. That's some of the food I dried over the summer." Mira stroked Frank's silky head. He shifted in her arms and gave her a contented look. "I told your mom she could have it, since I'll be living here."

Tabby turned toward her. "What all did you bring?"

"Yes, I'm curious as well," Della said behind Mira.

She turned and found both Della and Bill standing just inside the kitchen. How did they feel about deerskin bags in their spotless kitchen?

Judging by their expressions, they didn't mind.

"Venison jerky, dried apples, cherries, tomatoes, and raisins." She set Frank on the floor and pointed out the various bags, some containing more than one food. "There are also dried potatoes, turnips, carrots, and sweet potatoes. Some of the bags have peas, beans, wild onions, wild garlic, nuts, berries, oats, and different herbs. This bag over here has parch corn. You toast it in a skillet, then you have a crunchy, nutritious snack."

"What's in that last bag?" Tabby asked.

"Dried, smoked fish. It's not much to look at, but it tastes pretty good if it's cooked right."

"You definitely didn't have to worry about food, did you?" Bill said.

"Nope. Between my garden and what I could gather from the forest, I ate well." She smothered a yawn. "If nobody minds, I'd like to go to bed. This has been a very long day."

Della gave her an understanding smile. "Of course, Mira. We'll talk more tomorrow."

She bade everyone good night and headed for hallway, but she spotted the cat following her. She turned a questioning gaze on the Montaigne family. "Frank seems determined not to let me out of his sight. Would it be all right if he sleeps with me?"

"Certainly," Della said. "Just leave your door open a bit so can he get out in the middle of the night if he wishes."

"Okay." She scooped up Frank and received a loud purr in return. "Good night."

As she passed through the foyer, she noticed an unobtrusive door beneath the stairs. Why had Tabby bypassed it on the tour? She was trying to decide if she should open it when Tabby came up behind her.

"This is the powder room." She opened the door.

Mira peered in as Tabby turned on the light. The room was smaller than any she had seen so far in the house, about the same size as Harley and Marnie's bathroom. It wasn't nearly as plain as that room had been, however. The powder room was decorated in white and lavender with understated floral wallpaper and decorative lavender soaps in crystal dishes on the white pedestal sink.

"It's pretty."

"Yeah, but it doesn't get much use unless we have guests." She turned off the light and closed the door. "Tomorrow I'll have to show you the rest of the house and the stable."

"You mean there's more?" Mira stared at her. How much room did one family need?

Tabby laughed. "Lots more. I'll show it to you in the morning."

When Mira entered her room, she closed the door and set the cat on the bed. "Okay, Frank, after I change I'll open the door for you, and then I'm going to bed."

She dug through her meager wardrobe and pulled out a pair of soft flannel pajama pants she hadn't worn since losing her home. It had been much more practical to sleep in her clothes since she never knew when a hunter might stumble upon her little camp.

After changing into the flannel pants and a large T-shirt, she brushed her teeth and opened the door leading into the hall about six inches.

She turned out the lights and climbed into the big, soft bed, relishing the feel of sheets for the first time in months. Frank snuggled up against her, and she wrapped her arms around him, holding him like a teddy bear. He let out a contented sigh and purred them both to sleep.

Six

Something soft and furry pressed against Mira's face. She swatted it away, but it came back and pushed harder. Opening her eyes, she found bright green eyes staring back from a fluffy gray face. A loud purr and a soft meow accompanied another round of head butting.

"Good morning to you, too." She scratched under his chin and glanced around the dark room. "Frank, I'm not sure it's morning yet. Move over so I can see the clock."

She gave him a gentle shove. The glowing red numbers from the digital clock on the nightstand stared back. Frank rubbed his head on her nose, blocking her view again.

"Okay, you win." She sighed and sat up. "Six o'clock is morning, but this time of year it sure doesn't look like it."

The cat meowed again and looked pointedly at the door.

"All right!" She shook her head and smiled. Pure-bred cats were just as demanding as the strays she'd always owned. "Let me get dressed, and then I'll see if I can find your food."

Frank sat on the foot of the bed while she dressed in the clothes she'd worn the previous night. A few quick strokes of her brush, and she called her hair done. She crept out of her room, not wanting to disturb Tabby if she was still asleep.

As she went down the stairs, she glanced over her shoulder. Sure enough, Frank trailed her. A cat that big obviously never missed the opportunity for a meal.

Light shone through the open kitchen door, and quiet voices drifted into the hall. Were the Montaignes early risers?

Lucas sat at the table with two women in neat black uniforms. All three of them had partially eaten breakfasts in front of them.

"Miss Mira, you're up early." Lucas offered a friendly smile.

"*Somebody* decided he was hungry." She glanced at the cat winding around her legs.

"Frank! You naughty cat." The younger woman stood. "You know better than to wake the guests." She scooped him up and sent Mira an apologetic look. "I'm sorry he disturbed you, miss."

"Don't worry about it." She smiled, hoping to put the woman at ease. "I'm used to cats waking me up and early mornings. I lived on a farm for years, and the animals all liked to be fed before seven."

"I'm so relieved he didn't upset you, miss." She stroked the cat's head. "Let's go feed you, Frank."

The other woman stood as the first left the room. "I'm Charlotte, the cook. Can I fix you something to eat?"

"I guess so." The Montaignes had a cook?

"What would you like?"

"Anything is fine." How were you supposed to deal with a cook? She'd never had one.

"Honey, I'm all out of anything, so you're going to have to be a little more specific."

Mira drew a blank on American breakfast foods. She doubted the hummus she'd grown up eating was common in Ohio, but she couldn't think of another dish.

"Hey, Charlotte, isn't there still some sausage gravy left?" Lucas asked and glanced at Mira. "Do you like biscuits and gravy?"

Her brain kicked in again at the mention of one of her favorite American breakfast foods. "I haven't had biscuits and gravy in months."

"Well, have a seat, and I'll dish up a plate for you." Charlotte moved to the large gas stove.

Mira sat across from Lucas as the younger woman returned to her seat, minus the cat.

"Anita, here, is the live-in maid," Lucas said. "There were two, but Nancy left and Miss Della hasn't found a replacement yet."

"But she did arrange to have someone come in days to help," Anita added.

Charlotte set a plate of mouth-watering biscuits and sausage gravy in front of Mira. "Here you go, honey."

"Thanks." She inhaled the warm, slightly spicy aroma. "This looks delicious."

Charlotte sat down and watched her take the first bite.

Pure bliss filled Mira as she tasted the creamy gravy and flaky biscuit. "I think this might be better than Marnie's."

"Thank you." A pleased smile spread across the cook's face. "I'm glad you like it."

"I do." Mira took another bite.

"Who's Marnie?" Lucas asked.

"She was some kind of cousin to my mother." She understood his curiosity about the stranger the Montaignes had taken in. She'd be curious too. "I lived with her and her husband Harley after I came to this country."

Anita leaned forward. "Where are you from?"

"I was born in Palestine and lived there until I was thirteen." She hoped she wouldn't have to explain why she'd immigrated to live with her mother's cousins.

Silence fell, but Charlotte broke it after only a moment. "Why don't we get to work and let Miss Mira eat in peace?"

Guilt pinged Mira. "You don't have to leave on my account."

The cook reached across the table and gave her arm a pat. "I know, honey, but Anita and I have work to do. I'm sure Lucas has things that need his attention as well."

She and Anita rose and cleared their places, but Lucas stayed in his seat and drank his coffee. While Mira ate, he told her about the horses the Montaignes owned. They had eight, all of which had good pedigrees.

She finished the last bite, and Charlotte appeared beside her.

"Would you like some more?"

"No, thanks. That was plenty," Mira said with a smile.

Charlotte gathered the dishes and carried them to the sink. Lucas stood and picked up his own dishes then looked at Mira.

"Would you like to come down to the stable with me and see the horses? I bet old Dan would like to see you, too."

"Sure." She gave him a curious look as she rose. "Where is Dan? I haven't seen him since we got here."

"He lives with me above the stable. Miss Della doesn't like to have him in the house, so he's taken up residence in my apartment."

"Oh." After her years in West Virginia, she couldn't imagine not letting a pet dog in the house. Back in Palestine, however, any dogs had been forbidden to enter the house. Was Della's dislike of a dog in the house religious? It couldn't be cultural, since so many Americans didn't have a problem with it. "I need to go get my coat, and then I'll be ready to go."

"I'll wait here for you."

Mira ran up to her room and retrieved her coat. When she returned downstairs, she found Lucas waiting outside the kitchen, already wearing his coat. He led the way down the hall, past some closed doors, and opened the door at the end to reveal a mudroom. They passed through it and out into the cold predawn air.

A well-kept gravel walk led to a large stable. Lights shone through the windows. Lucas opened the door, and warmth wrapped around them the moment they stepped inside. The familiar scents of horses, hay, and leather eased Mira's tension.

A handsome man about her age with curly black hair, brown eyes, and an olive complexion similar to hers stepped out of one of the stalls.

"I got everybody fed. I'll start on the stalls in a few minutes." His gaze landed on Mira, and his expression changed to a mix of surprise and curiosity. "Hello."

"Ben Petros, Mira Hassan," Lucas said. "Mira's staying with the Montaignes for a while."

"It's nice to meet you." Ben's straight, white smile set her heart racing.

"Hey."

"Ben's a local college student who works here in the mornings," Lucas said. "He managed to arrange his schedule so that his earliest class is at noon."

Ben grinned. "I'd rather work with horses early in the morning than study the history of the modern world."

Lucas laughed and Mira smiled as she looked around, her thoughts on the mutt she'd befriended in West Virginia.

"Where's Dan?"

"He's in the tack room being lazy," Ben said. "Come on. I'll show you."

She followed him down the wide cement aisle between the stalls and peeked in at the horses they passed. "These are beautiful animals."

"Most of them are well-trained, too. The most recent arrival is another story. She's a Thoroughbred mare that's barely trained and can be spooked by her own shadow." He stopped beside an open door. "Here's the tack room."

Mira looked inside and the large, mixed-breed hound lying there thumped his tail on the floor. It warmed her heart to see evidence he still considered her a friend. She walked over and knelt beside him. As she rubbed his head, the tail picked up tempo.

"I see you and Dan know each other," Ben said from the doorway.

"Yeah, we met a few days ago when Bill was in West Virginia." She stood and dusted the loose dog hair from her hands.

"That's cool." He glanced toward the barn aisle. "I need to start mucking out stalls. If you want to hang around here for a while, you can put your coat on one of the hooks over there."

"Okay. Thanks."

He left to do his work, and she hung her coat where he had indicated. As she took in the expensive tack around her, it sank in that all the saddles were English style. The only kind she had ever used were the larger Western saddles.

Dan stretched into a standing position and followed Mira as she left the tack room. She found Lucas brushing a large bay.

"Ben said there's a horse what's been giving y'all trouble," she said, petting the bay's nose.

"She just needs a bit more training." He came around the horse to stand beside her.

"I might be able to help. I used to help Harley with the horses."

Lucas studied her. The bay sniffed her pockets as if it expected to find a carrot hidden in one.

"Well, I guess I can show her to you, but Dan has to stay in the tack room." He reached for the bay's halter and the crossties attached to it. "Maggie's more nervous than usual when he's around."

"Is that the mare's name?" she asked as he led the bay to a nearby stall.

"It's actually Magnolia Dream, but we call her Maggie," he said, coming out of the stall and securing the door.

They left Dan in the tack room with the door closed. Mira followed Lucas down to the end of the row of stalls. He grabbed a lead rope hanging on a hook screwed into the wall and cautiously opened the last stall. He entered with slow, deliberate steps, speaking in a low tone to the horse stamping her feet inside.

Mira stayed back as Lucas led the nervous animal out of her stall. He stopped a big gray in the center of the aisle.

"This is Magnolia Dream, a four-year-old Thoroughbred. Maggie is seventeen hands, barely trained, and as you can see, she has a nervous disposition."

The beautiful mare pranced a bit at the end of the lead rope. Everything about the horse reminded Mira so much of a pair of horses Harley had rescued. Maybe the same things would work on her that had worked on them.

She spoke soothing words in Hebrew as she stepped toward Maggie. The horse pricked her ears and calmed a little. With a careful, steady movement, Mira raised her open hand, palm up, and let the horse investigate.

Maggie calmed further, and Mira raised her other hand to rub the mare's forehead. She could feel Lucas's eyes on her as the horse lowered her head and allowed Mira to scratch behind her ears.

"I've never seen Maggie this calm," he said in a low tone.

She smiled and continued to pet the horse, showing she meant no harm. "You just have to know how to talk to her. Do you have a place to exercise her?"

"There's an indoor arena on the other side of these stalls." A crease furrowed his brow. "You're not thinking of riding her, are you?"

"No, I was going to ask for a longe line."

"There's one in the tack room."

"I'll hold Maggie, if you'll go get it."

Lucas looked at the animal continuing to relax under her gentle touch. "Okay, but if you need any help, just call out."

"All right, but I won't need help," Mira said with a smile as she took the lead rope from him.

He walked to the tack room as quickly as he dared without spooking Maggie. Mira went back to softly speaking Hebrew as she ran her fingers down the mare's soft neck. Lucas returned a moment later carrying a longe line and a long whip. Maggie began to dance at the end of the lead rope, her nostrils flaring and her eyes showing white.

Seven

"Lucas, please put the whip somewhere out of sight," Mira said in English before switching back to Hebrew for the horse's benefit.

He did as she asked, and she soon had the horse calmed again. Just like Harley's horses, this one appeared to have had a bad experience with a whip.

"Can you show me to the arena?"

"Why don't you let me take Maggie?" Lucas said, reaching for the lead rope.

She kept a firm grip on it. "I've got her. Just keep the whip out of sight, and we'll be fine."

"I put it behind a bale of hay." He didn't look happy, but he led her to a side aisle in the center of the building.

She continued to speak soothing words to the Thoroughbred prancing nervously alongside her. Lucas opened the gate to the arena and stood to the side as she led Maggie through. He started to follow, but Mira stopped him.

"The fewer people in here, the better. Just close the gate and don't worry."

"Sorry, I can't do that." He stepped into the arena and closed the gate behind him. "I'll stay out of your way, but I'm not leaving you alone with Maggie."

"Okay." She wasn't surprised he didn't trust her with the horse yet. He had no idea how much experience she had. "Give me the longe line."

Lucas handed her the long flat rope, and she traded it for the lead rope. She walked the horse to the center of the arena, reassuring her with promises of safety and gentle interaction. Lucas went to the low wall surrounding the arena and leaned back against it as he watched.

Mira walked in a circle to get the horse moving. Then she stood in the center, turning slowly as Maggie walked around her. She let out more line, widening the circle. Maggie's gait was uneven at first but quickly smoothed out.

She raised her free hand as she called out, "Trot!"

Maggie increased her pace, trotting in a stiff-legged, stumbling manner. After going around a few times, her trot evened out. Mira let her go around a few more times before increasing her speed to a canter. This time, Maggie only went around twice before her movements were smooth.

Seeing her in motion, Mira spotted the high quality of her breeding. She was a gorgeous animal with a powerful build and graceful movements. Mira cantered her another minute or two, and then gave a light tug on the longe line.

"Trot!"

At the pressure on her halter, Maggie came to a dead stop and reared.

Lucas straightened and took a step forward. Mira spoke calmly in Hebrew and crept toward the quivering horse, gathering the flat rope as she walked. Such a severe reaction to light pressure told her a lot about the horse's past. This poor creature had suffered at the hands of humans under the guise of training her.

When she reached Maggie, the horse reared again. Lucas moved toward them, and Mira switched to English, her eyes never leaving the horse.

"Lucas, I'm fine. Just let me work with her a while longer."

"If anything happens to you, it's my hide." The tension in his voice did nothing to soothe the horse.

"Nothing will happen as long as you don't interfere." She kept her tone calm, despite the adrenaline flowing through her veins. A frightened horse was an unpredictable horse. Still, she believed she would remain safe if she stayed vigilant. With a slow, gentle motion, she lifted her hand to the nervous horse's neck. "Easy, now, Maggie. I won't hurt you. Easy, girl."

It took several minutes of reassurance to clam her. Once she'd settled to only an occasional flick of her tail, Mira walked her around the arena, first in one direction, and then the other. Maggie balked a bit at the corners, but Mira's encouragement soon had her turning them with ease.

Mira decided to end the training session on a positive note and headed for the gate. Her heart picked up speed at the sight of Ben standing outside the arena with his arms resting on the wall. How long had he been watching her?

He stepped over to the gate as Lucas joined Mira.

Lucas handed her the lead rope and accepted the longe line.

"You've worked wonders with this horse," he said as Ben held the gate open to let them out. "I don't think I've ever seen her walk so calmly."

"Maggie's taken baby steps. She still has a long way to go." The praise lifted her spirit. Few in West Virginia would have appreciated her efforts, despite their effectiveness.

"She responds well to you," Ben said as they walked back to the stalls.

"She's responding to kindness." But that didn't stop the warmth his impressed tone caused. "I think she's been abused."

"It didn't happen here," Lucas said. "We would never hurt the horses."

"I know." The Montaignes were too kind to let anyone abuse their animals. "It was probably someone trying to train her fast and get her ready for sale. Unfortunately, now she has to be retrained and shown that training isn't anything to be afraid of."

"You've done a good job of that this morning."

"Maybe, but this isn't going to be fast or easy," Mira said as they stopped near Maggie's stall. "Do you mind if I give her a thorough grooming?"

"No, go ahead." Lucas reached for the crossties and clipped them to the mare's halter. "I think Maggie has earned a treat. I'll be right back."

Ben brought over a bucket of grooming tools as Lucas walked away. He set the bucket near Mira but far enough back that Maggie couldn't kick it.

"Watch her carefully. She sometimes acts up in

crossties."

"I think she'll be okay, but I'll keep an eye on her."

She was running a currycomb along the horse's side with a circular motion when Lucas returned with two carrots. He handed them to Mira with a smile.

"Maggie's worked hard," he said, cautiously petting the horse's forehead. "I figure she deserves a double treat."

"She does." She handed back one of the carrots and broke the other one into pieces about two inches long. "Why don't you give her one so she knows you love her?"

Lucas broke up the carrot as Mira fed chunks one at a time to the happy horse. As she went back to grooming, Lucas gave the mare more carrot pieces while praising her good behavior. He stroked the mare's face and neck as Mira worked her way around the horse. She traded the currycomb for a stiff body brush and thoroughly brushed the horse, flicking away dirt and loose hair. Lucas went back to work, but he stayed close enough to offer Mira assistance if she needed it.

A little while later, as she used a soft brush on Maggie, Bill and Josh entered the stable. They stared at the gray mare with her head low and eyelids drooping as she stood contentedly being groomed.

"Is that Maggie?" Bill asked, his tone stunned.

"Yeah." Mira smiled as she ran the brush lightly across the horse's face.

"What did you do to get her to behave so well?"

"Loved her and didn't punish her when she acted up earlier." She returned the brush to the bucket and turned toward him. "Once she found out I wasn't going to hurt her, she calmed down pretty quickly."

"The transformation is amazing." Bill reached out to smooth the relaxed animal's neck. When Maggie didn't even flinch, he grinned. "You've worked wonders on this horse."

"Maggie's a good horse. She's just been abused sometime before you got her."

Josh turned from studying the horse. "How do you know that?"

"The way she reacted to certain things. Harley took in a couple of abused horses and they reacted the same way, only they were a lot worse."

"Did you manage to get them straightened out?" Bill asked.

"Yeah, between me and Harley, we finally got them over their fears and spookiness, but it took a long time and a lot of patience." She stroked the mare's cheek and smiled. "Okay, Maggie, I think it's time for you to go back to your stall and have some hay and water."

She removed the crossties and put her hand on the mare's halter to lead her into the nearby stall. The light pressure on her halter made Maggie nervous, but she calmed when Mira spoke softly in Hebrew. After making sure the horse had plenty of clean water and hay, she stepped back into the aisle and closed the stall door. Then she went to the tack room and let a relieved Dan out.

"I wondered where he was," Bill said as the dog wagged his way over to greet his human.

Mira shrugged. "Lucas said Dan makes Maggie nervous."

71

"Yes, for some reason the dog upsets her."

"I can work on getting her used to him. But not right away. There are some other things I need to work on first."

"If I'm not careful, Miss Mira's going to put me out of a job," Lucas said as he joined them. "This girl has a way with horses."

"So we saw," Bill said with a smile. "How did she end up working with Maggie?"

As Lucas told him the events of the morning, Mira spotted Ben sitting on a stool near the tack room with a bridle in his hand. She walked over and sat on a nearby bale of hay to watch him clean the leather.

He looked up at her with a smile. "Do you find cleaning tack fascinating?"

"Only if someone else is doing it."

"I know the feeling," he said with a chuckle. "It's a tedious job, but someone's got to do it."

The sound of hooves caught her attention, and she looked up as both Bill and Josh led horses out of their stalls. She returned her gaze to Ben and he smiled.

"They like to go for a ride right after breakfast at least once when they're both here."

"That's nice." The well-lit stable seemed a little brighter when he smiled. "Harley and I used to go riding together when we got our chores done."

"Is Harley your brother?" Ben rubbed saddle soap into the bridle.

"No, he was my mother's cousin. I lived with him and his wife, Marnie, for a few years."

"Why are you speaking of them in the past tense?"

"They died at the beginning of March in an

accident." Despite the sad topic, she felt comfortable talking to him.

"I'm sorry to hear that." He worked quietly for a moment then glanced at her. "Why were you living with your mom's cousins? Where are your parents?"

"There were killed by a suicide bomber when I was thirteen." She forced herself not to think about that day. "My father's family had disowned him for marrying an American, so I had to come to this country to live with my mom's family."

"You've had a hard life."

"Maybe, but there have been a lot of good times, too." She might be comfortable talking to him, but she didn't want him to feel sorry for her.

"Where are you from? Before you came to the US?"

"Palestine. My father was Palestinian and my mother was from here in Ohio."

"Talk about worlds apart," Ben said as he finished the bridle.

"Yeah, but they loved each other."

He sighed and stood. "I have more work to do now, but maybe we can talk another time."

"I'd like that." She couldn't wait to get to know him better.

Eight

Della and Tabby took Mira into Dayton for a shopping trip after lunch. Mother and daughter had cornered Mira and forced her to reveal the contents of her wardrobe. When she admitted to owning two pairs of overalls, a pair of sturdy cargo pants, a sweater, a long-sleeved shirt, and two T-shirts, they planned the afternoon of shopping.

Mira wasn't sure she needed more clothing. After all, she'd survived this long with what she had. But the Montaigne women wouldn't take no for an answer.

During the short drive into the city, Della told Mira the events of the coming week—the week of Thanksgiving.

"On Monday evening, we're hosting a dinner party for some of Bill's business associates and a few close friends of the family."

Mira had never seen a dinner party, let alone participated in one. "I'll stay out of the way and out of sight."

"Oh, no, you won't. You'll be in attendance just like the rest of the family."

"But I'm not family."

"You're close enough. While you're living with us, you'll be treated as one of the family."

She didn't know how to respond. A lot of the people she'd met since moving to the United States hadn't even treated her as a friend, let alone family. And attending a dinner party? There had to be a way out of what was sure to be an awkward evening. "I don't have a dress."

Della laughed, extinguishing Mira's tiny spark of hope for escape. "We'll pick up something suitable. On Tuesday evening, Bill and I are supposed to attend a dinner, so you kids will have the house to yourselves."

Tabby shot an endearing smile toward her mother and returned her gaze to the road. "Can I invite some people over while you're gone? That way we'll have something to do and Mira can meet some people our age."

"That's a lovely idea, Tabby!" Della turned to Mira and lifted one expertly plucked eyebrow in inquiry. "What do you think, dear?"

Did it matter? "I guess it'd be okay."

"Great! I'll tell my friends when I see them tonight." Tabby looked at Mira in the rearview mirror. "Do you want to come with me? We're going dancing."

Mira had been to a few square dances since immigrating and knew several folk dances from Israel and Palestine, but she figured the dancing Tabby referred to was something entirely different. Like the kind of stuff she'd seen in movies and on TV—the kind of stuff she didn't know how to do because her parents had forbidden her to learn. Harley and Marnie had agreed with them. "I don't know."

"You think about it, dear, and let Tabby know later," Della said and continued with the week's schedule. "Throughout the day on Wednesday relatives will be arriving. On Thursday we'll have a big Thanksgiving dinner. Friday and Saturday will be fairly relaxed, and the visiting family will leave on Sunday."

Mira's mind whirled. Was every week that busy, or was it just because of the holiday? She couldn't imagine a life where she had some event most days. Her life had been much more laid back until now, and she didn't want to give that up.

They arrived at an upscale department store, and Della led the way inside. A saleswoman in a neatly tailored suit greeted them with a welcoming smile.

"Mrs. Montaigne, how lovely to see you again," she said in a well-modulated voice. "May I help you find something this afternoon?"

"Yes, Ashley." Della guided Mira forward. "This is Mira Hassan. She's in need of a new wardrobe."

"Very good." Ashley turned to Mira. "What are you looking for, Miss Hassan?"

Since when did store clerks call customers by name? Feeling completely out of her element, she glanced at Della. "Um..."

Della patted her arm and turned to the saleswoman. "Let's start with a dress or two."

"We have some lovely dresses," Ashley said as she led them to the correct department. "We also have some nice two-piece outfits, if you would prefer."

"Okay." Mira took in the wide selection of stylish clothing. What would the Montaigne women do if they knew she'd never worn anything so nice?

"Give me your coat, dear," Della said, holding out her hand.

She did so, and Ashley studied her before turning to a nearby rack to pull out a knee-length blue dress.

"This would look stunning with your coloring." Ashley held the dress in front of Mira and looked at Della for approval.

"That color is very becoming on you."

It was a beautiful dress, but the length was wrong. "It's too short."

The others stared at her as if she'd lost her mind.

"This is a popular length," Ashley assured her.

"It's beautiful, but I only wear long skirts." And not for the first time, she wished she could wear something shorter.

"Well, all right..." Ashley replaced the dress and moved to a different rack. She held up a long-sleeved dress in a fall pattern with an ankle length skirt. "Would something like this suit you better?"

Mira brushed her fingers across the soft fabric. "It's very nice."

Ashley smiled, her relief at finding something acceptable obvious. "If you'll follow me, I'll show you to the dressing rooms so you can try it on."

"Okay."

Tabby leaned close to Mira as they walked. "Why do you only wear long skirts?"

"Because of the scars. I survived the explosion that killed my parents, but my legs got hurt pretty bad."

"That's terrible!" A sheen of moisture in her eyes caught the light. "I'll help you find some awesome long skirts."

"Thanks, Tabby."

Mira followed Ashley into one of the small rooms and smiled as the saleswoman hung the dress on a hook and left. After she changed, she studied herself in the full-length mirror. The soft knit material flowed around her legs as she moved, and the dress flattered her slim figure. The fall colors in the fabric made her coppery hair glow. She'd never felt more beautiful.

She stepped out to see what the others thought.

"Mira, you look gorgeous!" Tabby clasped her hands in front of her chest. "That dress is amazing on you."

Della nodded, a pleased expression lifting the corners of her mouth. "You do look lovely. What do you think, dear?"

"I like it," Mira said, running her fingers along the skirt.

Ashley brought over a belt made of gold rings. "This would complete the look."

Mira held her arms away from her body while Ashley fastened the belt around her waist. Then she turned toward a nearby mirror and smiled when she saw the effect of the belt hanging loosely about her hips.

"I don't think I've ever seen anyone look so stunning in something so simple," Ashley said.

"We'll take both the dress and the belt," Della said. "Mira, why don't you go change? Then we'll find the other things you need."

Soon, they were searching through skirts and dresses again. Della insisted on buying another dress and two skirts with coordinating tops. Tabby helped

Mira find some casual clothing. Two pairs of jeans, a pair of khaki pants, and a half dozen shirts later, the women moved on to the shoe department.

Ashley helped Mira select a pair of fashionable boots that went with the skirts and dresses, and a pair of athletic shoes to go with the casual clothing. After a quick stop to find undergarments and sleepwear, Ashley left the women in the capable hands of Tanya at the cosmetics counter and carried the clothing off to be held until they were ready to leave.

After exclaiming over Mira's "amazing complexion," "gorgeous eyes," and "terrific cheekbones," Tanya put together a makeup kit to highlight her natural beauty without overwhelming it. Once Mira had picked out a collection of bath and skin care products with much assistance from the saleswoman, Della led the way to the jewelry counter.

All the fuss being made was overwhelming. Never had Mira been treated with such importance or had her every move in a store guided by doting employees. She said as much to Tabby.

"Mom just wants you to feel special," Tabby whispered. "She thinks every woman should have nice things. The reason the employees here are being so attentive is because Mom's a good customer. They want to make a good impression so she'll keep coming back."

"But your mom is spending so much on me." She tried not to remember the price she had seen on one of the skirts. She'd been so shocked that she'd refrained from looking at any more tags. The entire wardrobe she'd brought with her had cost less than half of that one piece of clothing.

"It's Mom's way of showing she cares. Besides, you've seen where we live. Trust me, she can afford it."

"If you're sure," Mira said as Della finished speaking with the man behind the jewelry counter.

"Mira, come over here and tell Philip what you like in the way of jewelry."

Philip looked expectant as she tried to figure out what to say. She decided to say what she was thinking and hope for the best. "I don't like to wear a lot of jewelry."

"Well, you must like something." He offered a charming smile.

"I guess a simple bracelet." She avoided glancing at Della for fear she would hurt the kind woman's feelings by being truthful.

Philip opened a drawer behind him. "Mrs. Montaigne described some of your new clothing, and I think I have just the thing."

She peeked at Della, relieved to find her smiling as she waited to see what Philip had in mind. Mira returned her attention to the counter as Philip placed a velvet-lined tray on it. Several plain gold bangles rested on the black cloth. He lifted four and held them so they resembled a single piece.

"What do you think?"

"They're pretty." Memories of her mother wearing a similar style caused a smile as she gazed at the glittering bracelets.

"Those would look so cool with that first dress you tried on," Tabby said. "You know, the one with the gold belt."

Mira glanced at Della and found her nodding.

"Those will be perfect, Philip." Her eyes scanned the glass counter. "May we see those pins and brooches?"

"Certainly." He set the bracelets down and pulled out the tray she indicated. "There are several lovely pieces here."

"Mira, do you see anything you like?"

She stepped closer and looked at the gold butter-flies, flowers, and leaves. One pin designed to look like an oak leaf caught her eye. She pointed it out to Della.

"That one is lovely," the older woman said with a smile.

Philip raised an eyebrow. "Shall I wrap it up for you?"

"Yes, please. Just place it and the bangles on my account."

"Yes, Mrs. Montaigne." He moved to take care of the sale.

They went in search of Ashley, who wasn't hard to find. After Della settled the bill, they carried the purchases out to the car. Mira breathed a sigh of relief as she sank into the back seat. She hadn't realized no idea that a couple of hours of shopping could be so exhausting.

Tabby backed out of the parking space and glanced at her mother while she waited for a break in traffic.

"Where to next?"

Della turned in her seat and met Mira's gaze. "Bill tells me you're interested in horses and work well with them."

"Yes, that's true." What did that have to do with Tabby's question?

"Do you have riding boots?"

"No, I don't." She was a little afraid of what Della planned do with that information, but she couldn't lie to the woman. Not after all Della had done for her.

Della faced the front again as Tabby took advantage of a window in the traffic. "We're going to Stuart's."

"Okay, Mom."

With any luck, Stuart's wasn't another fancy department store. Mira wasn't sure she could handle visiting another store that was so far out of her comfort zone.

She breathed a little easier when they turned into a shopping center filled with boutiques and other small shops. It resembled the kind of places Marnie and Harley had shopped when they went outside of Selma.

Tabby parked in front of the store in the center of the long, low building. She met Mira's gaze with a grin as they climbed out of the car.

"You're going to love this place."

Mira looked at the store and smiled at the sight of saddles and bridles displayed in the large plate glass windows. She never minded visiting a tack store.

A cheerful man in his fifties greeted them when they stepped inside the leather-scented shop. "Welcome to Stuart's. Can I help you ladies find something?"

"Yes," Della said, "we're interested in riding boots."

"For all three of you, or just one or two?" he asked as he led them toward the back of the store.

"I'm the one who needs boots." Surrounded by horse paraphernalia, Mira's nerves from the department store vanished.

"Well, then, take a look at what we have and pick your boots." He waved a hand at the display of boots. "I'll be back in a few minutes."

With Tabby by her side, Mira studied the selection of riding boots. She came to a stop in front of a pair that laced up rather than having to be pulled on.

"These look good."

"They are," Tabby said. "I used to have a pair almost identical to those. They were so comfortable."

The cheerful man rejoined them. "Did you find a pair?"

Mira showed him the boots she and Tabby had discussed.

"These will last you a long time." He tapped the toe of one. "They have high-quality construction. What's your shoe size?"

"Nine and a half."

He pulled a box off the shelf. "Go have a seat, and we'll see how these fit."

As soon as Mira donned the boots, she loved them. A short walk around the room confirmed their comfortable fit. She sat down to put on her own boots back on and smiled at the cheerful man. "They're perfect."

"Okay, I'll go ring them up."

As he walked to the front counter, she caught sight of Della studying a pair of form-fitting pants. She leaned over and whispered to Tabby, "What's your mom doing?"

"It looks like she's picking out a pair of breeches for you."

Mira groaned. "Please, no more clothes."

"I'll go talk to her." Tabby gave her a sympathetic look.

"Thank you." She prayed Della would listen to her daughter.

She tied her boots and meandered toward the front of the store, admiring the tack along the way. Della and Tabby met her close to the counter.

"You need a helmet if you want to ride," Della said.

Why would she need a helmet? "I've never worn a helmet before to ride. Harley taught me to ride carefully and how to fall so I don't hit my head."

"Well, I require everyone who lives in my house to wear a helmet."

"All right." Mira shrugged. It wasn't worth arguing.

Nine

After Tabby left to meet her friends, Mira wandered into the kitchen and found Charlotte and Anita studying her deerskin bags.

"Do you know what all this is?" Charlotte asked Mira, waving a hand at the bags. "I only ask because they arrived the same day you did."

"It's food I dried over the summer and early fall," Mira said as she joined them by the island. "There's also some herbs for healing and some for cooking and teas."

Charlotte gave a little laugh. "Now I understand why Miss Della had me go buy a bunch of storage containers and spice jars."

"Do you want some help putting this stuff in the containers?" She hadn't meant to create more work for the cook, especially since she could put it away just as easily. Maybe more so, considering she'd had to read the labels for Lucas.

"Yes, you'd better help." The glance Charlotte cast toward the bags told Mira she'd guessed right about the woman's inability to read Arabic. "Then you can label it so I know what it is."

Write out labels the average American could read? Embarrassment burned Mira's face. "I'll tell you what everything is, but you'd better label it. People tend to have trouble reading my labels."

Anita grinned. "My brother has the same problem. His handwriting is so bad that sometimes even he can't read it."

They gathered the plastic containers and spice jars, labels and a felt-tip pen. Mira and Anita transferred the food from the deerskin bags to the storage containers, and Charlotte neatly labeled each one. When they reached the herbs, Anita studied the Arabic labels on the pouches.

"This is really pretty." She traced her fingers over the curving lines as she turned to Mira. "Did you do it?"

"Yeah." Her heart lifted. Not everyone appreciated the work she'd put into the calligraphy. "I had to label the herbs somehow, and I like the look of Arabic."

"You can read and write Arabic?"

"Yes. I know Hebrew, too."

"That's really neat."

Charlotte looked up from the label she had just stuck to the last of the plastic containers. "I have an idea. Why don't you label everything in Arabic? Anita's right, it is pretty."

"Okay." Maybe she'd managed to find friends from her own social class in this unfamiliar world.

Anita placed the herbs in the jars, and Mira told them the name of each herb and what it was for while she wrote out a label in Arabic. Charlotte made the

English label and stuck them both to the jars.

Once they put everything away in the large, well-stocked pantry, Anita glanced toward the deerskin bags on the counter. Her expression turned thoughtful, and she headed toward the hall.

"I'll be right back."

Charlotte picked up one of the deerskin bags and turned it over as she studied it.

"These are beautiful." She ran her hand across the soft leather. "Did you make them?"

"Some of them. Marnie made the others." Mira joined her and folded a bag as memories of the woman who'd become a mother to her flooded her mind. Would she ever stop missing Harley and Marnie?

"Well, they're gorgeous," Charlotte said.

Mira looked at the bags more closely than she had in months. Since getting kicked out of the cabin, those bags had become a necessary part of life. Now, in this huge kitchen with fancy appliances, she tried to see them the way Charlotte did.

Each bag was more or less rectangular with a flap that folded over the top to close it. A single strip of leather formed the shoulder strap, and the top-stitching along the seams continued along the edges of the strap.

From there, Mira noticed the small differences in her bags and the ones Marnie had made. They'd both followed the same basic pattern, but Marnie's stitchwork was more even. Marnie had added a few painted flowers here and there for decoration. Mira had gone for a more Islamic flair with geometric patterns and calligraphy.

Seeing them now and paying attention to the details reminded her of why she'd chosen her style of decoration. It had nothing to do with religion. She missed her parents and her life in Palestine. It hadn't been easy, but it had been full of love.

Harley and Marnie had offered the same unconditional love, but many of Selma's residents had never accepted her as one of their own. Unlike the village in the West Bank, where she'd been accepted and treated like every other child her age.

Would she find acceptance in this new world of high society and wealth? Or would she meet with disdain because she was a poor immigrant with an Arab last name?

Sighing, she accepted that she had no way of knowing until she saw people's reactions. Until then, she would have to do her best to fit into a world that was as unfamiliar as West Virginia had been when she first arrived in the United States. Either she would learn the local customs and language well enough to fit in, or she would do her best and still be an outcast.

Regardless of which way it went, she was stuck there until she could find a way to support herself and move out on her own. With her lack of education, it could be a long wait.

She picked up another bag and folded it while Charlotte tucked the pouches from the herbs in a small bag. When they finished folding the bags, they placed them on a shelf in the pantry. Mira hated leaving them in the kitchen, but she had no good way to store them in her bedroom. Besides, they were intended for food storage, so keeping them in the pantry made more sense.

Anita returned carrying a cloth-covered book. "Miss Mira, is this yours?"

"Yes, it's my journal." She accepted it and smoothed a hand across the cover. "Where did you find it?"

"It was lying on the window seat in the library when I dusted in there this morning."

"I wondered where I left it." How had she forgotten to take it back to her room last night when she'd finished writing in it? Then again, she'd had a lot on her mind and Tabby had insisted on giving her a tour of the house. "How did you know it was mine?"

Anita's face flushed, and she clasped her hands together so tightly her knuckles turned white. "When I didn't see a title on the cover, I looked inside to see what it was."

"Don't worry about it." Mira smiled, hoping to relieve the maid's nervousness. She had no concerns about anyone spying on her innermost thoughts. Not in this house. "I'm not sure anyone around here could read it."

Anita laughed, a relieved sound that matched her expression.

Charlotte's gaze shifted back and forth between them. "Is your handwriting really that bad?"

Mira handed her the journal, unable to resist seeing her reaction. "Here. See for yourself."

She opened the book to the middle and thumbed through a few pages. Then she handed it back with a chuckle. "You weren't kidding when you said you know Arabic and Hebrew."

"No, I wasn't." Mira tapped the cover of her journal.

"I write in both so I don't forget the languages."

"That's a good idea." Charlotte appeared impressed. "How do you keep from forgetting how to speak them?"

"When I talk to animals, it's usually in Hebrew or Arabic." She'd learned a while back that animals preferred her native languages to English. They didn't seem to mind anyone else speaking to them in English, so she figured it had something to do with her accent. Or maybe it was just wishful thinking giving her an excuse to use the languages she missed hearing everywhere she went.

"Is that how you talk to Maggie?" Charlotte asked. "Lucas told me you sweet-talked the horse into behaving."

"I did talk to her in Hebrew, but mostly I listened to what she told me with her behavior and gave her the reassurance she needed."

How many people had Lucas told about the training session? For that matter, why was everyone so stunned? It wasn't as if she was doing anything unusual. She'd done the same thing with cats and dogs before immigrating, and she'd continued to do it with every animal she came across in West Virginia.

True, Harley had taught her a lot about working with horses, but she hadn't seen anything unusual about his methods. Then again, maybe she had and hadn't realized it. How many times had she seen someone take a harsh hand to a horse at the fairgrounds? Or swat a misbehaving dog with a rolled up newspaper?

"Well, whatever you did," Charlotte said, "Lucas said

it worked wonders."

"And good thing, too," Anita added. "I think Mr. Montaigne was about ready to sell her off."

"Sell her?" Mira stared at them. "Why would he do that?"

"She's crazy. Or she was, anyway." Anita shook her head. "Lucas took me out to the stable and showed her to me one time. That horse kicked the stall wall hard enough I was afraid she'd put a hole in it or break her leg. And all because Lucas tried to coax her into coming closer to the stall door."

Charlotte nodded. "He tried everything he knew to get that horse to settle down. So did his assistant. Some days it worked. Other days, it was as if they'd never worked with her at all. They did eventually get her to the point where she no longer kicks the stall whenever someone goes near it, but sometimes it still takes both of them to get her out of the stall so they can clean it."

"Well, it did, anyway." Anita sent Mira a smile. "From what Lucas says, moving her from one place to another is no longer a problem."

Mira held up her hands, hoping they would understand what really happened with the horse. "I'm not a miracle worker. She still has a long way to go and could easily slip back into her old habits at any moment."

"But you made amazing progress with her."

"Only because I listened to her and used the same tactics Harley taught me when we rescued a couple of horses in worse shape than Maggie."

"Mira, honey," Charlotte said, putting her hand on her hip, "No matter how much you try to deny it, you can't convince me you don't have a special touch when it comes to animals. I've heard how you charmed old Dan into becoming your best friend."

"A lot of that had to do with the venison jerky I fed him." She held up a hand to stop Charlotte's protest. "But I do get along well with animals."

She smiled at the memory of Harley saying something similar when he saw her interact with his animals. Her parents had believed she would grow up to work with animals because of how well she got along with them and how much she loved to be around them.

"I listen to what they tell me and use my instincts to give them what they need."

"That's a good talent to have," Charlotte said.

"Were you some kind of animal trainer before you came here?" Anita asked, her face full of curiosity.

"No, I was just a girl trying to get by in life. The only training I've ever done was on my own pets or the animals Harley owned. He taught me a lot about working with horses."

"I'd say you learned your lessons well." Charlotte studied her. "Have you considered talking to Mr. Montaigne and Lucas about helping out with the horses while you're here?"

"Not really. I think they're going to let me continue working with Maggie, but Lucas has Ben to help him with the regular chores." The thought of Ben warmed her heart. With any luck she could get to know him better without getting him in trouble by distracting him from his job.

"They'd be crazy to refuse your help with that

horse. You've made more progress with her in one morning than anyone else has in the entire time she's been in that stable."

Mira hoped Charlotte was right. Working with Maggie would give her a great excuse to spend a lot of time in the familiar atmosphere of the stable...and with Ben.

Ten

Shortly before sunrise, Mira went in search of food. She found Charlotte and Anita sitting at the kitchen table, dressed in casual clothing instead of their usual uniforms as they enjoyed cups of coffee. Charlotte shifted to stand, but Mira waved her back into her chair.

"Sit down and finish your coffee. It's your day off, and I'm perfectly capable of finding my own breakfast."

"All right." Charlotte resumed her seat with a shrug as Mira walked to the pantry.

She returned with the container of oats they had labeled the previous evening. After measuring water into a small saucepan, she rinsed off an apple from a bowl on the counter and cut it up into the pan as the water came to a boil. She tossed in a handful of oats and stirred it with a wooden spoon.

While the oats cooked, she searched through cabinets and drawers until she found a bowl and spoon. Once her oatmeal was in the bowl and she'd run water into the pan so nothing would stick, she carried her breakfast to the table and sat down.

Charlotte studied her with something that bordered on amazement. "I do believe you're the first person I've seen eat oatmeal here, other than the employees."

"I like oatmeal," Mira said as she lifted a spoonful of the creamy food. "Besides, it's a hearty breakfast, and I'm going to explore the woods for a while this morning."

Anita wrinkled her nose. "Isn't it kind of cold for that?"

"Not for me. I'm used to being outside in all kinds of weather."

"You take your walk in the woods if you want," Charlotte said, her expression stating her opinion of doing anything outside on a chilly morning. "I'm going to find something to do where it's warm."

Anita nodded. "Me, too."

"You don't know what you're missing." Mira finished her oatmeal and raised her eyebrows at her companions. "Do you think I could take Dan with me?"

"I don't see why not," Charlotte said, "but ask Lucas to make sure."

"Okay."

After drinking a glass of orange juice, Mira washed the dishes and headed upstairs to collect her coat. She also dug her water bottle out of her pack and refilled it at the bathroom sink. Hiking without food or water went against Harley's teaching. She donned her outerwear and slipped the water bottle in one of the large pockets. The pouch of venison jerky went in the other.

The lights were on in the stable when Mira arrived. Ben walked out of the tack room, and she offered a smile.

"Hi. I didn't know you worked on Sundays."

"I don't. Lucas wants to give a couple of the horses an outdoor ride, and he invited me along."

"Oh. Well, have fun." She shoved down the disappointment of not getting to talk to him for long. "I'm going to hike in the woods for a while. Do you know where Lucas is? I want to ask him if I can take Dan with me."

"He went to his apartment for a minute." Ben glanced toward the tack room. "I was just about to tack up the horses. Want to help?"

"Sure, why not?" She removed her outerwear and laid it on a nearby hay bale. "I should warn you, though, I don't have any experience with English saddles."

"They're not that different from Western saddles in terms of how you put them on a horse," Ben said as they entered the tack room. "I'll show you what to do."

"Thanks." Her heart fluttered under his warm brown gaze.

They were putting bridles on the horses when Lucas came in followed by Dan. The large mutt wagged his tail happily when he saw Mira, but he stayed away from the horses.

Lucas walked over and patted the neck of the black gelding beside Mira. "What brings you out here so early? The sun is barely up."

"I'm going to explore the woods, and Charlotte said to ask you if I can take Dan with me."

"Sure, you can take old Dan. He likes to hike in the woods."

"Thanks. Do I need a leash for him?"

"No, the property is fenced, and he'll stay close to you."

"Okay." Mira handed him the reins. "Have fun on your ride."

"Thanks. You and Dan enjoy your hike," Lucas said as she bundled up.

"We will." She looked at the dog lying nearby. "Come on, Dan. Let's go for a walk."

He clambered to his feet and wagged his tail as he followed her out into the cold morning air.

An hour later, as Mira headed back to the stable with Dan at her side, her right leg began to ache with surprising intensity. She stopped and shifted her weight to her other leg, hoping the brief break would help.

It didn't.

The dog looked up at her with a quizzical expression.

"Ouch. I'd forgotten how bad old injuries can hurt." She limped to a fallen log and sat on the cold bark. "We'll rest here for a few minutes until this leg of mine settles down."

Dan whined and sat in front of her with a wrinkled forehead. Mira scratched his head with one hand and pulled out the venison jerky with the other. The moment he saw the leather pouch, the dog swept the frozen ground with his tail.

"Yes, Dan, you can have some jerky," she said with a laugh. Then she cringed as a sharp pain shot through her leg. "Man, I wish this ache would go away."

She fed the dog a piece of jerky and chewed on a

small piece herself. Since she was sitting there anyway, she might as well have a snack. She handed Dan another bite and put the pouch back in her pocket. She opened her mouth to speak, but Dan sprang to his feet and took off through the woods.

"Dan! Get back here!" It was no use. He'd left her on her own. "Ungrateful dog. I give him a treat, and he decides to abandon me."

Distant barks drifted to her, and she figured he had found an animal to chase. She should have expected it, taking a hunting dog into the woods.

A cardinal landed in a tree close by, and she watched the brilliant red bird preen. She would head back to the house in a few minutes whether her leg quit hurting or not. The chilly air only made the ache worse.

As she prepared to stand, Dan ran up followed by two riders on horseback.

"You big goof," Mira said, rubbing the dog's velvety ears.

Lucas and Ben reined in their horses and dismounted. Both men walked over to Mira with concerned expressions.

"Are you hurt?" Lucas handed his reins to Ben and knelt in front of Mira.

Dan had pulled a Lassie and worried Lucas that much? "No, I just had an old leg injury decide to act up. I was about to head back to the house."

"Are you sure you're okay?"

"Yeah, an aching leg is nothing new." She stood to prove her point. "I don't know why Dan went to get you. I'll be fine."

"But you're not fine yet." Lucas stood and motioned for Ben to bring the horses closer. "You're not walking back."

Mira opened her mouth to protest, but her leg chose that moment to intensify the ache. She shifted her weight to her left leg and nodded. "Okay."

Lucas held the horse steady as Ben helped Mira onto its back and swung up behind her. Once Lucas mounted his horse, they headed back toward the stable with Dan running ahead.

"You doing okay?" Ben asked as she shifted in the small saddle.

"Yeah, but I'm going to guess there's a major weather change headed this way."

"There's snow moving in later today, and the storm is supposed to hang around until sometime tomorrow. How did you know?"

"My leg only aches like this when the weather changes, and especially if there's rain or snow coming."

"Is there anything you can do to make it feel better?"

"Believe it or not, horse liniment works really well."

"That's unique," Ben said with a chuckle. "There's liniment back at the stable. I don't think anyone will mind if you use some."

When they arrived, Ben helped Mira limp to the bench in the tack room while Lucas took charge of the horses. As she removed her coat and gloves, Ben retrieved a plastic bottle from a shelf. He brought it over as she set her hat and scarf on top of her coat.

"Here you go." He handed her the liniment.

"Thanks." She didn't want to lift her pants leg while

he was there. He didn't need to see the scars, but how could she ask him to leave when he was being so kind?

"Will you be okay if I go help Lucas with the horses?"

"Of course." She couldn't help a smile at his sweet show of concern. "I've been dealing with this since I was thirteen."

"Okay. I'll be back in a few minutes to see how you're doing."

As soon as he left, she turned sideways and propped her right foot on the bench. She pulled up the leg of her cargo pants and rubbed a small amount of liniment into her skin.

The familiar minty scent filling the air reminded her of the day Harley had taught her how to use liniment. She'd been having a bad pain day, with the bones in her legs aching due to a coming storm, and he'd told her about the old farmer's remedy for arthritis. She hadn't been sure about using a horse product on herself, but it had only taken that first application to make her a believer.

Between the warmth of the tack room, the liniment, and the massaging of her fingers, her leg soon began to feel better. She was still rubbing in the liniment when she heard a sharp intake of breath from the doorway. Mira yanked down her pants leg and looked over to find both men holding their tack and staring at her with wide eyes.

"What happened to your leg?" Lucas asked.

She fought down embarrassment over the patches of scar tissue crisscrossing her leg. "I got caught in an explosion when I was thirteen."

Ben and Lucas put their tack away and sat down, Lucas on the bench by her feet and Ben in a chair he set near her. When Mira saw the compassion in their eyes, she wanted to cry.

"Was it the explosion that killed your parents?" Ben asked.

She nodded and bit her lip, dropping her gaze to the bottle of liniment on the floor beside her. They were quiet for a moment, and then Lucas leaned over to pick up the liniment.

"Did this help?"

"Yes, it did." Why didn't he ask about the explosion the way most people did after seeing her scars? Not that she wanted to talk about it, but his lack of curiosity was unusual.

"Take it." He handed the bottle to her. "We have plenty more to use on the horses."

"Thank you." She barely kept her tears in check. So much kindness always got to her.

He stood and glanced at the dog lying in the middle of the floor. "I'm going to take Dan upstairs and get him some food and water. Ben can walk you up to the house whenever you're ready."

"Okay, and thanks again, Lucas."

He smiled and left the tack room, snapping his fingers so Dan would follow.

After they left, Mira finally worked up the courage to look at Ben. She found him watching her with a compassionate gaze she wasn't quite sure how to handle. Unable to bear it a moment longer, she glanced at the bottle of liniment in her hands.

"Why don't we go on up to the house?"

"Sure, I'll go grab my coat." Ben replaced the chair against the wall and left the room.

He returned as she finished zipping her coat. She stood and gingerly put more weight on her right leg. There was a dull ache, but she could ignore that.

Ben watched her with the same appraising gaze Harley had used when evaluating a horse's soundness. "You okay?"

"Yeah. I'm just moving slow so my leg doesn't start hurting again." She picked up the liniment. "Let's go."

They strolled up to the house, keeping the pace slow. Mira had only a slight limp, but Ben stayed close, ready to offer support if she needed it. When they reached the back door, she faced him with a mix of hope and nerves.

"Would you like a cup of coffee or something?"

"Sure." A surprised smile lit his eyes. "If you don't think the Montaignes will mind."

"Why would they mind?"

"Because I'm the stable boy."

"And I'm a near stranger from the hills of West Virginia," she said and opened the door. "Come on."

He grinned and followed her into the mudroom. Once their coats hung on pegs, Mira led the way into the hall. As they approached the kitchen, Della's voice drifted through the open doorway.

"Mira, is that you?"

"Yes, Della," she said, stepping into the kitchen. The whole Montaigne family sat around the table, finishing breakfast. "I invited Ben in for a cup of coffee."

The surprise on their faces disappeared behind friendliness, and Della smiled. "That's fine, dear. Bill made coffee a short time ago. It's on the counter."

Mira turned to Ben and murmured, "I told you."

They continued into the kitchen, and Mira set the liniment on the counter closest to the door. As she walked to the coffeepot, Della gasped.

"Mira, what happened?"

Eleven

Mira's gaze darted to her legs, but they were covered. She turned to Della, puzzled. "What do you mean?"

"You're limping, dear."

"Oh, that." She retrieved two mugs from the cabinet. "It's nothing. I'll be fine."

Bill gave her a doubtful look. "A person doesn't limp from nothing."

Ben cleared his throat. "It's an old leg injury, sir, that's acting up because of the snow moving in."

Bill ignored him and stared at Mira. She finished pouring the coffee and handed one cup to Ben. He smiled his thanks and took a sip. After taking a sip of her own coffee, she returned her attention to Bill.

"Ben's right. The explosion in Israel hurt my legs pretty bad. Sometimes when the weather changes, my right leg can ache something fierce. The coming snow is what made it hurt this time."

"And the horse liniment?" Bill said, waving his hand at the bottle.

"It helps." She shrugged and leaned back against the counter to drink her coffee.

The Montaignes went back to their breakfast, and Ben stood beside Mira silently drinking his coffee. Discomfort rolled off him in waves, and she spoke in a whisper.

"What's wrong?"

"Nothing really." He gave her a tight smile. "There's just a lot you have to learn about the way society works."

"What do you mean?"

"I'll tell you another time." He finished his coffee and handed her the mug with another smile, this one warmer than the last. "Thanks for the coffee. I'll see you later."

Before Mira could say anything, he left the room. She glanced at the Montaigne family and caught Tabby's sympathetic look. That couldn't be good.

Mira carried the mugs to the sink and washed them, her mind racing as she tried to figure out what she'd done to need sympathy. And what was with Ben's sudden change in mood?

As she dried her hands, Josh brought over a stack of dirty dishes. He had the same sympathetic expression as his sister.

"Mom wants to talk to you."

"Okay." She hesitated, but then asked what she'd wondered since Ben was so uncomfortable over drinking coffee. "Did I do something wrong?"

"Don't worry about it." He offered a reassuring smile.

Too bad Mira didn't feel reassured as she joined Bill and Della at the table. Tabby had disappeared.

"Do sit down," Della invited with a hint of a smile.

Mira pulled out one of the chairs and sat, feeling a little like a student called into the headmaster's office.

"It was kind of you to offer Ben a cup of coffee," Della said. "But, Mira, we just don't do things like that."

Her jaw dropped. "Why not? He'd been out riding in the cold, and he was kind enough to walk me back up to the house. I was just returning the kindness by offering him a cup of coffee. That's what Harley and Marnie taught me. If someone does you a kindness, the least you can do is offer them coffee, or iced tea in the summer."

"That may be, but things are done differently here. A person of means, especially a young lady of means, does not invite the stable help into the house."

"I'm not a person of means." Mira's temper burned hot as she stared at Della. "I haven't got a penny to my name."

"Mira, dear, you're living here now as one of the family. That means you count as a young lady of means."

"I'm not going to forget every ounce of manners I was ever taught just because I'm living in a big fancy house." She shoved back her chair and stood. "Please, excuse me. I'm going to go find something that makes sense."

She left the kitchen and went to the mudroom. As she pulled on her coat, she fought the urge to go pack her belongings and leave. She opened the back door and stepped outside, wishing she had more housing options than the Montaignes or a lean-to in the woods.

Taking a deep breath of the cold air, she headed for the stable. Inside its soothing, warm interior, she heard only the quiet sounds of the horses as they lazed the morning away. She walked to the last stall and found Maggie chewing a mouthful of hay.

The horse looked up and shifted her weight with a restless snort.

"Easy, Maggie." Mira spoke in Arabic, using her tone to soothe the horse. "It's just me. I worked with you and groomed you, remember?"

The horse settled down and walked over to the stall door. Mira reached up and scratched her forehead, receiving a soft whuffle in return.

"At least you like the way I do things. You've got it easy. You get fed, groomed, and exercised, and never have to worry about doing something that's going to upset some people and make others happy. I mean, what is so wrong with giving a friend a cup of coffee?"

The horse butted her shoulder with a large velvety nose. Mira gave a little laugh.

"I know. I barely know him and already I call him a friend. But I ask you, what is so terrible about befriending a man who works in a barn?" She sighed and rubbed behind the horse's ears. "I know I'm in a different world now. Things aren't so simple anymore."

The stable door closed, and someone walked down the aisle toward her. She glanced over to find Bill drawing near, and then she turned back to Maggie.

"Looks like it's time for round two."

"Mira, can we talk?" Bill asked.

She sighed and answered in English as she faced him. "I guess so."

"Why don't we sit down?"

Mira moved to a pair of hay bales and sat on one.

Bill sat on the other.

"Della may not have put it the best way, but she's right. We don't do things here the same way you did them in West Virginia."

"But I do. I've been here less than two days. I'm not going to change that fast. And if I have to be unkind to nice people to fit in around here, I'll go live somewhere else." Assuming she could figure out where to go.

"No one is asking you to be unkind. Eventually, you'll learn what the boundaries are, and then you won't commit any more faux pas."

"I don't know what that means."

"It means making a mistake. A faux pas is what inviting the stable boy into the house counts as."

"Back home, what I did counts as neighborly hospitality."

Bill sighed. "I know, but things are different here."

"Maybe I should go somewhere else. Somewhere that kindness includes everyone, not just people that have money."

"Kindness here does include everyone." He spread his hands to emphasize his point. "There are just different ways of showing that kindness. Besides, where would you go?"

"I don't know," she said, tears springing to her eyes. "I'm pretty much trapped here. There's nowhere else for me to go."

"Mira, none of us want you to feel trapped. We just want you to be happy."

"Then why do you want me to go against my nature?" She swiped at her eyes, irritated by the whole situation.

"I'm not asking you to go against your nature. I'm just pointing out the limitations society dictates and that we have to follow."

"They're stupid limitations."

Bill shook his head and sighed again. "I'll make a deal with you. You do your best to learn the limitations and try to stick to them regardless of how stupid they may seem, and I'll buy you a thermos so you can bring coffee to Ben whenever you want."

She considered his offer. It sounded fair enough, and the least she could do was try to get along since they were providing her with a place to live. "Okay. I'll do what I can, but I can't make any promises."

"All I ask is that you give it your best shot," he said, his relief at making progress strong enough she could almost feel it.

"Is Della going to get mad at me if I keep talking to Charlotte and Anita?"

"What Della doesn't know can't hurt her." He winked. "I won't tell her that you continue talking to them if you won't."

"Thanks, Bill." Maybe he understood more than she'd given him credit for.

"You're welcome."

Another thought sprang to mind. "What about Lucas? Will the stupid limitations let me openly talk to him?"

"Lucas is a different case. He manages the estate on a day-to-day basis."

"What does that mean?"

"It means Della won't mind if you invite him in for

a cup of coffee."

When they went back to the house, Mira headed up to her room and pulled a small book with a dark blue cover out of her duffel bag. As she sprawled on her stomach across the bed, Frank jumped up and sprawled beside her.

"Hey, you big lazy fluff ball." She gave him an affectionate scratch on the chin and received a happy purr in response. "I was beginning to wonder if I'd see you today."

Frank poked the cover of her book with a furry paw. She laughed as she looked into his inquisitive green eyes.

"It's a photo album, you silly cat." She moved his foot off the cover and stared at the paw that made her thumb look tiny. "Wow, you've got big feet."

Frank purred and shot a pointed look at the photo album, causing Mira to laugh again.

"All right, if you want to see the pictures that badly, we'll take a look." She opened the front cover and pointed to the first picture. "Those are my parents."

The ache of longing settled deep in her chest as she ran her fingers over the handsome Arab man with his arm around the pretty blonde woman leaning against him. They were so happy together, and she missed them so much.

She turned the page and looked at another photograph of the same couple, but this time the woman held an infant with wisps of copper-colored hair and the same complexion as the man looking on with pride.

Frank sniffed the picture, and Mira smiled. "That's

me a week after I was born."

She continued to study each photograph in the album, sometimes commenting to the cat, but mostly reliving her memories as the infant with the copper hair progressed through childhood. The last picture in the book showed Mira as a young teen standing between her parents. In the background, the Dome of the Rock glowed in the sunlight, showing every bit of its well-known splendor. Tears filled her eyes as she gazed at the happy trio.

"Not long after this was taken, we went to that café for lunch and..." Her voice trailed off, and she buried her face in Frank's soft fur. "Why did he have to set off his bomb in front of that café?"

As she cried, the gentle cat licked her hair a few times to comfort her. When her sobs quieted, she rolled away from Frank and stared at the ceiling. The cat crawled over and snuggled against her in such a way that she had no choice but to put her arm around him as if he were a stuffed animal. His rhythmic purr combined with the exhaustion of the emotional morning, and Mira drifted off to sleep.

Twelve

A sense of warmth and comfort woke Mira. Heat radiated through her right leg, and she found Frank stretched out against it. Every trace of its earlier ache had vanished. She sat up and petted the cat. He stretched and curled into a ball, giving no sign he ever awakened.

After doing some stretching of her own, she went into the bathroom and splashed some cool water on her face. Pain like that, especially mixed with the high emotion of looking through her photo album, was exhausting. A nap always cured her, but they tended to leave her feeling a little groggy.

She pulled her hair into a loose ponytail at the base of her neck and returned to the bedroom. As she passed the bed, she paused to rub the contented cat's soft side.

"See you later, Frank," she said and left her room.

Silence filled the second floor as she headed for the stairs. Maybe everyone was downstairs, or they could have gone out with friends. She hoped she could find someone to talk to, however. The last few days of being around people all the time had made her realize how much she'd missed having regular conversations while she lived in her lean-to.

When she arrived in the foyer, faint strains of music reached her ears. Was someone in the music room? She rounded the stairs and stopped as the sound of the violin grew louder. Whoever was playing had immense talent.

Mira leaned back against the wall and listened to the beautiful classical piece. Tchaikovsky, if she wasn't mistaken. Given her mother's love of classical violin, she'd spent her childhood listening to compositions by all the greats—Tchaikovsky, Mendelssohn, Brahms...

The music stopped.

Mira ducked around the stairs, out of sight of the hallway. Eavesdropping on someone's music time likely counted as one of the faux pas Bill had mentioned earlier.

Della appeared and continued down the hall toward the kitchen. Mira waited until her footsteps faded before slipping down the hallway and into the music room. The violin lay on the table, awaiting Della's return. The sight of the well-loved instrument brought back so many happy memories from her childhood in Palestine and more recently in West Virginia.

She listened carefully and heard nothing but silence. Tentatively, she reached out and ran her hand over the smooth finish of the violin. Oh, to be able to play again, even if only for a moment! Surely Della would understand, one violinist to another.

Mira glanced over her shoulder and found the open doorway empty.

Only for a moment, just a few quiet notes...

She picked up the bow and brought the violin to her shoulder in one fluid movement. Her eyes drifted shut as she drew the bow across the D string, and she relished the feel of the instrument, the faint vibration, as the note rang out clearly. Before she could think about the possible consequences of what she was doing, Mira began to play a haunting melody her mother had taught her.

As she played, she forgot she borrowed the violin without permission and lost herself in the familiar music. The notes flowed over and through her, soothing raw nerves and easing the pain of losing her parents and Harley and Marnie.

The sound of movement behind her snapped her back to reality. She whirled toward the doorway and found Della watching intently. Mira lowered the bow and violin, her face on fire as it sank in that she'd been caught.

"I-I'm sorry." She turned to put the violin back where she had found it. "I should have asked. But it was lying there already tuned, and it's been so long since I played..."

"Mira." Della's gentle voice stopped her.

She slowly turned around, still holding the violin.

"What were you playing? It was beautiful."

"It's something my mother taught me. I forget the name." Confusion filled her. She knew how touchy people could be about their instruments. "Aren't you mad that I played your violin without permission?"

"How can I be, after hearing you play so magnificently?" Della smiled and perched on one of the chairs. "Please play that piece again. It is so lovely."

"Okay." Mira lifted the violin again, disconcerted by Della's reaction. She drew in a calming breath and raised the bow.

As she played, the other family members came into the room and joined Della. Mira drew the bow across the strings one last time, and then lowered it and the violin. Now to find out what her small audience thought. A flutter of nerves attacked her stomach as she focused on them. Thankfully, they didn't keep her in suspense for long.

Tabby clapped her hands together, excitement lighting her face. "That was so awesome! How come you never told me you could play the violin?"

"I don't know." The exuberant praise embarrassed her, but she fought past it. "Just never thought it was important, I guess."

"Never thought it was important?" Tabby's eyes widened. "Mira, you play as well as Mom!"

"Thank you." She wasn't sure she believed it. She'd heard Della play. The woman had a lot of talent and training.

Della leaned forward. "Dear, do you own a violin?"

She would have to ask, wouldn't she? Mira sighed. "I don't know."

"You don't know?" Tabby stared at her as if she had just sprouted antennae. "Either you own one or you don't. How can you not know?"

"Tabby." The warning in Bill's tone stopped her.

"Sorry." She ducked her head.

"It's okay." Mira returned the violin and bow to where she had found them and took a seat with the family. "I don't know if I own a violin because I don't know what happened to my mother's. I couldn't find it when I packed to come to this country."

"Did it just get misplaced?" Bill asked.

"I don't think so. A close family friend helped me look. We searched the entire house, but there was no sign of it. I'm afraid my father's family took it while I was in the hospital. I know they took some other things."

His brow furrowed. "I thought your father's family disowned him when he married your mother."

"They did, but they decided to claim him again long enough to collect some of the things he owned. Just not long enough to collect me." Her hands clenched at the painful memory.

"How awful!" Tabby looked as if she was about to cry.

"There was nothing I could do," Mira said. "I was a thirteen-year-old orphan nobody wanted, except for one of my mother's distant cousins."

"Well, I want you." Tabby wrapped her in a hug. "I was always trying to get Mom and Dad to bring you home with us."

"I know." Her friend's words and embrace lifted her spirits. "You kept telling me you wanted me as a sister."

"And now I finally have you!"

Della glanced toward her violin, and then focused on Mira. "It's obvious to me that you've played since you moved in with Harley and Marnie."

"I thought you might notice that." Mira's smile faded as she continued. "Harley let me use one of his fiddles, but his family wouldn't let me have it."

"So, you haven't played since April?" Della's perfectly plucked eyebrows drew together in sympathy.

"There was a nice old man I've known since I moved in with Harley and Marnie who let me play his fiddle a few times. He taught me to play his way, and I taught him to play mine."

Della rose and walked over to a built-in cabinet with doors designed to blend in with the walls. She opened one of the lower doors and removed a black violin case from the shelf. After closing the cabinet, she brought the case to Mira.

"You may use this violin whenever you wish, until we can get you one of your own."

Tears stung Mira's eyes at the woman's kindness. "Thank you. I'll treat it as if it were my own."

"I know you will, dear," Della said, patting her shoulder.

Mira examined the violin. It was a high-quality instrument, similar to the one Della played. Her heart raced with the knowledge that for the moment it was hers. After giving it a quick tuning and rosining the bow, she played a couple of songs, including an old Appalachian tune she had learned from Harley.

The quality of sound the fine instrument produced reminded her of her mother's missing violin. She prayed she would be able to find it someday. She had so little to connect her to her parents, and the violin had been a large part of her connection with her mother. Thanks to Della, she now had a way to feel closer to her mother through the music they'd both loved to play.

During the impromptu recital, Tabby whispered

something to her brother. He glanced at Mira, and then gave his sister with a shrug and a nod. What were they plotting? As soon as Mira finished the song, she planned to find out.

The last notes faded away, and she replaced the violin in its case with a contented smile. Yes, having free access to the instrument would definitely make living there easier.

While Josh spoke quietly with his father, Tabby joined Mira with a grin. "I have a great idea. Why don't Josh and I call some people, and we'll all go out and see a movie or something this evening?"

Della turned from putting her own violin away and smiled. "I think it would be a wonderful way for Mira to meet some people the same age as you kids."

After she invited the stable boy into the house, they wanted her to spend an evening with what were sure to be more high society people? Mira glanced at Bill, certain he would understand her doubts, but he just gave her an encouraging nod.

No help there.

She turned back to Tabby with a bit of a smile, unable to think of a way out that wouldn't hurt the girl's feelings. "I guess it could be fun."

"Great! I'll go call a couple of my friends and set it up." Tabby bounded out of the room.

Mira had a feeling she would need all the energy she could get to survive Tabby's "great idea." She turned to Della. "Have I missed lunch?"

"Yes, but Charlotte left ingredients for sandwiches."

"If you don't mind, I think I'll go make one."

Della waved a hand toward the door. "Go right

ahead, dear. Feel free to use whatever you wish."

"Thank you." Mira returned her smile and headed into the hall.

As she ate a ham and cheese sandwich at the kitchen table a little while later, Bill and Josh joined her. Bill's features held a hint of sympathy as he spoke.

"You seemed a bit hesitant about agreeing to Tabby's idea."

"Yeah, maybe a little." She set her sandwich on the plate and studied them. They both seemed to understand her situation better than Tabby. Maybe they could help her survive the evening with a minimum of awkwardness. Or better yet, help her get out of it. "I don't know what to expect, and I don't want to mess up like I did this morning."

"That's what I thought," Bill said with a nod. "Tabby doesn't understand how difficult the transition into high society is for you. She thinks that since she has such an easy time with the social situations and graces that go with being well to do, you ought to have as easy a time. I'm not sure it's ever sunk in that our trips to West Virginia were a vacation for us, but you lived there all the time. Your life and ours have been completely different, but I don't think Tabby realizes it."

That sounded like her impulsive yet sweet friend. "She's always accepted me as I am, and I'm afraid she thinks everyone else will accept me just because she does. I know better than to believe that. I've had too much experience with people."

"I know. Josh and I were talking about that very thing a few minutes ago."

Josh leaned forward and crossed his arms on the edge of the table. "Yeah, and you don't need to worry about tonight."

"Why not?" Had he talked his sister out of the idea?

"Because I'll help you out. Once I find out who Tabby is inviting to come with us, I'll give you an idea of what to expect from them."

"Thank you." Relief washed through her. Josh had always understood that she was different from his family. With his help, she might survive after all.

Thirteen

Tabby bounced into the kitchen, her excitement showing on her animated face. "Janet, Paul, and Shannon are all coming. We're going to meet here about five and figure out where to go for dinner. After that, we'll go to the theater and see what's playing."

"Sounds like a good plan," Josh said.

Bill gave his seat to his daughter. "I'll let you kids talk."

As he left the kitchen, Tabby turned to her brother. "So, who are you going to invite?"

"Probably Adam and Ryan."

"That will be so perfect!" Tabby squealed and clapped her hands. "We'll have four guys and four girls."

"So we will." Josh looked like he wanted to laugh. "Why don't you tell Mira about your friends while I call mine?"

"Okay!"

As he pulled out his cell phone and headed for the opposite end of the kitchen, she turned to Mira.

"Paul is into investing. He's made a lot of money in

the last year by trading his stocks at just the right time. He's also really good-looking, but he and Shannon are dating. She's a model and does a bit of work in commercials. They just make the cutest couple!"

"What does Janet do?" What were these people like? Tabby didn't seem interested in telling her about their personalities.

"Janet helps her mother raise money for worthy causes. She is so good at planning dinners and charity balls and other events like that."

"So, what are they like?"

"They all enjoy the finer things in life. They also know how to have a good time. You can't beat their senses of humor, especially Paul. He is such a comedian!"

"Oh." She still felt anything but enlightened.

"Janet and Shannon both have a great sense of style. They can make the most awesome outfits with next to nothing to choose from. Like I said before, Janet does a lot of fundraising. Shannon donates to charities all the time."

"Do they volunteer somewhere?"

"A week or so before Christmas every year they take gifts to the patients at the children's hospital."

"What about the rest of the year?" Mira sensed Tabby's friends had as much depth as a dry creek bed.

"They donate money and Janet helps put on fundraisers," Tabby said as if she couldn't understand what more Mira expected them to do. "Shannon would do more fundraising work, but her modeling schedule keeps her busy."

"Oh, I see." With any luck, Josh would be able to

give her the information she really wanted. Tabby didn't seem to understand that Mira didn't care about income or fashion sense. What she needed to know was whether Tabby's friends would accept her or see her as a poor immigrant and possibly a terrorist like so many people she'd met since coming to the United States.

She finished her lunch while Tabby told her more superficial information about the people they were spending the evening with. By the time Josh finished his calls, Mira still had no idea if she would get along with Tabby's friends or if she would have to put up with disguised—or blatant—ridicule.

Not a comfortable position to be in.

She pushed her empty plate aside as Josh returned to his seat.

Tabby stopped the flow of useless information and turned to her brother. "So, are Adam and Ryan both coming?"

"Yes, they are."

"They aren't going to talk about boring save-the-world stuff all night, are they?"

Josh laughed. "Probably not. I told them we're going out with your friends."

She smacked her brother's shoulder and faced Mira. "I'll let Josh tell you about his friends. I'm going to figure out what to wear."

A new worry niggled its way into Mira's mind as she watched Tabby leave. "Do I need to dress up this evening?"

"No, we'll be dressed casually." Josh chuckled as she brought her gaze back to him. "Tabby just takes forever to decide which pair of pants goes best with whatever shirt she finally decides to wear."

Mira laughed. Somehow, it didn't surprise her. "From what she told me about Janet and Shannon, they're probably already trying to figure out what to wear tonight, too."

"Probably." His grin faded as he studied her. "So, what did Tabby tell you about her friends?"

"Not a lot, actually." She spread her hands on the table and studied them. Would anyone mind her Middle Eastern complexion? "What she told me made them sound kind of shallow."

"They are."

She looked up at him with surprise. He wasn't even going to try to deny it?

"Shannon, Janet, and Paul are more concerned with looks than anything else," Josh said. "Their most recent form of entertainment is terrorist watching."

That didn't bode well for them accepting her. "What does that mean?"

"They go to Middle Eastern restaurants and see if they can spot someone they think looks like a terrorist. For some reason, they think it's cool to see these so-called terrorists."

"What do they do when they see one?" Would they see her as a terrorist? Did Tabby, since she was friends with these people?

"Nothing, except stare and talk about what the guy might have done or be planning to do." Josh gave Mira a serious look, and she knew he'd noticed her concern. "I think it's wrong to judge people by their appearance or where they're from. I'd rather get to know them before I decide what they're like."

That provided a bit of comfort, but... "What about Tabby and your friends?"

"Adam and Ryan feel the same way I do. Tabby doesn't usually judge by looks, but she goes along with her friends so they'll think she's cool."

"Hmm." Mira tried to absorb what he was saying. It sounded like most of the guys would stand up for her if necessary, but would Tabby speak out against her friends? Her thoughts continued to whirl. "Is my knowing Arabic going to cause a problem?"

"I seriously doubt it, although if they find one of their so-called terrorists, they may want you to translate what he's saying if it's in Arabic. Depending on where we eat, they may also want you to order just to hear you speak what they call the 'terrorist language.'"

Disgust burned hot, and she struggled to control her temper. "In other words, they'd use my native language as a form of entertainment."

"They might, and then again they might not," Josh said with a shrug. "Who knows? Maybe they've gotten bored with terrorist watching and have moved on to something else. Tabby's friends can be a bit unpredictable."

"What if they haven't gotten bored with it?"

"Then we do our best to ignore their rude, idiotic behavior. And if it gets too bad, we can always leave. Ryan and Adam would go with us, and Tabby can spend the evening with her friends."

Having an escape plan eased some of her worry, but she didn't know anything about his friends yet. "Ryan and Adam wouldn't mind if I was with you guys?"

"No, they're looking forward to meeting you." He smiled as she tried to figure out why they would want to meet her. "I've told them both about you. They know you love the outdoors and animals, and that you're a kind person who's willing to work hard to help someone in need."

He'd said that about her? Her mood lightened. "What are Adam and Ryan like?"

"Ryan is a bit of a comedian, but he knows when to be serious, too. He's studying to be a lawyer, like his father. He helps stock the shelves at the local food pantry a couple of times a month and visits the nursing home his grandfather was in. His grandfather died about three years ago, but Ryan likes to talk to the residents at the nursing home. He says they have a lot of interesting stories to tell."

"They probably do. I always liked talking to old people. They've lived through so much and know so many neat things."

Josh grinned. "Ryan says the same thing about the people in the nursing home."

"What about Adam? What is he like?"

"Adam loves to be outdoors almost as much as you. He's studying to be a botanist. Actually, he just got back from spending six months in South America studying the plants down there. He also has a soft spot for animals. When he can, he volunteers at the animal shelter, but he doesn't have a lot of time because of school."

"Are they nice?" She hoped he wouldn't be offended, but after hearing about Tabby's friends, she needed some kind of reassurance.

"Yes, they are."

Mira stood and carried her dishes to the sink. Even though she was more hopeful about her chances of survival, she needed to relax before dealing with people who enjoyed "terrorist watching." As she washed the dishes, she glanced over at Josh. "Do you think anyone would mind if I spent some time with Maggie? I'd like to reinforce the progress she made yesterday."

"That sounds like a good idea." He joined her and leaned back against the counter. "If I go with you, I don't think anyone will mind. The main concern with Maggie is that she'll act up and hurt whoever is working with her. That's why there are always two people when she's out of her stall."

"Okay." She set her plate in the drainer with the glass she'd used and dried her hands. "I'm ready when you are."

Fourteen

Maggie acted up a few times when Mira started walking her around the arena, but she settled down after a few turns. After about twenty minutes of working on lead training, Mira ended the session on a good note and led the horse through the gate Josh held open.

"It looks like she remembers what she learned yesterday," he said as the docile mare walked past him.

"She does," Mira said as they headed toward Maggie's stall. "And now that she learned it again today, hopefully she'll remember it tomorrow."

"I'm sure she will."

They put the mare in crossties to groom her. While they brushed the happy horse, they talked about the coming evening and the events during the rest of the busy week. Josh made everything sound so simple and non-threatening, but Mira couldn't deny the flutter of nerves as she considered meeting the Montaignes' relatives and being included in their dinner party.

About four o'clock, Mira and Josh hung their coats in the mudroom and stepped into the main part of the house. Tabby rushed down the hall.

"There you are!" She latched onto Mira's arm. "I've been looking all over for you. Where were you?"

"Out in the stable, working with Maggie. Why were you looking for me?"

"So we can figure out what you're going to wear tonight," Tabby said as though it should have been obvious. "We're going to have to hurry. You only have an hour to get ready."

"I think I can be ready in an hour." Mira cast an amused glance at Josh, who grinned.

She followed Tabby to her room and took off her boots while Tabby closed the door and went to the closet.

"I'll help you find the right thing to wear."

At least it would save Mira the trouble of figuring out the best clothing for the evening. "Why don't you just pick out what you think would be appropriate while I take a quick shower?"

"Okay. I'll put together the perfect outfit," Tabby said, already studying the clothes they had bought the previous day.

Mira tried not to roll her eyes as she closed the bathroom door. Fifteen minutes later, she stepped back into her room, wrapped in a voluminous terrycloth robe and toweling her hair dry.

Tabby turned toward her, surprise raising her eyebrows. "That was fast."

"It usually doesn't take long." Mira fought to hide her amusement. She had a feeling a quick shower in Tabby's world lasted at least half an hour.

"Well, I found the perfect clothes for you." Tabby

129

held up a pair of blue jeans and a gray hoodie with a college logo on the front. "What do you think?"

"Where did the sweatshirt come from?" She'd never seen it before.

Tabby laughed and set the clothes on the bed. "I stole it from Josh."

"Does he know?"

"He handed it to me. After you get dressed, come to my room and bring your makeup."

"Okay."

Mira watched her friend leave, closing the door behind her. Makeup? For a casual evening out with friends? Not where she came from, but Tabby knew more about this stuff than she did.

She quickly dressed, adding a T-shirt to Tabby's "perfect" outfit. After pulling on her athletic shoes, she combed and braided her hair. Then she grabbed her makeup kit and headed for Tabby's room.

Tabby capped her lipstick and motioned her over. "I'll help you with your makeup."

Mira joined her at the cluttered dressing table. "I know how to put on makeup, but I don't really like the stuff."

Judging by Tabby's shocked expression, it had never occurred to her that anyone could not like makeup. "Well, you should wear at least a little."

If that's the way she felt...

Mira unzipped her cosmetics bag and pulled out a tube of tinted lip gloss and mascara. "How about this?"

"That's it? That's all you're going to wear?"

"Just watch." She faced the mirror and hoped Tabby would approve of her minimalist look. After applying the bare minimum of the cosmetics, she turned back to Tabby. "Will this work?"

She studied Mira's face and nodded. "I like it. With your complexion, you don't need much makeup."

"Thanks." One challenge down, innumerable more to go. Mira smiled as she zipped the cosmetics bag closed. "Now what?"

"Now, we relax and wait for people to get here." Tabby turned on her stereo, keeping the volume low. "I should warn you about my friends' latest obsession."

They sat facing each other on the window seat, and Mira raised her eyebrows. "You mean terrorist watching?"

"Yeah." A blush crept into Tabby's cheeks. "I see Josh told you about that already."

"Yes, he did. You do realize I find the whole thing insulting, right?"

"I was afraid you might. That's why I wanted to warn you about it. I tried to convince them to lay off for tonight, but they found a new restaurant they want to check out. Do you like Middle Eastern food?"

Had Tabby forgotten where she was from? "Sure. I grew up eating it. My mother liked to fix the foods my father had grown up eating."

"That's cool. Do you have a favorite food?" Tabby's wide-eyed curiosity made her look younger than nineteen, despite the coating of makeup.

"Lots of them, but I guess the one I like most is *mujaddara*."

"What is it?"

"Lentils, onions, and *burghul*. I mean, bulgur." Just the memory of the comfort food made her mouth water. "My mother always served it with tabbouleh."

"It sounds...interesting." Clearly, Tabby had never had it. She glanced at her clock and stood. "We better head downstairs."

She turned off the stereo and led the way to the living room. They found Josh sitting on a sofa with Frank on the cushion beside him. The cat meowed when he saw Mira but didn't even attempt to move.

"Too much work to come say hi?" She walked over and smoothed the cat's large head. "You poor baby."

"Frank is the laziest cat I've ever seen." Josh's laughter faded as he studied her. "So that's why Tabby wanted my shirt."

"Do you mind?" She plucked at the warm material as uncertainty filled her. "I still have time to change."

"It's fine. That shirt makes you look like thousands of college students."

"But only the cool ones," Tabby said with a teasing twinkle in her eyes.

They sat down, and Mira listened while Josh and Tabby discussed their classes and various events on their respective campuses. As Tabby talked about her English professor, who lectured barefoot and sitting cross-legged in the middle of his desk, the doorbell chimed.

"I'll get it!" She sprang to her feet.

Mira listened to her bound across the foyer. When she heard voices and the sound of the front door closing, she shot a nervous glance at Josh.

He offered a reassuring smile. "You'll be fine."

She had her doubts about that, but she shifted her attention to the doorway as two men around Josh's age appeared. He stood to greet them as Tabby plopped onto a chair.

"Hey, man, you should come home more often," the tall blond joked. "We don't see you enough."

"Like you can talk," Josh said with a grin. "You just got back from a six-month vacation in South America."

"Ha! Vacation my foot. Have you ever tried to go anywhere in the jungle? Between the vines and the bugs, I'm lucky I didn't get lost or go crazy."

"That's why I'm the smart one," the other man said. He ran a hand through his dark hair and gave them a superior look. "The only bugs I have to deal with are annoying pre-law students."

"Like you." Josh laughed.

"Very funny," he said with a roll of his eyes, and then he smiled at Mira. "You going to introduce your friend?"

Tabby hopped up, pulled Mira to her feet, and led her over to the three men.

"This is Mira Hassan," Josh said. "She's staying here for a while."

At least he hadn't said why she was staying there. She smiled but didn't speak, so Josh continued.

"Mira, this is Adam Turner." He indicated the blond with a wave of his hand. "He may drive you nuts talking about plants, but that's one of the hazards of hanging out with a future botanist."

Adam chuckled. "Josh has obviously forgotten that I can talk about other things."

Josh dropped a hand on his other friend's shoulder. "Ryan Farnsworth is the future lawyer. In the meantime, if you need legal advice, call his father."

"Yeah, and unless you're a major corporation, he'll refer you to one of the underlings in the firm." Ryan turned to Mira with a friendly smile. "It's a pleasure to meet you, Mira."

The doorbell sounded again, and Tabby went to answer it. Adam focused on Josh and Mira.

"So, do we know what we're doing tonight?"

"Tabby said her friends found a new restaurant they want to try." Just the thought made her accent thicken. Not what she needed to help her relax.

"That sounds ominous," Ryan said.

Before Mira could assure him it was, Tabby returned with a young man and two young women around her age. The man wore chinos and a button-down white shirt. The two girls were dressed in form-fitting jeans and sweaters. All three ran appraising gazes over Mira.

"You must be Mira Hassan," the young man stated with an air of self-confidence that bordered on arrogant. "I'm Paul Washburn the third."

Mira smiled, hoping it hid her discomfort, as Tabby hurried to introduce her other friends.

"Mira, this is Janet Foster and Shannon Crosse."

"How do you do?" Janet asked, primping her curly auburn hair.

"It's nice to meet you," Mira said.

"Oh, I love your accent!" Shannon gushed with an enthusiasm that rivaled a flight attendant's. "It makes you sound so mysterious. Where are you from?"

"Most recently, West Virginia. Before that, Israel." She had a feeling admitting to growing up in Palestine would work against her with these people. It had happened more than once in West Virginia.

"I toured Israel with a friend of mine once," Janet said.

Maybe they weren't as clueless about the world as she'd thought. "What did you think?"

"Oh, it was okay, I suppose," she said with a noncommittal wave of her hand. "But I was glad to get home again. I mean, how can you know what those people are really thinking?"

Those people? Did Janet fail to notice that Mira was one of *those people*? She caught the sympathetic looks Josh and his friends gave her before staring at the floor. This was going to be a long night.

"You know," Adam said, "it can be just as hard to know what people are really thinking in this country."

"Whatever." Janet dismissed him with a wave as she turned to Tabby. "So, are we going to that new place?"

Ryan looked a little too innocent. "What does it serve?"

"Middle Eastern food with names no one can pronounce."

"Why do you want to eat food you can't pronounce?" Ryan asked, his innocence growing.

Anyone with the slightest bit of sense could see he hoped to make a fool of her. Mira seriously doubted Janet noticed.

"You never know who you might see in one of those places," Shannon said with a hushed tone.

Mira's curiosity about the restaurant got the better of her. "What country is the food from?"

"Beats me." Janet gave a careless shrug. "One of those Arab countries I assume."

"Why don't we get going?" Tabby shot a guilty glance at Mira. At least she had the good sense to realize how wrong her friends' idea of entertainment was.

Everyone donned coats and gloves and headed outside. They would travel in two groups—one in Adam's dark green SUV, the other in Paul's silver SUV. Mira opted to ride with Josh and his friends. The less time she had to spend with Janet, the better. Otherwise, she might start giving the girl her true opinion. It was tempting to do it anyway, but she didn't want to cause trouble for Tabby.

She ended up in the back seat beside Ryan. As they followed the other car through the falling snow, Mira stared out the window. How would the rest of the evening go after its less than ideal beginning? Could she keep her temper in check if Janet and Shannon started their prejudiced nonsense at the restaurant?

Fifteen

They could see Dayton ahead when Ryan turned to Mira. "Are you okay?"

"It's nothing I haven't dealt with before." She glanced at him. Josh's friends seems okay, but she wished the evening was already over so she wouldn't have to deal with Tabby's so-called friends.

"It's nothing you should *have* to deal with."

"Maybe not, but when you speak a different language and have an Arab last name in this country, you learn real fast that what should be and what is are two completely different things." An idea struck, one that might turn the discomfort and embarrassment back on Janet and Shannon. "What do you say we make this evening a learning experience?"

Josh turned to meet her gaze over the back of the seat. "Sounds good to me."

"What do you have in mind?" Adam asked.

"Well, they're suspicious of Arabs, so I'll speak Arabic to the people at the restaurant." A possible snag in her plan came to mind. "I assume they'll speak Arabic where we're going?"

"Absolutely," Josh said. "Tabby's friends couldn't have their fun if everyone at the restaurant only spoke English."

"I wonder if her friends will let me order." Based on Tabby's reaction to her description of mujaddara, just about anything she ordered would be met with suspicion.

"You can offer." Ryan gave her a pleading look. "My only request is that you order something edible for us."

"Don't worry, it will all taste good." It occurred to her that they might not enjoy Middle Eastern seasonings. Not everyone she'd met in the US had. "At least, I'll think it tastes good. I don't know what you like."

"I try to avoid brains, tongues, and feet. But I'll eat just about anything else."

Adam grinned into the rearview mirror. "What about squid and octopus?"

Ryan shuddered. "I don't like things that squeak when I chew, either."

"I'll keep that in mind," she said with a laugh.

They tossed around ideas about what they could do to get Tabby's friends to stop their insulting idea of fun. The discussion lifted Mira's mood and enabled her to anticipate the possibility of eating some of the foods she'd enjoyed throughout her childhood—the same foods she hadn't eaten in seven years.

By the time they arrived at the restaurant, she had a plan for what she would do if the employees were willing to play along. She also had the full support of Josh, Ryan, and Adam. Depending on how the evening worked out, she might need all the support she could get.

They parked beside Paul's car and the group headed for the entrance. A hand-lettered sign in the window made Mira smile. She glanced at Josh, who was walking beside her.

"They serve Palestinian food here," she said, pointing to the Arabic words. "That means I know the same version of Arabic as the owners."

He grinned and spoke in an undertone. "That could help."

"Especially if they have a good sense of humor."

As soon as they stepped into the small restaurant, a cheerful Middle Eastern man in his fifties greeted them with a smile. "Welcome! How many?"

"Eight," Paul said, an obnoxious amount of authority in his voice.

"Very good." He called something over his shoulder, and a teenager with similar features pushed two tables together to accommodate the group. "My son will have the table ready in a minute."

Soon, they were seated and looking at plastic covered menus printed in both English and Arabic. Mira smiled as she scanned the list of familiar dishes. This made her plan so much easier.

"What do you think this stuff is?" Janet asked, running her finger down the menu.

Mira peered over the top of her menu, taking full advantage of the opening Janet provided. "I know what it is. When I lived in Israel, I ate these same things."

"Why don't you order for us?" Ryan asked, playing his part well. "I'm sure you know what's good."

Tabby fell for the bait. "That's a great idea!"

"Okay. I'll be right back." Mira carried her menu to the counter at the back where the cheerful man and his son were working.

The son saw her first. "Are you ready to order?"

"Yes, I'm ordering for everyone," Mira said in Arabic.

"Ah, you speak Arabic," the cheerful man said in the same language as he stepped closer.

"My father was Palestinian, and I was born in the West Bank."

Behind her, Shannon spoke in a stage whisper. "Ooh, she's talking in their language! I wonder what they're saying."

The son rolled his eyes and continued folding napkins. His father glanced at Shannon, his mouth tightening. Then he returned his gaze to Mira and continued to speak his native language. "What can I get for you and your...friends?"

She glanced at the menu in her hand and laid it on the counter. "I'm hoping you can help me teach the obnoxious ones in the group a lesson."

"What do you mean?"

She quickly outlined her idea and the man grinned. The son grinned as well, showing he understood Arabic even though he continued folding napkins as if he wasn't paying attention.

"I like your idea," the father said with a chuckle. "My name is Omar, and this is my son Abdul."

"I'm Mira, and I appreciate your help. Now, I better order and get back to my friends."

She placed the order, and Abdul carried it back to the kitchen. As Mira turned to go back to the table,

Omar stopped her.

"I have some friends who would love to help. They have seen your companions in other restaurants and were not impressed."

"I just met most of them a little while ago, but I'm not impressed with some of them, either. Just remember which of my friends are in on the joke."

"Of course. We'll bring your meal out soon."

"Thank you," Mira said and returned to her seat.

Suspicion marred Paul's face as he studied her. "What was that all about?"

"Yeah," Shannon said. "It doesn't take that long to place an order."

Mira shrugged and reached for her water glass. "We were just talking."

"About what?" Paul demanded.

"Oh, all sorts of things."

"It must be nice to have a conversation in Arabic after so long," Josh said, giving her a convenient excuse for the conversation with Omar.

"It is." She had enjoyed speaking Arabic and having someone understand her. It was beside the point that she likely would have spoken English, if not for her plan.

A loud burst of laughter came from the kitchen. She grinned when everyone turned toward the swinging doors. Ryan caught her gaze, and she winked. As they settled back in their seats, Mira wiped all traces of mischief from her face.

"I wonder what's so funny," Tabby said.

"Someone probably told a good joke," Adam said.

Abdul and Omar came out of the kitchen carrying

trays. Abdul placed the dishes he carried in front of Tabby, Paul, Janet, and Shannon. Omar placed the contents of his tray in front of the others and spoke to Mira in Arabic.

"My brother loves your joke. Be prepared for him to come out and switch plates around during the next course."

"Okay, and thanks again for your help," she said with a smile. She turned to her friends and switched to English. "This is *mutabbal* and hummus with *taboun*."

The group studied the food they were about to eat. Adam asked the question obviously on everyone's mind.

"Can you give us the English translation?"

Mira swallowed a laugh. Josh's friends were playing right into the plan, and they did it so naturally. "Mutabbal is an eggplant dip, and hummus is a dip made with pureed chickpeas. You dip the taboun—the bread—in it."

She began to eat, and the others followed her example. It tasted like home. Josh and his friends seemed to enjoy it as much as she did. Tabby and her friends appeared surprised at the food's high quality.

After a while, Abdul arrived to collect the dirty dishes and carry them back to the kitchen. A moment later, he and Omar returned carrying trays once again. They placed the fragrant food in front of their customers and were headed back to kitchen when a man near Omar's age suddenly rushed out. He spoke to Omar for a moment, and then hurried to Mira's table.

Apologizing profusely in Arabic, he switched the

plate in front of Mira with the one in front of Shannon. After studying the rest of the plates, he nodded in satisfaction. He spoke to Mira in an apologetic tone, his words anything but an apology.

"Omar's friends will arrive soon carrying black cases. They'll provide entertainment later."

He went back to the kitchen with his brother and nephew, and Mira waited for the inevitable questions. She didn't have to wait long.

"Who was that guy?" Janet asked in a suspicious tone.

Tabby leaned forward, her expression curious. "What did he say?"

"That was the cook." Mira hoped they couldn't see how pleased she was that they were falling for her plan like leaves from a tree in autumn. "Apparently, there was some kind of mix up in the kitchen. He made a plate with extra mujaddara especially for me, but it accidentally went to Shannon."

"Are you sure?" Shannon studied her plate as if it would attack her.

"Positive. He explained it as he switched the plates."

Paul stared at her, clearly unwilling to believe the exchange had been so innocent. "What did he say right before he went back to the kitchen?"

"He told me there would be a surprise later." She pointed to the dishes as she explained what they were. "This is mujaddara. It's lentils, bulgur, and onions. The salad with it is tabbouleh. That's made with tomatoes, cucumbers, parsley, onions, and mint. And this platter has *musakhan*, a chicken dish."

Josh studied the musakhan. "Is it on bread?"

"Yes, that's taboun." She took a bite of the mujaddara the cook had switched and savored the familiar flavors. "This is almost as good as my mother's."

Shannon still looked at her plate as though the contents would bite her. "I bet this is poisoned."

"I don't think so." Ryan reached over and traded plates with her. "Now you don't have to worry. If anyone gets poisoned it'll be me."

Adam and Josh laughed as he took a bite of the mujaddara while Tabby and her friends watched with anxious expressions. After he swallowed, he looked at Mira and smiled.

"You're right. This is good. Although I have no idea how your mother's tastes."

When Ryan suffered no ill effects, the others began to eat. More customers trickled in, including several men carrying black cases. Their arrivals were spaced a few minutes apart, but they all went straight to a table in the back corner.

Mira had a hard time not laughing as the men appeared to have a serious discussion while glancing toward her table. Whoever these guys were, they played their part beautifully. She would have to thank them and Omar later.

Shannon leaned toward the center of the table and spoke in her annoying stage whisper. "Do you think those guys are terrorists?"

"Maybe." Janet glanced toward the crowded table in the back. "They could have explosives in those cases."

They continued to speculate as they ate. Mira did her best to ignore them as she listened to Josh and his friends hold a normal, non-prejudiced conversation about Thanksgiving plans, but it was difficult.

After a while, Paul focused on her. "You lived in Israel, right?"

"Yes." Why the sudden interest? Especially since he hadn't seemed to care when she'd mentioned it to Shannon earlier.

"Did you ever see a suicide bomber?"

The simple question brought forth a flood of memories. She refused to give into her emotions as she met his gaze with an unwavering one of her own. "I did once, in Jerusalem."

"What was it like?" Janet leaned forward with an excited expression.

"Terrifying and very painful." Disgusted by their uncompassionate stupidity, Mira stood. "Excuse me."

She walked toward a short hall in the back of the restaurant. A sign printed in Arabic above the doorway announced there were restrooms. She stepped into the ladies room and closed the door behind her, fighting against the threatening tears.

She had hoped to teach Tabby's friends a lesson about judging others based on a stereotype, but she doubted it would ever work. They seemed incapable of understanding terrorism was a real thing. Judging by Janet's reaction to Mira's admission of seeing a suicide bomber, they viewed it as a game and had no regard for others as long as they had their fun.

Mira took several calming breaths while she tried to decide whether to be angry at their lack of caring or feel pity for their ignorance. She settled on pity, because it seemed easier to deal with.

After splashing cold water on her face and patting it

dry with paper towels, she stepped back into the hall. One of Omar's friends stood nearby. He appeared to be only a little older than Josh.

"I heard what your friends asked and your answers," he said gently in Arabic. "Are you okay?"

"Yes, but those aren't my friends," Mira said in the same language, anger lurking just below the surface as she thought of the things they'd said and done in the short time she'd known them. "They are friends of a friend."

"I see." His kind face took on a thoughtful expression. "Would you like to teach them a lesson?"

"You don't mean to hurt them?" She knew how hot-tempered some Arab men could be when a woman was threatened. She still had vivid memories of her father defending her mother against his brother the only time Mira had met her uncle.

To her relief, the man chuckled. "No, of course not. I only mean to set them up. I have a friend with a wicked sense of humor when it comes to stereotypes and educating the willfully ignorant. If I call him, he'll be here in ten minutes. It's hard to say exactly what he'll do, but I can guarantee it will make a lasting impression."

Since nothing else had gotten through to Tabby and her friends, maybe his friend could. "Sure, go ahead and call him. By the way, I'm Mira."

"I'm Akram," he said with a friendly smile. "I'll talk to you again later."

"Okay. Thanks for your help." She headed back to her table, feeling a little better about the evening.

Sixteen

Mira returned to her seat and saw Akram speak with Abdul. The teenager went to every table in the room, except theirs, and spoke briefly with the diners. Josh gave Mira a concerned look.

"Are you okay?" he asked in an undertone.

"I'm fine." She wasn't quite there yet, but thanks to Akram, she was better.

They continued their meal, and moments later, a Middle Eastern man around Josh's age entered the restaurant. He wore a heavy coat that hung open to reveal a heavy vest. He nodded to Akram and took a seat near the front of the room.

Mira ignored him, but Tabby and her friends watched him with suspicion and fear. As they whispered terrible possibilities, Josh gave them a curious look.

"What's all the whispering about?"

"Didn't you see the way that guy nodded to the terrorists in the back?" Shannon's voice was quieter than her previous stage whispers. "He's got to be one of them."

"Maybe he's just a friend of theirs and wanted to

acknowledge them without interrupting," Adam said.

Janet shook her head. "Not dressed like that."

"What do you mean?" Ryan asked.

"That vest has got to be wired with explosives." Janet cast a fearful glance at the man in question.

Abdul walked up to Mira and spoke quietly in Arabic. "Akram wants you to come to his table."

She stood and gave the group an apologetic look. "I'll be right back. Someone wants to talk to me."

She followed Abdul to the table in the back corner. He headed into the kitchen, leaving Mira with Omar's friends. She turned to Akram and waited.

"It looks like my friend decided to go with his bomber impression." He lifted an eyebrow. "Did they take the bait?"

"Oh, yeah." If only he knew how well they'd taken it. She grinned, taking care not to let her dinner companions see. "He's done a great job of scaring them."

He chuckled and nodded. "It's about to get better. Step around here so you can see."

She cleared all traces of amusement from her expression and stepped behind him. Tabby and her friends shifted nervous glances from Akram's friend to Mira and back. Josh, Ryan, and Adam sent curious glances in Mira's direction and went back to their conversation.

Akram made a big show of checking his watch and nodding at his friend. The man in the vest nodded in return and stood. Every eye in the restaurant was on him as he covered the short distance to Tabby and her friends. They watched fearfully as he stuck his hand in his pocket.

Shannon shrieked and covered her head with her arms.

"He has a bomb!" Janet screamed and ducked.

Tabby and Paul stared in silence as he pulled a cell phone out of his pocket.

His serious face broke into a big grin, and he said, "No, I have a phone."

Everyone in the place burst into laughter and applause, except Tabby and her friends. They gaped at the fake bomber. Then Paul scowled and rose from his chair.

"What kind of stunt are you trying to pull?"

The young man held up his hands and took a step back. "Hey, man, it was just a joke."

"I don't see anything funny about scaring these girls half to death."

Akram's friend looked at Janet and Shannon, who glared back. Then his gaze shifted to Tabby. Tears glistened in her eyes, and his expression softened.

"Hey, I'm sorry. I didn't mean to scare you that much."

"Well, you did," Janet said in a hateful tone.

Mira headed for the table to give the poor guy some support. He was there at her request, after all. Akram joined her as she stopped by her empty chair.

"He played the joke because I had Akram ask him to," she said, aware that she would lose any chance at friendship with Janet, Paul, and Shannon. Their version of friendship wasn't worth anything, anyway.

Shannon's eyes narrowed. "Why would you do something like that?"

"Akram heard your questions about suicide bombers and my answers." Mira held a steady gaze on her, feeling her temper rise at the memory. She shoved it back down. Losing her cool would only make the situation worse, not improve it. "He told me he had a friend who uses humor to destroy stereotypes, and I thought it might help you understand how insulting and prejudiced your current idea of fun is."

"This is insane," Janet said as she stood and waved her hand at Akram and his friend, as well as Omar's other friends. "You've probably been planning it for weeks."

Mira shook her head. Didn't the girl realize she'd only been in Dayton two days? "No, this all came about after we got here this evening."

"I can't believe you set us up."

"I only meant to prove that you shouldn't go by stereotypes when deciding what other people are like." Mira caught sight of the other diners nodding.

Janet turned on Josh and his friends, disgust twisting her features. "You're in on this, too? I should have known."

Josh shrugged and leaned back in his chair. "You have to admit that your choice of entertainment leaves a lot to be desired."

"I don't have to admit anything, especially to *you*." Janet turned to her friends. "Let's get out of here."

Shannon stood and pulled on her coat. As Paul followed suit, he looked at Tabby, who made no move to stand.

"Are you coming?"

She shook her head, not meeting his gaze. "I think

I'll stay here. I can get a ride home with the others."

"Whatever."

After Paul and the two girls left, Omar came out of the kitchen carrying a tray laden with dessert plates holding small slices of golden cake topped with almonds. Abdul followed with a second tray. They set their loads on the counter, and Omar smiled at everyone in the restaurant.

"I have *harisseh* for everyone. It's on the house to thank you for being such good sports during the unusual events this evening."

The diners gave a cheer, and Abdul began to clear dishes from the tables. Akram went back to his table, but his friend sat next to Tabby. Mira resumed her seat and sent him a smile.

"You do a great suicide bomber impression. I'm glad I knew it was all an act."

"Thanks." His smile faded as he turned to Tabby. "Are you okay? I'm really sorry if I scared you that badly."

"I'm fine." She glanced at him with a sheepish expression. "Just feeling bad about the way my friends and I acted tonight and a few other times."

"Don't worry about it." He gave a relaxed shrug. "I think all of us have had friends do things they shouldn't have. We've probably gone along with some of those things and lived to regret it, too."

"Thanks for understanding." Her countenance brightened.

"No problem. By the way, my name's Sa'id."

"I'm Tabby." She pointed out the others seated around the table. "That's my brother Josh, his friends

Ryan and Adam, and Mira."

"It's a pleasure to meet all of you," Sa'id said with a smile. He turned and waved a pair of young women over. "I'd like you to meet my sister Yasmina and Akram's sister, Zeina."

The two dark-haired women smiled as Tabby introduced the group at the table again.

"It's not often we see new faces in here," Yasmina said as she and Zeina accepted the offered seats. "Usually, it's just people from the neighborhood who have been coming here since Omar and his brother opened the place a couple of years ago."

The restaurant's atmosphere brought back good memories of Palestine, and Mira smiled. "I may have to start coming here more often. It reminds me of home."

Zeina gave her a curious look. "Where is home?"

"A little village in the West Bank. But I've lived in this country since I was thirteen."

Her eyes widened. "Akram and I have family in the West Bank. Which village did you live in?"

Mira gave the name, and Zeina broke into a big grin. "That's where our grandmother lives!"

Just then, Abdul arrived with plates of harisseh. He served everyone at the table as Akram and Omar's other friends finished removing their instruments from the cases they had brought in.

Yasmina smiled. "You're in for a treat. These guys are really good."

Josh leaned over and spoke softly to Mira. "What am I about to eat?"

She laughed. "Harisseh. It's a cake made with corn

flour and soaked with a flavored syrup. Going by the scent, I'd say this syrup has orange blossom water in it."

"That sounds good."

"It's delicious." Mira smiled and took a tiny bite of the sweet cake.

Over dessert, with the live music as a backdrop, Mira and Zeina reminisced about Palestine and the people in Mira's hometown. They discovered many of Mira's childhood friends were family to Zeina and Akram.

The connection brought about a sense of belonging that Mira hadn't experienced since leaving Israel. Although Harley and Marnie had welcomed her with open arms, most of the people in the rural area had put up with her presence because they had to. Here, in this little neighborhood restaurant, Mira found the sense of community she'd missed since immigrating.

After the music, Akram joined them and looked at the empty dessert dishes with a smile. "I see you enjoyed Ibrihim's famous harisseh."

Mira smiled and nodded. "Yes, we did. It was one of the best I've ever had."

Omar's cheerful face brightened even more as he brought a serving of harisseh to Akram. "My brother will be pleased to hear that."

"Please tell him the entire meal was delicious," Adam said.

"I will." Omar left the table with a spring in his step.

Tabby leaned forward. "Akram, you and your friends play beautifully."

"I'm glad you enjoyed it." His dark eyes sparkled.

"Oh, I did! Very much."

"You'll never guess who Mira knows," Zeina said with an excited expression aimed at Akram.

"Who?"

"Teta Nida."

His eyes widened as he turned to Mira. "How did you happen to meet our grandmother?"

She smiled, remembering the old woman she'd known since the day she was born. "I lived down the street from her. She used to tell me about her grandchildren in America, but I never thought I'd meet them."

"Teta will be so surprised when we tell her!" Zeina said.

Akram studied Mira, and his expression turned questioning. "Are you, by any chance, Khalil Hassan's daughter?"

The sound of her father's name set her heart pounding. "How did you know that?"

"Teta used to tell us about you, too." His smile faded into a sympathetic look. "I was sorry to hear about your parents. I was also sorry to hear about the way your father's family treated you."

"It didn't surprise me." Sadness had long ago replaced the anger of past hurts. "They never even knew me, only knew *of* me."

"They dishonored their family name by refusing to take in a family member in need. Especially since that family member was a child."

"My mother's family took me in," Mira said, certain he had heard about it already. "Harley and Marnie treated me as their own child."

"I'm glad to hear it," Zeina said with a glance at her

brother, who appeared ready to say more on the subject of family honor. "You know, there's a Bible study that meets every Monday evening at our church. We'd be more than happy to have you guys come."

Josh exchanged a glance with his sister. "We'd love to come, but our parents are having a dinner tomorrow night. Tabby, Mira, and I are expected to be there."

"I have to be there, too," Ryan added.

"I have a dinner meeting with some botanists and other grad students," Adam said regretfully.

"Well, maybe you can come another time." Disappointment tempered Zeina's smile.

"Maybe." Josh turned to Adam. "You have a dinner meeting three days before Thanksgiving?"

"It was the only time we could all get together. I just got back a few days ago, and one of the other guys was in Florida until yesterday. We saw some interesting species, and the botanists want to pick our brains as soon as possible."

Tabby rolled her eyes. "I was beginning to think he would make it through the whole evening without talking about plants. I guess I should have known better."

"Hey, at least I didn't tell you about the species." Adam defended himself with a grin as everyone laughed. "But you might be interested in this little flower I saw..."

"No, please! Nothing educational!" Tabby's protest would have been more effective if she hadn't been giggling.

Josh laughed. "That's an odd thing for an education major to say."

"Hey, I'm on vacation." She smiled and shrugged. "I'll think about educational things next week."

The group broke up soon after. As Josh paid the bill, Zeina borrowed a pen and a scrap of paper. She wrote down her name and number, as well as Yasmina's, and handed the paper to Mira.

"Give one of us a call whenever you have some free time and we'll get together."

"Okay." She noted their names were written in both English and Arabic. She glanced at Tabby. "What's the number at the house?"

Mira borrowed the pen and copied it onto a paper napkin as Tabby recited it. She added her name and passed it to Zeina.

"Now, you can call me if you want. I'm free most of the time."

"Thanks," Zeina said with a smile. "Are you doing anything Tuesday?"

"Not for most of the day. I'm not sure about the evening, though."

"Well, maybe we can do something in the afternoon."

"That sounds like fun." Two days in her new town, and she already had friends. Despite what had led her to the restaurant, going there had been a great idea.

Seventeen

Ben's smile brightened the predawn gloom the moment Mira walked into the stable.

"Morning, Mira. You must really like getting up early."

She laughed as she unzipped her coat and tried not to notice how wonderful her name sounded when he said it. "It's habit from living on a farm for years. Of course, I could say the same of you. What time do you get here?"

"Six." He glanced toward the tack room. "I'm supposed to be cleaning a saddle right now."

"Well, I don't want you to get into trouble because of me. Do you mind if I watch while you clean it? That way we can still talk, and Lucas can't say you're not working."

"Sounds good to me."

She followed him to the tack room. Talking to him first thing in the morning made the whole day brighter. Beautiful brown eyes, warm smile... Yes, just seeing him lifted her spirits. He didn't seem to mind her showing up either, which added to her good mood.

She hung up her coat and sat on the bench while Ben moved one of the saddles to a stand in the middle of the room. As he rubbed saddle soap into the smooth leather, Mira asked a few questions about the horses in the stable. He answered each one and asked a few of his own about her life before coming to Dayton.

By the time he finished the saddle, Mira was certain she'd been correct when she'd called him a friend. He seemed interested in learning more about her, but he didn't press her if she wasn't comfortable with the topic—like why she was staying with the Montaignes. It could have been because he didn't know her that well yet, but she sensed he wanted to respect her privacy.

Lucas came in as Ben replaced the saddle. He studied them for a moment before focusing on Mira. "I assume you'd like to work with Maggie this morning?"

"Only if it's okay with you," she said, rising from the bench.

"You're the only who's ever gotten that horse to behave so well. Who am I to stand in the way of curing her erratic behavior?"

"Thanks, Lucas." She retrieved the longe line from the shelf and turned to Ben. "I'll talk to you later."

"Okay, Mira," he said and grinned. "Good luck with Maggie."

She laughed, wishing he was the one going with her instead of Lucas. "Thanks, but the trick to Maggie is understanding, not luck."

She followed Lucas out of the tack room and considered his thoughtful expression. Did he mind that Ben had talked to her while he worked? She doubted it since she hadn't interfered with Ben completing his work. But what else could give Lucas that expression?

Nervous stamping came from the stall at the end of the row, and Mira shoved aside all thoughts but the task ahead.

Warmth surrounded Mira as she stepped into the house with Tabby. The trail ride through the snow had been exhilarating, but the icy wind made her glad she could spend the rest of the afternoon indoors. As they removed their coats and boots in the mudroom, Anita appeared in the doorway.

"Miss Mira, Zeina Talhami called while you were out. She would like you to return her call."

"Thank you, Anita." Mira smiled and wished they could speak like friends. Unfortunately, Tabby was too much like her mother. She wouldn't understand how Mira could befriend a maid.

Anita disappeared down the hall, and Mira turned to Tabby. "Where's a phone I can use?"

"You can use the one in my room."

"Thanks."

Upstairs, Mira retrieved Zeina's number from her room. Tabby showed her the phone and left. Taking a deep breath to calm her nerves, Mira dialed and listened to it ring.

Finally, a man answered. "Hello?"

She hadn't realized Zeina was married...or was it her brother? Her father? "Is Zeina there?"

"Yeah, just a second." Not her father. No father said "yeah."

A moment later, Zeina's friendly voice came over the line. "Hello?"

"Hi, this is Mira."

"Mira, hi!" Zeina said, and Mira could hear the smile in her voice. "I'm glad you got my message. What are you doing tomorrow afternoon?"

"Nothing, except maybe working with one of the horses." The more she worked with Maggie, the better. The horse was showing progress, but she needed frequent reminders that training wasn't scary and no one would hurt her.

"You want to get together and do something?"

"Sure. What time?" She could work with Maggie in the morning and visit her in the evening.

"I have the entire afternoon off, so any time would work." The man said something in the background, and Zeina laughed. "Akram's complaining because he has to work until two."

"We can make it closer to three if that would be better." Was Zeina's family traditional enough that she needed a chaperone to go out? It hadn't seemed that way last night, but Mira knew how strict some traditional parents could be, even the non-Muslim ones.

"That would be great. Do you want to come to my apartment or meet somewhere?"

Okay, so maybe Akram just wanted to hang out with them. If Zeina's parents required her to have a chaperone, she wouldn't have her own apartment. "I don't have a car."

"That's fine, we can come to you. What's your address?"

Mira recited the Montaigne's address, thankful she had asked Tabby about it earlier. "I will warn you, the place is huge."

Zeina laughed. "That's all right. We all have to live somewhere. We'll be over between two thirty and three."

"Okay. See you tomorrow." Now she had to hope the Motaignes didn't mind her inviting friends over. They'd told her to think of the house as her home, but had they meant it or just said it to be polite?

Mira fiddled with the gold chain belt hanging low around her waist as she followed Tabby away from their bedrooms. Why had she agreed to go through with this dinner party? Even though she looked the part in her fall print dress, she didn't feel it. Too bad Della hadn't given her a choice about attending.

They met Josh at the top of the stairs, and Mira struggled to appear as calm as he and his sister did. He scanned them and offered an approving smile.

"You two look beautiful."

"Thanks. You look pretty good yourself," Tabby said, plucking the sleeve of his tailored suit. "I bet Maryann will approve."

"Probably. She gave me this tie."

They went down the stairs and into the living room. Mira held Tabby back as Josh crossed the room to talk with his father.

"Who is Maryann?"

"Maryann Halliday, Josh's girlfriend."

"Is she related to Richard Halliday?"

"Richard is her father. Richard's wife is Donna."

"And they'll all be here tonight?" It would be nice to have Richard see her in something other than battered overalls and an oversized sweater with just as much wear.

"Right. Ryan and his parents will be here, too. Their names are William and Caroline. William's firm takes care of all the legal work for Montaigne Enterprises. David Barton and his wife, Rita, are coming as well. He's the vice president of the company. Dad invited someone else so there will be an even number, but I'm not sure who it is."

Della joined them and smiled. "He invited Gregory Markham, the head of Montaigne Enterprises' European offices."

Excitement lit up Tabby's face. "I didn't know Mr. Markham was in the country."

"Yes, there are some meetings scheduled for this week that he needs to attend. Your father thought he might enjoy coming to dinner and seeing all of us again."

"It will be so nice to see him." Tabby faced Mira, her eyes sparkling. "Mr. Markham lives in Paris, since that's where the headquarters for Europe are, but he grew up in England. When I took French in high school, he tested my vocabulary and pronunciation every time he visited. It was a lot of fun and helped me learn French."

"That was nice of him," Mira said.

"Shall we move into the parlor?" Della raised her voice to include the men. "Our guests will be arriving soon."

She led the way across the foyer and into the more formal parlor. Bill and his kids stood near the center of the room to talk. Mira stayed beside the fireplace and tried not to worry about what the evening would bring. Della approached with an encouraging smile.

"You look lovely, dear."

"Thank you, Della." She smoothed the skirt of her dress and met her gaze. "I should warn you that I've never attended a dinner party like this before."

"You'll be fine. I've placed you across the table from Tabby. Just follow her example."

"Okay," Mira said as the doorbell chimed. She moved to answer it, but Della placed a gentle hand on her arm.

"Anita will let the guests in."

"Oh." Did people this rich do anything for themselves other than on the servants' day off?

A moment later, Richard Halliday entered the parlor, followed by a woman about the same age as Della and a younger woman around Josh's age. After speaking briefly with the Montaignes, Richard focused on Mira.

"Mira, it's good to see you. How are you enjoying your new life?"

"It's very different from what I'm used to." she said, uncomfortably aware that everyone in the room listened to her answer. "I'm having to learn a lot of things, but it's been nice."

"I'm glad to hear it." Richard glanced toward the women he'd arrived with, and they joined him with curious expressions. "I'd like you to meet my wife, Donna, and our daughter, Maryann. This is Mira

Hassan."

"Mira, I'm so happy to meet you." Maryann's smile rivaled Tabby's for exuberance. "Josh has told me so much about you."

"He has?" She hadn't realized Josh knew much about her to tell.

"Yes, he has." Maryann cast an affectionate look toward her boyfriend. "He told me once that he sees you as a sister."

"That's nice to know." How had she never realized she'd made such an impression on the Montaignes during their annual trips to West Virginia?

"You made a big impression on Richard last Friday," Donna said.

"I don't know how, but okay," Mira said with a small laugh.

"You don't know how?" Richard's voice was rife with astonishment. "You lived alone in the woods for nearly eight months."

"Only because I had nowhere else to go." She shifted her weight, hoping they would find a new topic soon—one that didn't have anything to do with her.

Fortunately, the doorbell sounded again. A man with streaks of gray in his black hair entered the room, and Tabby walked over to greet him.

"Bonjour, Monsieur Markham."

"Bonjour, mademoiselle," he said with a smile and a flawless French accent. "And how are you this evening?"

"Wonderful! Mr. Markham, I want you to meet a friend of mine." She led him to Mira. "This is Mira Hassan."

"A pleasure, Miss Hassan." He took her hand and brought it to his lips. "I am Gregory Markham."

Heat rushed to Mira's cheeks. She had never dealt with such courtly behavior before. As she struggled to think of something to say, she glanced at Della. Would she offer any kind of guidance or maybe a rescue?

Della stepped over and played the part of gracious hostess. "May I offer anyone a drink?"

"That would be wonderful, Della," Gregory said. "Thank you."

Bill went to the small bar at the opposite end of the room and filled the drink orders. Mira hung back to regain her composure. How long would this evening last?

The other guests arrived, and soon the party moved to the formal dining room. Mira took in the elegant china, crystal goblets, and sparkling silver as a swarm of butterflies attacked her stomach. If this counted as an "informal" dinner party, she was afraid to see a formal one.

Eighteen

By emulating Tabby, Mira made it through the meal without breaking the rules of etiquette. Afterward, the group split into two smaller parties. The older group retired to the parlor, while the younger group, at Tabby's insistence, went to the music room. Once they had gathered in the center of the room, Josh faced her and raised an eyebrow.

"Okay, why did you bring us in here?"

Tabby grinned. "I want Ryan and Maryann to hear Mira play the violin."

"Hear *me*?" Mira's heart pounded. A little warning would have been nice. "Why?"

"Because you're good."

"She's right," Josh said. "You are good."

"Well, I guess I could play something." Did she even know anything high-class enough for Maryann? Whatever she played would probably be fine for Ryan.

"Oh, please do," Maryann said with almost as much enthusiasm as Tabby.

While Mira tuned her borrowed violin, she listened to Tabby gush about her ability as a violinist. Didn't the

166

girl realize there were better violinists out there? Mira was more of a fiddler than a classical violinist anyway. She rosined her bow and lifted the violin to her shoulder, hoping Tabby wouldn't be too disappointed if Ryan and Maryann weren't impressed with her playing.

Tabby made everyone sit down, and Mira began to play one of her favorite tunes. It had a title that was sure to cause comment given the present company, but that was half the fun. When she lowered her bow, Maryann applauded and Ryan looked impressed.

"I like that," Ryan said. "What's it called?"

"'Farewell to Whiskey.'"

A soft gasp came from Maryann, but Ryan laughed. "I take it that's not something you say from personal experience."

Mira grinned. "No, it's just a song Harley taught me when he found out I could play the fiddle."

Maryann's composure returned, and she asked, "How many pieces do you know?"

"I have no idea. A lot."

"Do you know any classical pieces?"

It figured she would prefer classical to folk. "A few, but most of what I know is folk music, mainly from Appalachia."

Ryan leaned forward as she adjusted the tuning on one of the strings. "Where is the rest of it from?"

"The Middle East."

"Ooh, can you play one?" Tabby's wide eyes reminded Mira of Dan begging for venison jerky.

It took all her effort not to laugh. "I guess I can."

She considered the folk songs she'd learned in

Israel. Which one would Tabby enjoy most? It probably wouldn't matter if she chose a simple song any child could play, but she picked a more challenging one and began to play again. Judging by her listeners' expressions, she might be a better violinist than she'd thought. At least she hadn't embarrassed herself by coming across as a backwoods hack with no sense of music.

She played two more pieces—a short classical piece and an Appalachian folk song—and lowered the instrument. "Okay, that's enough for tonight."

"You have a lot of talent," Maryann said as Mira put the violin away. "Are you studying with someone?"

"Ah, no, not right now." She obviously didn't know the circumstances surrounding Mira's sudden move.

"You should consider finding someone. With your talent, you could go far in the music world."

"I'll think about it." Someone as high class as Maryann Halliday was that impressed her ability? Mira had always thought she was just a good fiddler, not a great violinist.

"I can get some names of violinists who would be willing to take on a student, if you'd like."

"I'll have to give it some thought before I make a decision." Were all rich women pushy? Mira wished people would quit trying to turn her into what they thought she should be and let her be herself.

Josh stood and held out his hand to Maryann. "Let's go to the conservatory."

"All right." She took his hand with a smile and gracefully rose from her chair.

"We'll be back," he said as he led his girlfriend out

of the room.

Ryan stood as well. "Mira, I hear you worked wonders with Magnolia Dream."

Finally, a topic she could talk about for hours. "She's a lot calmer. Of course, she still gets spooked easily, but at least she'll walk on a lead most of the time."

"I'll have to see this transformation sometime. The last time I saw her, she tried to kick down the stall door."

"Mira," Tabby said, her smile indicating she'd had another of her "great" ideas. "Why don't you go introduce Ryan to the new and improved Maggie?"

Go to the stable during a dinner party? "Will your mom mind?"

"No, I'll deal with her. Go on out to the stable. I'll let the others know where you went."

"You aren't coming?" Yeah, Tabby'd had another idea. This one involved matchmaking, and Mira had fallen for it hook, line, and sinker.

"Nope," Tabby said cheerfully and turned to Ryan. "There's a coat in the mudroom that you can borrow."

"Thanks." Once she bounded out of the room, he turned to Mira. "Shall we?"

"Why not?" At least it would put her in comfortable territory.

She led the way down the hall past the kitchen to the mudroom door. Ryan reached around her and opened it before she could lift her hand. She smiled and stepped inside.

"I think that's the one Tabby was talking about." She pointed out a dark brown coat.

"All right." He made no move to reach for it. Instead, he waited for Mira to pick up her coat. Then he took it from her and held it as she slipped her arms into the sleeves.

"Thank you." Where had all this gentlemanly behavior come from? Back in West Virginia, she'd been lucky if any of the guys would talk to her. Forget about them opening doors and holding her coat for her.

Ryan pulled on the borrowed coat, and they went out into the snowy night. The path had been clear earlier in the day, but now a light dusting of snow covered the gravel. They walked side by side down to the stable and entered the warm, dimly lit building. Quiet, peaceful sounds of horses settling down for the night filled the hay-scented air.

"Maggie's down at the end of the row," Mira said, leading the way down the aisle. As they drew near the stall, she spoke softly so she wouldn't startle the horse. "Hey, Maggie, it's just me. I brought a friend to see you."

A soft nicker came from inside the stall. After a moment of shuffling, the large gray head appeared over the top of the stall door.

"Hi, sweetie." Mira rubbed the mare's forehead and glanced at Ryan. "Come say hi."

He stepped closer and held out his open hand, palm up. Maggie thoroughly sniffed it, and then poked him in the shoulder with her nose. Ryan shot a surprised smile toward Mira and reached up to stroke the mare's neck.

"You've worked a miracle with this horse. I've never seen her so friendly and calm."

Would people ever realize the horse's improvement had nothing to do with miracles? "I let her know she's safe and that people love her. I don't punish her when she acts up, either, because I know it's just because she's scared."

"How long have you been working with her?"

She did some quick counting. "Three days, but I'm out here as often as I can be."

Ryan quit petting the horse and turned toward her, his gaze full of admiration. "That's amazing, considering the amount of progress she's made since the last time I saw her."

"Maybe," she said with a shrug, embarrassed by his praise.

They spent a few more minutes with Maggie before strolling back up the aisle. At the door, Ryan stopped and faced Mira.

"Can I ask you a personal question?"

"I guess." Everyone else seemed to lately.

"Why did you suddenly come to visit Josh's family so close to Thanksgiving? I'm kind of surprised your relatives let you come the week of a major holiday."

Mira opened her mouth to respond, but closed it again with a sigh and looked at the floor as she tried to figure out how to answer. What could she say that didn't involve lying or telling him more than most people knew?

Finally, she settled on telling him the truth and hoped it wasn't a mistake. "My relatives didn't let me come. They don't care where I am."

"What about the ones you live with?" Poor Ryan looked confused. "Josh told me how much they love you."

So much for the conversation sticking with comfortable topics. "They, um, aren't living. Not since early this year."

"I'm so sorry." Sympathy filled his gaze and his voice. "Do the Montaignes know?"

"Yes, I told them Friday." She took a deep breath and prayed he would understand. "I guess since you're one of Josh's closest friends, you should know that I live here now."

She told him the basics of her story, and he listened in silence. When she finished, he reached out and touched her arm, prompting her to look at him. As she gazed into his hazel eyes, she found the same compassion she had seen in Josh and Bill.

Ryan offered a sad smile. "I'm glad Bill brought you here. I'm sorry it's under such difficult circumstances, but I'm happy I finally got the chance to meet you."

"What do you mean, finally?" She had to have missed something.

"Josh has been telling me about you for years. The more he told me, the more I wanted to meet you."

"How come you never came to West Virginia with the Montaignes?"

"Those trips were their family time." He stared at her for a moment, the warmth in his eyes making her heart pick up its pace. "Mira, you are so beautiful. Not just on the surface, but deep inside as well."

He liked her.

It took her a moment to recover the ability to speak, but her brain had stopped working. "I don't know what to say."

"That's okay." Ryan gave her hand a gentle squeeze. "We should probably go back to the house."

Mira walked silently beside him up the gravel path. She was still trying to understand what his comment meant to their fledgling friendship when they entered the mudroom. He helped her remove her coat, but even the gentlemanly behavior couldn't distract her mind from its efforts. She hadn't figured it out by the time they crossed the hall and entered the parlor by its other door.

Bill raised his eyebrows when he saw them. "So, Ryan, what do you think of Maggie?"

"The transformation is amazing, especially in so short a time. Mira definitely has a way with horses."

"It's not just horses," Richard said as he joined them. "You should have seen the way she charmed my hunting dogs."

That began a discussion on past hunting dogs and trips. Mira wandered over to Tabby, who had been watching her curiously since she walked in the door with Ryan.

"What has you looking so strange?" Tabby whispered.

"Ryan told me I'm beautiful inside and out," Mira whispered back, her heart lighter than it had been in a long time. "And it was after I told him why I'm here."

Nineteen

It was almost seven when Mira awoke to whiskers tickling her face. She opened her eyes to find Frank staring at her.

"You're better than an alarm clock." She reached up to scratch under his chin, and the cat purred loudly. "Since I'm awake, let's go find some breakfast."

She climbed out of bed and dressed in her overalls and a long-sleeved shirt. Frank led the way to the kitchen where Mira received a warm smile from Charlotte.

"Good morning, honey. Mr. Montaigne is already in the family dining room if you want to join him."

"Okay." Mira turned to leave.

"What would you like for breakfast?"

"Um..." She thought for a moment then glanced over her shoulder. "I guess whatever Bill is having."

"Scrambled eggs, toast, and bacon it is," Charlotte said and went back to the stove.

Mira continued on to the small informal dining room. Bill read the newspaper at the head of the table and looked up with a smile.

"Good morning, Mira." He folded the paper and set it aside. "Did you tell Charlotte what you want for breakfast?"

"Yes, I did."

"Well, have a seat, then." He lifted an eyebrow as she sat down in the chair to his left. "Did you enjoy the dinner party last night?"

"It was good, I guess. I've never been to anything like it before, so I was a bit nervous."

"You handled yourself well. Although, you did seem a little uncomfortable with Gregory Markham at first."

"His greeting was...unique. During dinner I realized it fit his personality perfectly."

Bill's chuckle filled the room. "Yes, Gregory does tend to be a bit formal and overly proper at times, but he's a good man and a genius at business."

Charlotte came in carrying a tray bearing two identical plates, orange juice, and coffee. After serving them and making sure they had everything they needed, she left the room. They ate quietly, and then Bill leaned back in his chair to drink his coffee.

"So, do you have any plans for the day?"

"I'm going to work with Maggie this morning." Mira took a sip of her own coffee. The rich black brew was a perfect way to end the meal. "And I might work with her for a bit after lunch, if that's okay."

"Of course," Bill said with a smile. "As long as you enjoy working with her, feel free to do it whenever you want. The only thing I ask is that Lucas, Ben, Josh, or I be in the arena with you and Maggie. It isn't that I don't have faith in your ability to handle horses, but Maggie can be unpredictable. It's for your safety that I want one of us men in the arena with you."

"I understand." His concern for her brought back memories of her own father and Harley. "It's nice to know that help is there, but I hope I never need it."

"I hope you don't need it, either." He looked at his watch and finished the last of his coffee. "I'd better get moving. I have to leave for the office soon."

Mira shifted in her seat. This was her last chance to mention the rest of her plans for the afternoon. "I didn't have a chance to tell you yesterday, but I invited a couple of people to come here this afternoon. Zeina Talhami and her brother, Akram. I met them Sunday. I hope it's okay."

"It's fine, Mira." Bill gave her a reassuring smile. "This is your home now. Any time you want to invite people over, go right ahead."

"Thanks, Bill." Relief washed through her. Since he approved, she could only hope Della would agree.

He stood and pushed his chair under the table. "I have to go. I'll be home between five and six, and if your friends are still here, I'd be happy to meet them."

"Okay." She smiled, her heart warming with the certainty he would tell Tabby the same thing.

After visiting most of the horses and talking to Ben for a few minutes, Mira found Lucas in the feed room filling out a form. Dan lay at his feet, snoring.

"Good morning," he said. "Going to work with Maggie?"

She grinned. "You're a mind reader. I came to let

you know I'm about to bring her out of her stall."

"Hang on just a minute." He finished the form and hung the clipboard on a nail in the wall. Then he looked at the dog on the floor. "Dan, to the tack room."

The dog raised his head and revealed his teeth in a huge yawn before slowly climbing to his feet and plodding out of the feed room.

Lucas shook his head as he watched the process. "I swear, that dog gets lazier every day."

Mira laughed. "Maybe he just wants to sleep later."

"Maybe," he said as they followed Dan.

Maggie was skittish on the way to the arena, so Mira skipped using the longe line and walked her around on a lead rope. Once the horse had relaxed enough, Mira led her in a zigzagging pattern from one end of the arena to the other. After doing that a few more times to reinforce following whoever held the lead, she led the horse to the gate.

"I wonder what has her so jittery this morning," Lucas said as he swung the gate open.

Mira led the horse through. "I don't know, but she's calm enough now. I'll give her a good grooming to relax her even more, and then if you don't mind, I'd like to try her on the longe line after lunch."

"Sounds like a good plan. What time do you have in mind?"

"Maybe about one? That way I can give Maggie a short training session and still have time to clean up before my friends arrive."

"One o'clock is fine with me."

"Great." She smiled as she put the mare in crossties.

After taking Dan for a walk in one of the pastures to make up for locking him in the tack room, Mira went up the gravel path to the house. She left her coat and snowy boots in the mudroom and headed upstairs to change into a pair of dry pants. The snow had drifted in the pasture, making some places over a foot deep. Of course, those were the places Dan had wanted to walk.

As she reached the foot of the stairs, she heard Della call to her from the living room.

"Mira! I'm glad you came in. You *must* meet my nephews."

She stepped into the living room, painfully aware that she was sock footed and her overalls were soaked from the knees down. Two handsome, blond-haired men in their mid-twenties sat on a sofa near the fireplace. Della perched in a chair facing the door, and Josh and Tabby occupied a sofa perpendicular to their cousins.

Della ran her gaze over Mira and gasped. "You're soaked! What happened?"

"I took Dan for a walk in one of the pastures." Heat flooded her cheeks, and she tried to cover her embarrassment with a wry smile. "The snow was a bit deeper than I expected."

"Well, hurry and change into some dry clothes. I'll introduce you when you get back."

"Yes, ma'am." She caught Josh smothering a grin as she turned to leave. So like a brother.

She ran up the stairs and down the hall to her

room. A few minutes later, she went back downstairs dressed in her green cargo pants, brown long-sleeved shirt, and athletic shoes. When she reentered the living room, Della smiled and nodded her approval.

"Mira, these are my nephews Wayne and Brandon Zivney," she said as the two young men stood and turned toward the door. "Their father is my older brother, Aaron. Boys, this is Mira Hassan."

"Hello." She smiled, hoping it would ease the discomfort of meeting more people who were far above her social class.

It didn't help.

"So, you're the infamous Mira I've heard so much about from my cousins," Wayne said as he scrutinized her.

"I guess so." Was that good or bad? And did he have to stare at her like that?

Tabby patted the empty seat beside her. "Mira, come sit down."

"Okay." She sat next to Tabby, feeling out of place. Almost as if she was invading a family gathering.

Once Wayne and Brandon had seated themselves again, they continued to study Mira.

"What do you do for a living?" Wayne asked. "Or are you in college?"

He certainly didn't waste any time hitting uncomfortable topics. "I'm not in college, and I don't have a job right now. What about you?"

"Brandon and I both work for our father at Zivney Industries." Wayne's voice overflowed with pride.

"What does Zivney Industries do?"

He stared at her, his eyes wide with disbelief.

"You've never heard of Zivney Industries?"

"Ah, no." Had she said the wrong thing?

Brandon shot his brother a warning look and turned to Mira. "We design computer software, mostly for business, but we've recently expanded into the games market. Perhaps you've heard of *Bastion of Destruction*. That was our first game and very popular."

"Sorry." She offered an apologetic smile, uncomfortably aware of Wayne watching her. "I don't use computers very much."

Brandon chuckled. "I don't know what I'd do without my computer."

"Probably go insane," Josh said. "I know I would."

"That's what you get for being a computer science major." Tabby rolled her eyes. "I could live without a computer."

"Sure. That's why you have to check your e-mail at least twice a day and check your social media accounts more often than that."

"So, Mira," Wayne said, a pompous tone to his words, "how long are you visiting Aunt Della and Uncle Bill?"

She glanced at Della. They'd never discussed what she should tell their relatives. "I, um…"

"Mira is staying with us for a while." Della gave him a disapproving look. "And it is rude to ask such a thing of someone else's guest."

"Sorry, Aunt Della." A light flush crept into Wayne's face.

"You're forgiven." She graced him with a smile.

"Mira, where are you from?" Brandon asked. "I notice you have an unusual accent."

"I was born in Israel." That admission seemed safer than admitting to being half-Palestinian. Wayne reminded her too much of Paul. "I lived there until I was thirteen, and then I moved to West Virginia."

"That must have been quite a shock, moving to someplace so different."

"Oh, it was." She didn't bother to explain that the circumstances surrounding her move had been more of a shock than the move itself.

"Did you speak English before you came to America?"

"No, I just spoke Arabic and Hebrew." The need to be honest hit. "Well, I knew a few words of English, but nothing useful."

Wayne raised his eyebrows. "You're trilingual?"

"Yeah, I guess I am." She'd never thought of that. Maybe she wasn't as uneducated as she felt most of the time. "Do you know any languages other than English?"

"I'm fluent in Spanish. That's why Dad has me working with a group in Mexico on developing software for Latin America."

"That sounds like an important job."

She regretted her words as soon as he straightened with a smug expression reminiscent a peacock showing off for a peahen. "Oh, it is."

He went on to explain what his job entailed in such great detail Mira was sure she could do his job without much more training.

After a while, Della excused herself to go check on lunch preparations. Brandon and Josh somehow managed to turn the conversation away from Wayne, an amazing accomplishment given the size of his ego. No doubt it would be a difficult week with Wayne around. Mira wasn't sure how long she could listen to his bragging before she lost her patience and took him down a notch or two.

Twenty

After lunch, Josh and Brandon went into the city. Wayne and Tabby tagged along with Mira to the stable. Lucas met them at the door.

"Are you still planning to longe Maggie?" he asked with a glance at Tabby and Wayne.

"Absolutely." Mira smiled. "Tabby and Wayne came along for the sake of something to do."

"That's fine. I left Dan upstairs, so we don't have to worry about him."

"Great." She headed for the tack room to hang up her coat, and the others followed. "Wayne, have you seen Magnolia Dream?"

He hung his coat on one of the pegs. "Isn't that the psychotic Thoroughbred?"

"Yes, but she's not psychotic." She retrieved a longe line from a shelf and turned to face him. "Maggie's just been abused and is frightened of everything."

"And this is the horse you're putting on a longe line?" Wayne looked so doubtful it was almost comical. "Last I heard, she reared at the sight of a lead rope."

"She's over that now," Tabby said as they headed for

the stall at the end of the aisle. "Mira's done a great job of calming Maggie down. You're going to be so surprised at how well she behaves."

As much as she hated to dampen her friend's enthusiasm, Mira had to shake her head. "Maybe not. She was pretty nervous this morning, so she may not behave real well this afternoon."

They reached Maggie's stall, and the horse stuck her head over the door. She tossed her head a bit, but a few quiet words from Mira calmed her.

Mira clipped the longe line to the mare's halter and opened the stall door. Wayne and Tabby stood back as she led the horse into the aisle. Lucas watched for any sign of trouble, but he stayed out of the way.

"Wayne, meet the much improved, but far from cured, Maggie," Mira said.

"She is much calmer than the last time I saw her." He studied the horse, who shifted her weight and stared back.

"She's also getting nervous standing here." Mira stroked the mare's neck. "Let's go see if a little exercise calms her down."

Lucas walked beside her as she led the mare to the arena. Wayne and Tabby followed at a safe distance and sat on the small set of bleachers off to one side. Mira walked Maggie in an ever-expanding circle. Once the mare walked calmly, Mira increased the horse's pace to an uneven trot.

When Maggie's stride evened out, Mira brought her back down to a walk and then put her back up to a trot. She repeated the exercise a few more times until Maggie made smooth transitions. As Mira considered whether to try her at a canter, a voice called out from the other side of the stalls, near the entrance to the stable.

"Hello! Anybody here?" the feminine voice asked.

Mira slowed Maggie to a walk, and Tabby stood. "I'll go see who it is."

As Tabby left, Lucas watched Maggie walk calmly at the end of the longe line. "You know, I'm surprised at how well Maggie's behaving."

"Me, too." Mira let out a little more rope, allowing the horse to widen the circle a bit farther. "After this morning, I didn't know what to expect, but I sure didn't expect her to be this calm."

"Hey, Mira, look who's here," Tabby said as she returned with Zeina and Akram.

Mira smiled and gave the longe line a light tug. "Whoa, Maggie."

The mare jerked her head a little as she came to a stop but otherwise gave no adverse reaction to the pressure on her halter. Mira quickly gathered the flat rope and led the horse to the low wall surrounding the arena. "So, am I running really late, or are you guys early?"

Zeina laughed. "We're early. Akram got off at noon instead of two, so after we grabbed some lunch, we decided to come on over here. I hope you don't mind."

"No, it's fine." Maggie started to fidget, so she laid a calming hand on the horse's neck. "This is Magnolia Dream, better known as Maggie. She's a bit nervous today, but she's behaving pretty well so far."

Zeina studied the horse with a smile. "She's pretty."

"She's a four-year-old Thoroughbred," Mira said as

the horse in question tossed her head and backed up a couple of steps. "She's also getting fidgety."

"Why don't you go ahead and finish whatever you were doing?" Akram said. "Maybe that would help."

She stroked Maggie's neck to calm her. "Do you guys mind waiting?"

"Not at all." Akram answered for his sister as well. "We're the ones who showed up early."

"Okay, you can sit with Tabby and Wayne," Mira said as she led Maggie back to the center of the arena. She faced the bleachers and noticed the seat near the top was empty. "Where did Wayne go?"

"I don't know." Tabby shrugged as she sat down in a middle row. "He walked past me a couple of minutes ago saying he needed to get something."

"That's weird," Mira said as she moved the longe line to the other side of the horse's halter. She put thoughts of Wayne out of her mind and focused on the horse in front of her. "Okay, Maggie, let's go the other way this time. We don't want you to become one-sided."

The others laughed as she walked the mare to get her started, letting out a little of the rope at a time. As Mira took up a stationary position in the center of the arena, Wayne appeared at the gate. He had one hand behind his back and reached to open the gate with the other.

Had he lost his mind? Mira kept Maggie at a walk and hoped Lucas would keep him out of the way. "Wayne, what are you doing?"

"You're not working her properly." He started to bring his hand out from behind his back.

In a flash, Mira knew what he was hiding behind him and kept her voice as calm as possible to avoid upsetting the skittish horse. "No. Keep it out of sight."

"It's just a whip," Wayne said and held it up.

Maggie caught sight of it and whinnied shrilly as she jerked to a stop. She backed away from Wayne, tossing her head.

"Get it out of sight!" Mira focused on the frightened mare and hoped Wayne was smart enough to listen. "Easy now, Maggie. You're okay."

She crept toward the horse, gathering the longe line and speaking in soothing tones. Lucas stepped closer to offer assistance if needed. As Mira approached the quivering horse, Wayne lifted the whip again.

"What is so bad about a whip?" he asked, waving it a little.

Maggie reared. On her way back down, she kicked out with her forelegs. One hoof caught Mira's lower right leg. She gasped at the pain and bit her lip to keep from crying out and frightening the horse further.

Lucas closed the distance and took the longe line from Mira as she shifted all of her weight to her left leg. "Are you okay?"

"No," she whispered, tears blurring her vision.

Lucas glanced toward the worried group near the bleachers. "Come help her."

Akram entered the arena as Lucas led Maggie to the far end. He put Mira's arm across his shoulders and helped her hop out of the arena. Each step sent a new wave of pain through her leg, and she fought with everything in her not to make a sound that might spook Maggie. As they passed Wayne, she glared at him through her tears.

"You are an idiot."

He looked stunned as Akram helped her to the bleachers. Mira sat sideways on the bottom bench and stretched her right leg out on it, leaving her left foot on the floor. She leaned back until she lay flat and covered her eyes with her arm as if it could block out the pain searing up the bone in her lower leg. Someone straddled the bench above her head.

"Mira?" Tabby said hesitantly. "Are you okay?"

She lowered her arm and stared up into her friend's worried eyes. Then she felt her pants leg move. She sat up to see Akram lifting the cuff. "No, don't."

He stilled his hands and met her gaze. "It's okay. I worked my way through college as an EMT."

"But I have scars," she protested softly in Arabic, fresh tears filling her eyes.

"It's all right." His compassionate expression said he knew where they'd come from.

Zeina knelt beside her and put an arm around her shoulders. "Let him look. A few scars won't bother him or me."

Mira leaned against her, hating the position Wayne had put her in. Yet she knew she needed her leg checked. Sighing, she nodded. "Okay."

Akram lifted her pants leg. The place where the hoof had hit was already turning purple and swelling. He lowered the material, his expression serious. "You need to get that X-rayed."

Mira shook her head. "I don't like hospitals."

"There's a good chance it's broken. You need to have a doctor look at your leg."

Tabby whispered to Zeina, "What are they saying?"

Mira straightened and glanced back. Had her friend forgotten English?

Before she could ask, Zeina smiled. "You're speaking Arabic," she said in the same language, and then switched to English for the benefit of Tabby, Lucas, and Wayne as she repeated the conversation.

"I'll go get Mom," Tabby said after hearing Akram's opinion. She hurried off with Wayne close behind.

Maggie had calmed by then, and Lucas led her out of the arena. "I'll be back just as soon as I get this critter settled in her stall."

Once he was gone, Mira leaned against Zeina again. "I really hate hospitals."

"Why?"

Akram glanced at Mira's leg. "She spent a lot of time in one when she lived in Israel."

Despite her certainty that he knew the story behind her scars, Mira's heart raced. "How did you know?"

"Teta told me," he said with a small smile.

"She never told me." Zeina studied Mira. "What happened?"

"There was a bombing. That's what gave me the scars, too."

Before Zeina could respond, Tabby returned with her mother and Lucas. Della rushed to Mira's side, and Zeina moved out of the way.

"I am so sorry about this." Della smoothed a strand of hair away from Mira's eyes. "I've told Bill many times that horse was dangerous. I kept telling him we needed to get rid of it before someone got hurt."

Mira shook her head. "No, Wayne—"

She broke off as she struggled to remember the English words she needed.

"Wayne?" Confusion formed a furrow between Della's eyebrows. "He's bringing the car around."

"No! No, I—" She let loose a string of Arabic as tears of frustration sprang to her eyes.

"What is it, dear?" Della asked.

Mira shook her head and looked helplessly at Akram and Zeina. If they wouldn't translate for her, she wouldn't be able to communicate until she relaxed enough for her English skills returned.

"She can't think of the English words," Akram said to her relief. "What she was trying to tell you is that it's not Maggie's fault. Wayne was waving a whip around after Mira told him to keep it out of sight. The horse spooked and kicked."

"Oh, I see." Della's expression grew thoughtful, and she turned to her daughter. "Tabby, why don't you go get Mira's coat for her?"

"Okay, Mom."

She left, and Della walked over to Akram. "I know it is a terrible imposition, but would you be willing to come with us and translate for the doctor?"

"Of course," he said without hesitation. "I'm happy to help."

Tabby returned carrying Mira's coat and helped her put it on. A moment later, Wayne walked in. He had enough wisdom to stay well away from Mira as he turned to Della.

"I pulled the car up as close to the door as I could."

"Thank you, Wayne."

Twenty-One

Lucas and Akram acted as human crutches for Mira and helped her to the champagne luxury sedan parked outside. She sat in the back with her right leg stretched out across the seat. Akram rode in the front seat beside Della as she drove to the hospital. The vibration of the car was excruciating, and Mira spent the drive plotting ways to make Wayne understand just how much pain she was in because of his stupidity.

When Della pulled up at the emergency entrance, Akram went inside and returned a moment later pushing a wheelchair. He took Mira to check-in while Della parked the car. Having a guy she'd just met know so much about her would have been more awkward if he wasn't the grandson of Teta Nida, the old woman who had been like a grandmother to her in Israel.

The emergency room had few patients, so Mira went back almost immediately. Akram's presence helped her stay calm since he could understand her and knew her history. Not everyone understood why she still struggled seven years after the bombing that had killed her parents, but he seemed to get it.

Probably because his grandmother had given him more details than anyone else in this country knew.

The doctor arrived, and Akram translated Mira's answers to his questions. When the doctor examined her injured leg, her response needed no translation.

"I'm going to order some X-rays," the doctor said as he made a note on Mira's chart. "Someone will be here soon to take you to radiology."

He left the room, and Mira leaned back against the gurney as she willed the pain to subside.

Della patted her shoulder in a comforting manner. "How are you doing?"

Mira struggled to find the right words. "I hate hospital."

"I know, dear, but sometimes they're necessary."

"Yes," Mira said and sighed.

"You know," Akram said, "I've met some very nice people in hospitals."

Mira responded in Arabic, not caring if Della got upset that she couldn't understand. "So have I, but have you ever been in one for six weeks and spent most of that time crying because of the pain or sleeping because of the pain medication?"

"No, I can't say that I have," Akram said in English. "The most time I've spent in the hospital is when I was eleven and had my appendix removed, but that was only two days."

An orderly arrived and took Mira to the radiology department. As the radiologist positioned her leg for X-rays, she told him her opinion of the pain he was causing and him for causing it. Fortunately, he didn't understand Arabic.

By the time the doctor arrived to discuss what the X-rays showed, Mira wanted nothing more than to go home and take a nap. She had forgotten how exhausting extreme pain could be. The doctor smiled as Mira adjusted the ice pack a nurse had given her.

"I have good news," he said. "Your leg isn't broken, just badly bruised."

Della breathed a sigh of relief. "That *is* good news."

He nodded and returned his attention to Mira. "I want you to use crutches for the next couple of days and stay off that leg as much as possible. Keep it propped up and use ice to keep the swelling down. Take ibuprofen for the pain. If it isn't any better in a week, or if it gets worse, see your regular doctor. Do you have any questions?"

"Do you want to know what a badly bruised leg feels like?" she muttered in Arabic.

Akram smothered a laugh as the doctor turned to him for a translation. "She, uh, doesn't have any questions."

The doctor nodded as he focused on Mira again. "Okay, I'll sign the discharge papers, and you can go home. I must say, after seeing the X-rays, I'm surprised you can walk well enough to work with horses. It looks like your leg was basically shattered at some point."

"It was." Mira spoke in heavily accented English. "When I thirteen."

"It's a miracle you recovered fully from an injury like that." The doctor scribbled his signature on a form, and then he handed it and some other papers to her. "Remember to stay off that leg for a few days."

"Okay," she said as he left.

They rented a pair of crutches at the pharmacy. Mercifully, Della also bought ibuprofen and a bottle of water. Mira had a feeling the over-the-counter pain medication would be her best friend for the next few days.

By the time they reached the Montaigne estate, the painkiller had kicked in and Mira's leg had only a dull ache. A worried Lucas met the car when Della pulled up to the front door.

"What did the doctor say?" he asked as Akram helped Mira out of the car.

"Bad bruise," she said, standing on her good leg while she adjusted the height of the crutches.

"I'm glad that's all it is," Lucas said, clearly relieved. "How long are you on crutches?"

Mira shrugged. "Few days."

"That's not too bad." Lucas accepted the car keys Della handed him. "Miss Della, your husband is in his office waiting for you. He wants to know how Miss Mira is doing."

"I'll go talk him. Do you know if Josh and Brandon have returned?"

"Yes, I believe they're watching a movie with Tabby, Wayne, and Tabby's friend."

"Thank you, Lucas," Della said in a dismissive tone.

He slid behind the steering wheel and drove around the side of the house. Della led the way inside. Anita came around the corner as Akram closed the door. She took their coats and although she sent worried glances toward Mira, she didn't say a word. Della told her about the injury and the need to have ice packs ready at all times.

"Where are the children?" Della asked.

"Upstairs in the game room, ma'am," Anita said.

"Thank you, Anita." Della had the same dismissive tone she'd used with Lucas. The maid disappeared back the way she had come, and Della turned to Mira. "Can you get upstairs all right? I can have the others come down here."

"I can go upstairs." English got easier to speak with every passing moment, something she was grateful for. Regressing in her language skills had been frustrating beyond words.

"In that case, I'll go speak with Bill," Della said and headed down the hall behind the stairs.

Akram followed Mira as she began the slow, tedious task of going up stairs on crutches. "You seem to be remembering your English."

"Yeah, I remember most of it now. The pain isn't as bad, and I'm over the terror of thinking my leg was broken again." When they finally reached the second floor, she faced Akram with a sigh. "I hate crutches almost as much as I hate hospitals."

"You're only on them for a couple of days," he said unsympathetically. "You'll live."

"You are so mean to me," she said with a smile as she led the way toward the game room door.

Akram laughed. "Don't let Zeina hear you say that. She might yell at me for picking on you."

"Somehow, I doubt that." Zeina would likely be just as unsympathetic about the crutches.

"Mira?" Tabby called from the game room. "Is that you?"

"Yeah," she said as she and Akram entered the

room. Everyone looked concerned when they saw the crutches. "My leg's not broken, just bruised. I'm supposed to stay off it for the next few days."

Tabby's expression cleared. "That's a relief. I was so afraid you were going to come back in a cast or something."

"Nah, I'm too stubborn to let a little thing like getting kicked break my leg." She didn't want to admit she'd been afraid of the same thing. She'd been warned years ago that there were weak spots in the bone.

"Do you guys want to watch the rest of this movie with us?" Josh asked.

Mira glanced at Akram and received a nod. She turned back to Josh. "Sure."

Tabby and Zeina moved over on the sofa they shared, making room for Mira. Akram brought a footstool over so Mira could prop up her leg, and then he sat in the matching armchair.

They laughed their way through the rest of the comedy, making the occasional comment on the bad special effects and the stupidity of the main character. When the credits began to roll, Josh turned it off.

"What shall we do now?"

"Mira could introduce me to her friend," Brandon said with a glance at Akram.

"That's right, you weren't here earlier." She held her hand out toward Akram. "This is Akram Talhami, Zeina's brother. Akram, that's Brandon Zivney, Wayne's brother and Josh and Tabby's cousin."

Akram studied Brandon. "Are you related to Aaron Zivney of Zivney Industries?"

"He's our father. Wayne and I both work for him."

"I've done some consulting work at Zivney Industries."

Wayne leaned forward. "Who do you currently work for?"

"Digital Realms. I'm in charge of the graphics for our latest game."

Zeina rolled her eyes at Tabby and Mira. "Now they've done it. Akram will be speaking computer jargon soon."

Tabby laughed. "So will Josh. What do you say we leave the guys to their inevitable computer discussion and go find somewhere less technical?"

"Sounds good to me." Zeina glanced at Mira. "How about you?"

"Sure, why not?"

Tabby turned to the men, who were discussing graphics cards. "We'll see you guys later."

"Okay," Josh said without looking at her.

She grinned and the women headed out of the room. Once in the hallway, Tabby and Zeina laughed.

"What do you bet that in an hour or so one of them looks up and wonders where we went?" Tabby asked.

"Probably," Zeina said with a grin. "I know that when Akram gets started talking about computers, the real world kind of fades away."

"Trust me, the other three have the same problem." Tabby led the way around the corner in the hall.

Mira smiled, remembering young men with a similar problem. "I knew some guys in West Virginia that once they started talking about crops and livestock it was almost impossible to get them to stop."

"It's got to be a guy thing," Zeina said.

"I don't know," Tabby said as she opened the door to her room. "I've met some girls who can be pretty focused. Or maybe obsessed would be a better word."

They laughed as they followed Tabby inside. She turned on her stereo to provide quiet background music, and then perched in the window seat. Zeina sat in the chair. Mira got Tabby's permission to stretch out on the bed with her right leg propped up on a pillow.

Zeina gave her a curious look. "Tabby says you just moved here recently."

"That's right." What else had Tabby told her? "I came here Friday."

"What do you think of Dayton so far?"

"It's not too bad. Bigger than what I'm used to and things seem to move a lot faster."

"Where did you live before you came here?"

"Just outside a small town in West Virginia. Most of the town's population lives on farms or in cabins in the woods."

"Dayton would be quite a change from that."

"Oh, it is," Tabby said. "But the area Mira's from is so pretty and peaceful."

Curiosity filled Zeina's face. "Have you spent much time down there?"

"My family used to spend every summer there. We have a cabin near where Mira lived. My parents were good friends with her cousins, so I got to meet her the first summer she was here."

Mira laughed at the memory. "That was an interesting experience. I could barely speak English, but somehow we managed to have a lot of fun together."

"And get a bad case of poison ivy doing it," Tabby

added with a grin.

They talked about their childhood adventures for a while. Zeina was in the middle of relating a disastrous attempt to make a cake when Mira covered yawn.

"Are you tired?" Zeina asked.

"A little. The pain and the stress of going to the emergency room wore me out." She sat up and stretched her arms above her head. "If y'all don't mind, I think I need a nap."

"That's fine. Mr. Montaigne invited Akram and me to stay for dinner so we'll probably still be here when you wake up."

Mira recalled the schedule Della had given her and turned to Tabby. "I thought your parents had a dinner to go to tonight."

"They did, but after Dad heard about you getting hurt, he decided they would stay home with us instead."

"They don't have to do that." Guilt washed over her for ruining their plans.

"I know, but they want to."

"All right, if they insist." If they wanted to give up their evening because their nephew got her kicked by a horse, that was their decision. She stood with the aid of her crutches. "I'll see you guys later."

She went to her room and found Frank lying in the middle of her bed. He blinked sleepily and meowed.

"Move over, cat." She sat on the edge of the bed and laid her crutches on the floor. "You're getting a nap buddy."

Twenty-Two

Mira laughs as her father teases her mother about the bright purple musical note earrings she bought earlier. A couple of her mother's friends watch with amusement across the outdoor table at a restaurant in Jerusalem.

"Hey, Dad, can we go see the Western Wall after lunch?" Mira asks.

"We're way ahead of you," he says with a smile. "Your mother and I had already planned to take you there."

"Thank you!" She jumps up from her seat and throws her arms around him in a hug.

"You know, we can see the Western Wall from our apartment," Hannah Cohen says.

"Really?" Mira straightens and studies her mother's friend. "What does it look like at night when it's dark out?"

"They have bright lights aimed at the wall. And even at night, people visit the wall to pray."

"That is so cool," she says as a man in a heavy coat stops close by.

A deafening bang shatters the air. Mira is thrown to the ground, and her father falls on top of her. Pain sears through her legs, and she cries out...

Mira's eyes shot open, and she gasped. Her heart pounded as her gaze darted around the room. Where had her father gone?

When she spotted a large gray cat staring at her with a startled expression, she remembered where she was. It had only been a dream.

Tears spilled from her eyes as the pain of losing her parents in such a violent manner hit her harder than it had in a long time. Not only had she become an orphan in an instant, she'd spent the next several weeks fighting for her life and recovering from traumatic injuries with no one for moral support other than the doctors and nurses. No one from the village had been allowed entry into Israel, and the only people she'd known in the country had died with her parents.

A knock on the door made her jump, and she sucked in a breath as she sat up. "Yes?"

The door swung open, and Josh peered in. "Dinner is in a few minutes."

"All right." She took another shaky breath and tried to dry her eyes without drawing attention to the action.

She knew she'd failed when Josh's brow furrowed. "Are you okay?"

"I'm fine." She forced a smile that felt about as genuine as counterfeit currency. "Why do you ask?"

"It's obvious you've been crying. That tends to indicate something is wrong."

She scooped Frank into her arms, his warm furry body providing much-needed comfort. "I'm okay. I just had a bad dream."

"Must have been some dream." Josh clearly didn't believe she was all right as he came the rest of the way into the room. "Do you want to talk about it?"

He deserved some kind of explanation, but talking about that day hurt. She hugged the cat close as her eyes flooded. "I guess you could say it was more of a memory of when my parents were killed."

He sat down beside her on the bed. "I bet that was terrifying."

"It was." She set Frank in her lap and stroked his silky fur, trying hard not to think about what she said. "We were talking about the Western Wall, and then there was an explosion. My father fell on top of me, but the pain in my legs..."

Her voice trailed off as she remembered. Josh held her as she cried, and Frank licked her face, trying to comfort her. Once the tears stopped, she drew in a shuddering breath and wiped the moisture from her cheeks as she straightened.

"I'm sorry." She couldn't believe she'd broken down in front of him like that. "It's been so long since I had that nightmare. I guess it caught me by surprise."

"You don't have to apologize. I can't begin to understand how frightening that day must have been. I would imagine that you still feel almost as scared when you remember it."

"I do. And it's not just the fear. Losing both my parents so suddenly and in such a horrible way is still hard to think about, even after seven years."

"I'd believe it. That was a very traumatic event."

He didn't know the half of it.

Brandon appeared in the open doorway. "Hey, did you guys get lost? Everyone's downstairs waiting."

"Sorry." Mira set Frank beside her and swung her

legs over the side of the bed. "You guys go ahead. I'll be down in a few minutes."

"We'll wait," Josh said as she picked up her crutches and swung her way to the bathroom.

As she closed the door, she heard Brandon speak quietly to his cousin.

"Is she okay? She looks like she's been crying."

She didn't hear Josh's response as she turned on the water and washed her face. A few minutes later, she opened the door and reentered her bedroom. Both men waited near the door to the hall. They let her set the pace toward the stairs, and she offered them a smile.

"You guys didn't have to wait for me."

"Sure, we did," Josh said.

"Yeah, it would have been rude of us to make you come downstairs alone," Brandon added.

Mira gave a little laugh. "Going down stairs on crutches takes a while. We're all going to be late if you walk with me."

"Don't worry about it." Josh grinned, humor twinkling in his eyes. "We'll just say we're fashionably late."

"You know, there's one thing I've never understood about the phrase 'fashionably late,'" she said as they descended the stairs.

"What's that?" Brandon asked.

"How can being late be fashionable? I was always taught that being late is rude."

He paused and exchanged a glance with Josh before continuing down the stairs. "I have no idea. Aunt Della would be the best person to ask. She knows all kinds of things like that."

"I'll wait for a quiet moment." She already knew she would never ask. With her luck, admitting ignorance about a common phrase would break some stupid rule of society she'd never heard of. The fewer of those rules she broke in front of Della, the better.

They finally reached the first floor, and Mira swung along at a more normal pace. Brandon led the way to the family dining room, where the others were already seated and waiting. Josh held the empty chair beside Zeina for Mira. Then he and Brandon took the other two empty seats at the table.

"I'm sorry we're late," Mira said.

"That's quite all right, dear." Della waved off the apology as Anita and the temporary maid served the meal.

Small talk dominated the conversation as everyone shared their plans for Thanksgiving and discussed past holiday celebrations. About halfway through dinner, Mira spotted Wayne watching her. Was he trying to figure out how angry he'd made her by ignoring her instructions in the stable? She would be more than happy to tell him if she ever had a chance to talk to him alone.

His gaze darted away from her. A moment later, he excused himself from the table and left the room.

He stayed gone long enough for Mira to wonder if he would return. Had she scared him off? She hadn't meant to. Her irritation had started to fade the moment the doctor said her leg wasn't broken.

When he resumed his seat at the table, he started a conversation with Akram. Mira considered saying something to him, but she decided against it.

Everything she could think of was better left to a private conversation without an audience.

Shortly after Anita served slices of apple pie, the dull ache in Mira's leg intensified to a painful throb. She laid her napkin beside her dessert plate and reached for her crutches. As she shifted to stand, a sharp pain shot through her leg causing her to wince.

Bill set his fork down. "Are you all right, Mira?"

Everyone looked at her, making her wish she'd never moved.

"I'm fine," she said, rising and adjusting her hold on her crutches. "The ibuprofen wore off, and I need to take some more. I'll be right back."

She went down the hall and entered the kitchen where Charlotte and Anita were cleaning up.

"Hey, is there any ibuprofen down here that I could take?" Mira asked as they turned toward her. "I don't want to have to go all the way upstairs to take some."

"Sure, honey." Charlotte dried her hands on a kitchen towel lying on the counter. "I'll go get it for you."

"Thanks, Charlotte."

The cook disappeared into the pantry and returned a moment later carrying a small plastic bottle. She handed it to Mira as the doorbell chimed. Anita went to answer it, and Charlotte filled a glass with water.

"Here you go," she said, handing it over. "Is your leg bothering you much?"

Mira swallowed a couple of tablets before answering. "Some, but once the ibuprofen kicks in it won't be too bad. I'll probably ice it before I go to bed tonight."

Anita returned carrying a colorful bouquet of

flowers in a cut glass vase. Charlotte walked over and leaned close to sniff the blossoms.

"These are gorgeous!"

"They're for Mira," Anita said with a big smile.

"For me?" Shock coursed through her. "Who would send me flowers?"

"Read the card and find out." Anita set the vase on the island in front of her.

Mira slipped the card out of the envelope and looked at the handwritten message. She studied it for a moment, wishing for all she was worth that she could decipher the words. Admitting defeat, she set the card on the counter beside the vase.

"Well?" Anita said. "Who are they from?"

"I don't know." Heat crept into Mira's cheeks.

Anita's eyebrows drew together. "Doesn't it say?"

"I don't know." Why did her biggest shame have to be thrust into the light?

Charlotte scrutinized her. "What do you mean, you don't know?"

Mira heard footsteps in the hall and hoped it was Bill. Anyone else in the family learning her secret was beyond humiliating. "I can't read it. I can read Arabic and Hebrew just fine, but I never learned to read English."

"Oh, honey." Charlotte came and put an arm around her. "I can help you learn, if you'd like."

"Thanks, Charlotte." The relief was overwhelming. Unlike so many people back in West Virginia, her friends here weren't the type to ridicule her for not knowing how to read English.

"Would you like me to read the card to you?" Anita

asked.

"That won't be necessary."

Wayne's voice made Mira cringe.

He came the rest of the way into the room. "Would you excuse us?"

Charlotte gave Mira a quick hug before leaving the kitchen with Anita. Mira stayed where she was, staring at the countertop as she worked to wipe all traces of embarrassment from her face. Wayne walked around to the other side of the island and stood directly across from her.

"I sent the flowers to you."

He what? She looked up, stunned, as he reached for the card and began to read.

"Mira, I am so sorry you got hurt because of my stupidity. Please forgive me. Wayne."

She studied the four different kinds of flowers filling the vase. Did he know what kind of flowers he'd sent? She shifted her gaze back to Wayne. "Is that really what it says?"

"Yes, and I mean every word of it." The sincerity in his voice matched the expression in his eyes.

She glanced at the flowers again, warmth spreading through her. "I should have known."

"Excuse me?" His brow furrowed.

"Feverfew, calendula, Echinacea..." She touched the blooms as she came to them. "They're healing plants."

"Healing plants?"

"Yes, they're all plants used for healing various ailments." She touched another flower. "This is a zinnia. You had no way of knowing, but Marnie planted zinnias in front of the cabin every spring."

"I sent healing flowers to apologize and try to fix a friendship I ruined before it had a chance to start?"

"Yes, that's exactly what you did." Mira met his gaze with a smile, all of her previous irritation gone. "And I think it's sweet. Thank you."

"You're welcome." He studied her, uncertainty shining in his eyes. "So, can we start over?"

She tilted her head and considered the possibility. "Yeah, I think we can. Just listen to me the next time I'm working with a horse."

"Trust me, I will," Wayne said with a relieved smile. He glanced toward the hall. "I guess we should go back into the dining room."

She hesitated, her eyes drawn to the card he'd laid on the counter. "Um, the others don't know I can't read English. You, Anita, and Charlotte are the only ones here that know."

"I won't say a word. But if you want to know what something says, just ask."

Twenty-Three

After Zeina and Akram went home, Mira wandered into the music room and sat in a straight-backed chair next to the table holding her borrowed violin. In a matter of minutes, she had the violin tuned and the bow rosined. She played bits and pieces of music, not completing any one song, her thoughts as fragmented as the bone in her leg had been before the doctors pinned it together.

Bill same into the room as she began yet another piece. She lowered the violin, and he pulled up a chair and sat facing her.

"How is your leg doing?" he asked.

Mira shrugged. "Okay, I guess. It aches, but it does that sometimes anyway."

"Della tells me the doctor was surprised that you can walk because your leg was shattered at some point." Bill's curiosity about the healed injury was evident in his gaze.

"Yeah." She set the violin and bow on the table beside her. "The explosion in Jerusalem broke my leg in several places. The doctors had to pin the pieces together so the bone would heal straight. They said my legs had been so damaged that I would never walk again. I decided to prove them wrong. When I arrived in this country, I was in a wheelchair. With Harley and Marnie's help and a lot of physical therapy, I learned to walk with crutches."

"I didn't realize you had been here that long when we first met you."

"I'd lived in West Virginia for the better part of a year. I was supposed to be using crutches when I met you, but when I saw Tabby and Josh walking and running, I decided I wanted to be normal too. So, I only used the crutches at home and didn't bring them to your cabin."

"I had wondered about your limp. All Harley would tell me was that you had been in an accident."

"Yes, I know." She smiled when his eyebrows rose. "He told me you asked."

"Somehow, knowing Harley, that doesn't surprise me," Bill said with a fond smile. "So, how are you adjusting to life here in Dayton?"

"I don't know," Mira said with a shrug. "Okay, I guess. Things are a lot different here. Believe it or not, it's the little things that are the hardest to get used to."

His eyebrows drew together in puzzlement. "What do you mean?"

"Well, having someone else wash my laundry for me instead of doing it myself, for one thing." She'd been so surprised when Anita came to collect towels and dirty clothes that morning. "And having someone else do all the cooking and cleaning. I always helped Marnie with that stuff, and I helped my mom before that. It's strange not doing it."

Bill nodded, his expression full of understanding. "Yes, I can see how it would be difficult to adjust. We have a completely different way of life from the one you're used to."

"Yeah. I'm trying to learn how things work around here, but it's hard." Mira sighed. Just the thought of how much she still needed to learn was exhausting. "I think the hardest part is knowing that for the first time I can remember, I won't be in the kitchen helping cook for a holiday."

"Well, if there's something you would like to make, just tell Charlotte. I'm sure she'd be willing to share the kitchen with you."

"I know, but it's not the same." She sighed again, missing her previous life more than usual. "I appreciate everything you and Della are doing for me, but I miss home and I miss my family. The problem is I don't have a family or a home to go back to."

Tears stung her eyes at the admission, and Bill laid a comforting hand on her shoulder. "Mira, you do have a family, right here. Josh and Tabby both think of you as a sister."

She already knew that; she'd heard it often enough. "What about you and Della?"

"Today, when Maggie kicked you and you needed x-rays, both Della and I were as worried about you as we were about Josh when he fell out of a tree and broke his arm." Sincerity filled his gaze, and he lowered his hand. "We feel as protective of you as we do Tabby and Josh. Mira, you've become another daughter to us."

Silence filled the room as she considered his

statements. "So...you're kind of like a father to me and Della is kind of a mother?"

A hint of a smile lifted the corners of his mouth. "Yes, if you would like to consider us as such."

An interesting idea, especially given Della's statements when she introduced her nephews. "Do I tell people I live here? Or do I say I'm visiting?"

"I don't see any reason not to say you live here."

"Then why did Della tell Wayne and Brandon that I'm just visiting?"

"I don't know." The perplexity in his voice matched the confusion on his face. "I'll speak with her about it later."

"So, what do I tell people like your relatives that are coming?"

"Tell them whatever you're comfortable telling them. Like I told you this morning, this is your home now."

If she were truly in her own home and had a bunch of relatives coming in for a holiday, what would she do? "Can I cook lunch tomorrow?"

Bill's eyebrows shot up toward his graying hair. "Why, I suppose that would be all right, but I don't want you to feel like you have to."

"It's not that. I've been eating fancy meals since I came here, some of which I couldn't identify. Don't get me wrong, it's all been really good, but I'd like to eat something simple and familiar."

He nodded. "Okay, just leave a note on the kitchen counter to let Charlotte know you'll be cooking. That way she'll know not to prepare anything."

"I'll go do that," Mira said and began to loosen her bow.

"All right." He stood and met her gaze. "I have some work to finish, so I'll be in my office for a little while if you want to talk more."

"Okay." She closed her violin case. "Oh, Bill?"

"Yes?"

"How many people will be here for lunch?" She stood and adjusted her crutches.

"You'd better plan on at least fifteen people. I know for sure there will be ten, but I'm not sure how many of our relatives will arrive in time for lunch, if any."

"Okay. I'll make plenty," she said as they left the music room. Her thoughts were already on how to write note in a language she couldn't read. *Wayne.*

Bill went into his office, and Mira stepped into the library. Empty. Where was Wayne likely to spend the evening? She made a quick search of the downstairs and found it empty as well. As she slowly went up the stairs, laughter drifted out of the game room. She peeked inside and found Brandon, Tabby, and Josh playing a board game, but Wayne was absent. She backed away from the door, thankful the others hadn't seen her.

Heading down the hall, Mira tried to figure out the least embarrassing way to ask Wayne to write the note for Charlotte. By the time she reached the room he was sharing with his brother, she still hadn't come up with anything. Taking a deep breath, she knocked on the door. Wayne opened it and his eyes widened.

"Hey, Wayne." She shifted under his gaze, fighting back a flutter of nerves. "I hope I'm not bothering you."

"Not at all. I was just checking my e-mail," he said, waving toward the open laptop on the desk. "What's up?"

"I have a favor to ask."

"Okay..."

She drew in a calming breath. "Could you write a note for Charlotte to let her know I want to cook lunch tomorrow? Bill told me to leave a note on the counter, but she wouldn't be able to read anything I write."

"Sure, no problem." He smiled and opened the door wider. "Come on in and tell me what you want to say."

Mira followed him to the desk and watched as he pulled out a piece of paper and a pen. "I'm not sure what it should say. I just need to let her know she doesn't need to plan anything for lunch."

Wayne thought for a moment. "What about this? 'Charlotte, I'd like to fix lunch for everyone. Don't worry about planning anything, I already have something in mind. Mira.'"

She nodded. "That sounds good."

"All right." He quickly wrote the note and handed it to her. "There you go."

"Thanks, Wayne." She looked at the writing on the page, her mind racing. "How hard do you think it would be for me to learn to read and write English?"

"I have no idea." He glanced toward his computer. "Would you like to start learning now?"

Mira bit her lip, desperately wanting to say yes. Not knowing how to read English was driving her nuts. "I don't want to bother you."

"It's not a bother." He pulled out the desk chair. "Why don't you sit here, and I'll show you a few words?"

"Okay." She settled in the offered chair and laid her

crutches on the floor.

Wayne pulled over another chair and sat beside her. He closed the e-mail program and opened another program. "This is a word processing program. It's for writing letters, reports, or whatever." He looked at Mira and lifted an eyebrow. "Have you ever used a computer?"

"Only a few times since coming to the US. I used one often before I immigrated."

"Okay, I was just wondering." He typed something and glanced at her. "What do you think that says?"

She studied the screen for a moment. "That's my name."

Suspicion crept into Wayne's gaze. "I thought you said you couldn't read English."

She laughed. "I can't, but my name is on my driver's license so I know what it looks like."

"You have a driver's license?"

"Yeah. Harley and Marnie wanted me to have the freedom to go into town whenever I wanted, so they helped me get a license."

"That's cool." Wayne glanced at his computer. "Why don't I show you a few more words?"

He left her name at the top of the screen as he typed. Mira stared at her name and realized she had seen it somewhere other than her driver's license and translated birth certificate. She just couldn't remember where.

Wayne pointed out some of the words he had typed, but he stopped talking when she didn't respond. "Is something wrong?"

"I don't know," Mira said, turning toward him. "I

know I've seen my name somewhere other than on my driver's license, but I can't remember where."

"Maybe on your birth certificate?"

"Yeah, but I've seen it somewhere else." The memory lurked just beyond the edge of recall, leaving her frustrated. "I wish I could remember."

"Hm... That is a bit of a puzzle," Wayne said, his gaze sympathetic. "Maybe if you think about something else for a while you'll remember."

"Maybe."

For the next twenty minutes, Wayne typed simple words and helped Mira learn how each letter sounded. Excitement filled her as she sounded out the last two words by herself. Maybe she could learn to read English after all.

"You're a good teacher," she said as Wayne exited the word processing program.

He smiled as he closed his computer. "You're a fast learner. How come you didn't try to learn to read before this?"

"I had too many other things to learn. And I'm not sure how well Harley and Marnie could read."

"Well, as quickly as you picked up on it tonight, you'll be reading as well as I do in no time."

Oh, how she would love that! "I don't know how I can thank you for helping me out."

He waved away her gratitude. "Don't worry about it. I always thought it would be cool to be a teacher. I should thank you for giving me the chance to find out if I was right."

Did that mean he'd enjoyed helping her? "I still feel like I ought to do something to repay you."

"Well, since you feel the need to do something, go out with me," Wayne said with a perfectly straight face.

Her heart skipped a beat. She had to have misheard him. "What?"

"Go to dinner with me and maybe a movie or something."

She'd heard right. Her pulse picked up speed like a raccoon with a coonhound on its trail. "But how does that thank you?"

"It would be an honor to spend one evening alone with someone as beautiful and intelligent as you." He flashed her a charming smile. "That would be the most perfect way to thank me."

He couldn't be serious...could he? Regardless of his intentions, she'd insisted on doing something for him. "I guess I could."

He grinned, pleasure lighting up his blue eyes. "Great! How does Saturday sound?"

Too soon? "Okay, I guess."

"I'll make reservations."

"Okay." Mira picked up the note she had laid on the desk, ready to escape and figure out what had just happened. "I better take this to the kitchen."

Wayne took the note from her. "I'll do it. That way you don't have to navigate the stairs again tonight."

"Thanks. I appreciate it." One more reason to repay his kindness by going out with him.

She grabbed her crutches and led the way out of the room. Tabby, Josh, and Brandon stood talking at the other end of the hallway. All three looked surprised to see Wayne and Mira together.

She put a smile on her face as she reached them

and hoped they couldn't see the heat creeping into her cheeks. She would rather not have to explain her sudden date with Wayne.

"Hey, I'm going to turn in for the night," she said. "I'll see y'all in the morning."

The men bade her good night, but Tabby followed her to her room. Mira sat on the edge of her bed and laid her crutches on the floor as Tabby closed the door.

Someone had placed her flowers on the desk. The memory of Wayne's apology brought a smile Mira quickly hid. Tabby would ask too many questions if she showed any emotion.

"I see you and Wayne are getting along now," Tabby said, coming to sit beside Mira.

So much for not having to explain anything tonight. "He apologized, and when he's not trying to impress anyone, he's a pretty nice guy."

Tabby studied her. "There's more, isn't there? You look kind of strange."

"Well, something kind of strange did happen." She still couldn't believe what had happened, but suddenly she wanted to tell someone.

"What?"

"Wayne asked me out." Mira laughed when Tabby's eyes widened and her jaw dropped. "Now you're looking strange."

"He asked you out?" Tabby repeated as though she couldn't believe it. "What did you say?"

"I said okay, and he said he'd make reservations."

"When's your date? And where are you going?"

"We're going out Saturday, but I don't know where we're going. Wayne said something about dinner, but other than that I don't know what we'll do."

"This is so cool!" Tabby squealed and gave her a hug. She sat back and gazed at her thoughtfully. "A little weird, but cool."

Not the most comforting statement when she was already nervous about her date. "How is it weird?"

"Wayne started out being annoying. Then he acted stupid, and you got hurt because of it. Every time you saw him after that, you looked like you wanted to kill him. Then you left during dessert, and Wayne followed you, and you both came back civil toward each other."

"Wayne sent me those." Mira pointed to the vase of flowers sitting on her desk. She might as well own up to the reason for their sudden friendship. "They arrived during dessert. He and I talked and decided to start over."

A teasing sparkle appeared in Tabby's eyes. "Since you have a date Saturday, I'd say starting over worked out pretty well."

Heat flooded Mira's cheeks. "Yeah, I guess it did."

"So, what were you doing in his room?"

"We were just talking, and he showed me something on his computer." Mira lifted an eyebrow. "You're asking a lot of questions. Is it really that interesting, or are you just being nosy?"

Tabby's face flushed. "I'm just being nosy, but it's only because my cousin wants to take one of my best friends on a date."

"In that case, I guess you have a right to be nosy."

Twenty-Four

Mira walked into the kitchen early Wednesday morning and received a big smile from Charlotte.

"I got your note, honey. May I ask what you have in mind?"

The cook seemed curious rather than irritated, and relief flowed through Mira. "Stew and biscuits. I figure I might as well use some of the food I brought, and I think everyone will like the stew."

"That sounds good. I hope you don't mind if I watch you cook. I've never made stew with dried ingredients."

A lot of people hadn't. Mira herself had only learned the recipe from Marnie a couple of years ago. "Of course I don't mind. Since everything's dried, I'll have to put it on to cook soon if we want it ready in time for lunch."

"Leave me one burner to cook breakfast, and the rest of the stove is yours."

Mira laughed. How did this woman make stew? "I only need one burner, Charlotte. Well, I need a big pot, too."

"Do you want it before or after breakfast?"

She checked the clock on the wall and saw that it was already after seven. "I'll get the stew started and then eat."

Charlotte set a huge pot on the stove. "What else do you need, honey? I'll get it for you so you don't have to try to carry it on crutches."

"Let's see..." She ran the simple recipe through her mind and considered the ingredients she'd brought with her. "I'll need the jerky, potatoes, carrots, onions, peas, sage, thyme, and rosemary. I'll also need salt and pepper and a lot of water."

"Okay, I'll be right back." Charlotte disappeared into the pantry.

She returned carrying a stack of plastic storage boxes. After setting them on the counter next to the stove, she went back to the pantry to retrieve the herbs. Mira opened the box of venison jerky and began breaking it into small pieces, which she tossed into the pot. Charlotte set the bottles of herbs on the counter and picked up a piece of jerky.

Mira glanced at the cook as she tossed a handful of bite-sized pieces of dried meat into the pot. "You don't have to help."

"I know." Charlotte continued breaking up the jerky.

Mira smiled and shook her head. Well, she'd never complained about having help in the kitchen, and she wasn't about to start now. Not when she had to make enough stew for fifteen people.

They continued breaking up the jerky until about three pounds of the dried meat sat in the bottom of the pot. Mira threw in a couple of pounds each of carrots, peas, and potatoes, then tossed in a handful of dried onions. Charlotte carried over water as Mira added salt and pepper and crumbled some of the thyme, sage, and rosemary into the pot as well. Soon, water covered the dried ingredients, and Mira stirred the pot with a sturdy wooden spoon as she waited for it to come to a boil.

"I can tell you've cooked for a large group before," Charlotte said as Mira set the spoon aside and covered the pot.

She turned the burner down to a simmer and smiled. "Yeah, every fall during harvest, and the occasional holiday."

"Do you come from a large family?" Charlotte asked as she went to work browning sausage in a large cast iron skillet.

"No, I'm an only child. But every fall, all the farmers in the area help each other bring in the crops. It's the responsibility of the women on each farm to provide meals for the men. It's amazing how much they can eat during the harvest."

"What about the holidays? Did you have a lot of relatives come to visit?"

"Not really," Mira said, taking a seat at the counter. "Mostly it was other families in the area."

Bill walked into the kitchen, preventing further conversation. He took an appreciative sniff of the herb-scented air and looked at the cook.

"Charlotte, what do I smell?"

"It could be the sausage gravy I'm working on," she said, turning to face her employer.

He sniffed again and shook his head. "It isn't

sausage."

"Then it must be the venison stew Miss Mira is preparing for lunch."

"Well, it smells wonderful."

Hopefully, everyone would think it tasted just as good. Mira shrugged off the faint worry and smiled. "That's just the rosemary, sage, and thyme. In a couple of hours, you'll smell the venison, too."

"I may not make it until lunch," Bill said with a chuckle.

"What can I fix for your breakfast, Mr. Montaigne?" Charlotte asked.

He glanced at the sizzling skillet beside the steaming pot on the stove. "The sausage gravy you mentioned sounds good."

"It will be about fifteen or twenty minutes, then," Charlotte said. "I still need to make the biscuits to go with it."

"That's fine."

Mira turned on her stool to watch Charlotte retrieve a glass mixing bowl from one of the cabinets. "Do you want me to make the biscuits?"

"No, I'll make them, honey. You go sit down, and I'll bring your breakfast just as soon as it's ready."

"Okay." She grabbed her crutches and slid off the stool.

She followed Bill into the family dining room and took a seat on one side. After a brief exchange of small talk, Bill picked up the newspaper lying at his place at the head of the table.

As she looked at the paper, Mira suddenly remembered where she had seen her name. Shortly after

Harley and Marnie's accident, she had been looking in Harley's desk and found a folder in the bottom of one of the drawers. There had been newspaper clippings and important-looking papers inside, several of which had contained her name. She'd planned on taking the papers to her friend Sally the next day to find out if they were as important as they looked, but that night Harley's relatives had come to clean out the desk. They had taken every scrap of paper, including the folder with the newspaper clippings.

Charlotte brought coffee in and served Bill first. After placing a cup of the steaming brew in front of Mira, she headed back to the kitchen. Mira watched Bill lower the paper and take a sip of coffee.

As he replaced his cup on the saucer, he gave her a questioning look. "Everything okay, Mira? You look like you have something on your mind."

She drew in a steadying breath, hoping he could help her. "Do you know of any important-looking papers that would have my name on them?"

"Not right off hand." His eyebrows drew together. "Why?"

"I was going through Harley's desk after he and Marnie died, and I found a folder full of newspaper clippings and important-looking papers. I kept seeing my name in those papers. Last night I saw my name and remembered seeing it somewhere before, but I couldn't figure out where. This morning I remembered the papers."

Bill studied her. "Do I want to know why you seem surprised to remember what your name looks like?"

A blush burned across her face, and she looked at

her coffee, unable to meet his gaze as she made the admission. "I, um, can't read English. Before those papers, the only places I'd seen my name in English were on my driver's license and my translated birth certificate when I first came to the United States."

"I see." He folded his paper and set it aside. "How did you come to see your name last night?"

"Wayne was teaching me a little about reading English, and he showed me my name." How would Bill react to that piece of information? Not too badly, she hoped.

"Wayne was teaching..." His voice trailed off, and he waved his hand as if to chase the thought away. "Never mind. We can talk about that later. Where are the papers now?"

"I don't know. Harley's kin came and cleaned out the desk the same day I found the papers."

While Bill sipped his coffee with a thoughtful expression, Charlotte brought their breakfast in and set it on the table.

"Thanks." Mira studied the fluffy biscuits smothered with creamy gravy. "This looks delicious."

The cook beamed. "Thank you, Miss Mira."

"You're welcome, Charlotte." She met the woman's gaze, her mind drifting to lunch. "Could you do me a favor?"

"Of course. What do you need?"

"The stew probably needs some more water added. Could you add enough so it's at the same level it was before?"

"Sure, honey."

"Thank you," Mira said as the cook left the room.

She turned back to Bill and found him watching her with a smile. "Charlotte seems to like you."

"I guess so," she said with a shrug. "She's nice to me at least."

He ate a few bites of his breakfast before continuing their previous conversation. "Do you remember seeing any dates on those papers?"

Mira ate a bite of gravy-covered biscuit and tried to remember. "A few. Some were dated a few years before I came to this country. Some of them were dated the same year, and I think a couple were more recent than that."

"Well, at least some of those papers probably had to do with Harley and Marnie taking guardianship of you. Do you know if you're a US citizen?"

"I'm pretty sure I am since my mom was American, but I was still recovering from the explosion and losing my parents when I came here." She shoved away the encroaching memories and focused on the current conversation. "Everything from my first year with Harley and Marnie is kind of hazy."

"That's perfectly understandable." Bill took another sip of coffee. "I would guess that any papers pertaining to your citizenship were in that folder. It's the papers dated while you were still in Israel that I can't even guess on."

Mira sighed; it had been worth a shot. "I was afraid of that. I wish I knew what those papers were."

"I'll tell you what," Bill said, determination filling his voice. "Next week, I'll see if I can find out what they might have been."

Her heart skipped a beat. "You can do that?"

"I can *try.*" He obviously didn't want her too optimistic about his chances. "I don't guarantee I'll find anything, but I'll do what I can."

That was still more than she could have hoped for. "Thank you. I appreciate it more than you know."

Mira spent most of the morning in the kitchen, loving the familiarity of the scents and the warmth of the atmosphere. She added water to the stew a few times and managed to convince Charlotte to let her help with the preparations for the next day's feast.

About the middle of the morning, as Mira made a pie crust, Della brought a middle-aged couple into the kitchen. Charlotte stood nearby working on another pie, and Mira was grateful for her presence. This new couple looked like they could buy half of Dayton and not feel it at all.

Della led them closer. "Mira, I'd like you to meet my brother, Aaron, and his wife, Brenda. They're Brandon and Wayne's parents."

She shoved her first impression aside and gave them a friendly smile. "It's nice to meet you."

"Della tells me you play the violin," Aaron said.

She hoped he didn't want a recital. Playing for him would be more intimidating than playing for Maryann had been. "Yes, I do, but I'm better at folk music than classical violin."

"I'd like to hear you play sometime, if I may." So much for no recital. "Thanks to Della, I learned to appreciate the violin."

Mira breathed a mental sigh of relief at the chance to move the topic away from herself. "She plays really well."

Della raised her elegantly curved eyebrows. "When did you hear me play?"

Oops. She'd forgotten Della didn't know about that. "The other day. The same day you found out I can play."

Charlotte took the completed pie crust in front of Mira and began to pour in the spiced pumpkin filling.

Mira watched for a second. "You know, I could have done that."

"I'm sure you could have, Miss Mira," Charlotte said, never pausing in her task. "Why don't you go talk with Miss Della and Mr. and Mrs. Zivney? I'll keep an eye on the stew for you."

She didn't want to leave the comfort and security of the kitchen, but she knew she didn't have a choice. "Okay, Charlotte. I'll be back to make the biscuits."

"Yes, Miss Mira."

Mira dusted the flour from her hands and removed the apron protecting her sweater and blue jeans. As she reached for her crutches, Della turned to her brother and sister-in-law.

"Shall we retire to the living room?"

"Some tea while we talk would be lovely." Brenda shot a pointed look at the cook.

"That does sound nice," Della said. "Charlotte, please have Anita bring tea to us."

"Yes, Miss Della."

"Thank you, Charlotte."

Mira hung back as the others left the kitchen. "Should I be worried that Mrs. Zivney hasn't said a word to me?"

"I don't think so," Charlotte whispered back as she reached for a teapot. "Now, go on and be sociable."

"Yes, ma'am."

As Charlotte threatened to swat her with a dish towel, Mira grinned and left the room as quickly as her crutches could carry her.

Twenty-Five

Mira caught up with the others outside the living room. Aaron excused himself to go talk with Bill, leaving the three women alone. Della and Brenda gracefully seated themselves on one of the sofas, and Mira—somewhat less gracefully—lowered herself into a facing chair.

As the two older women spoke of fundraisers and mutual acquaintances, Mira wished could have stayed in the kitchen. This type of thing was so far out of her realm of experience that she couldn't even see it.

After Anita served the tea and left the room, Brenda said, "So, Mira, tell me about yourself."

The woman's superior tone took Mira to a whole new level of discomfort. "I'm not sure what you want to know."

"Who are your parents?" Brenda said as though speaking to a small child. "Where are you from?"

She dreaded the interrogation she feared would follow her answers. "My parents were Khalil and Louise Hassan. I was born in Palestine, but most recently I lived just outside Selma, West Virginia."

Suspicion crept into the woman's cool gaze. "What caused you to immigrate?"

What business was it of hers? Mira fought back her irritation and answered with a matter-of-fact tone. "The deaths of my parents. A couple of my mother's cousins in Selma took me in."

"I see." Brenda cast a glance at Della. "How is it you happen to be here for Thanksgiving instead of with your own family?"

"I haven't got family what cares to see me." If the woman didn't like her West Virginia speech patterns, too bad. Mira didn't feel the need to make her speech fit in like she usually did. Not for someone who had decided to interrogate her moments after they met. "Bill and Della invited me to come here, so I did."

"And how did you happen to meet Bill and Della?"

"They have a cabin a short ways from Harley and Marnie's farm." She caught Brenda's questioning look and resisted the urge to sigh. Why didn't Della rescue her from this uncomfortable conversation? "Harley and Marnie were the cousins what took me in. They always made sure the Montaigne cabin was kept in good repair, and Marnie would freshen it up a day or two before the Montaignes arrived."

Della finally intervened. "I've told you about the cabin and Marnie's welcome gifts. She made some of the most delicious baked goods I have ever tasted."

Brenda nodded and returned her gaze to Mira. "Am I to assume these people are no longer living, since you refer to them in the past tense?"

"Yes, ma'am. They were in a bad accident back in March."

"And you have no other family to speak of?"

Why wouldn't the woman let it drop? Thinking about dead relatives and being alone in the world was the last thing Mira wanted to do the day before a major holiday. "No, ma'am."

"So you are running this farm by yourself." Brenda arched one eyebrow.

From one uncomfortable topic to another. "Uh, no, ma'am."

"You have hired help?"

The woman looked and sounded so impressed Mira wished she could say yes, but she couldn't lie, especially with Della listening to every word. "I don't live there any more."

The suspicion returned. "So, where do you live?"

"More tea, anyone?" Della appeared more uncomfortable than Mira felt.

Hadn't Bill talked to her about admitting the truth? Mira ignored Della's shaking head and met Brenda's gaze, noticing Wayne had inherited his mother's eyes. "I live here right at the moment."

Brenda turned to her sister-in-law in dismay. "Della, you and Bill have taken in a homeless immigrant? She'll probably take everything she can get her hands on and disappear into the night."

"Brenda!" Della gasped, a hand fluttering to her throat. "How can you say such a thing? Mira is a sweet, trustworthy girl."

Mira's also had enough. She stood and put her crutches under her arms as she allowed her rising temper to peek through. "Would you excuse me? There's something I need to do."

She glared at Brenda and made her way to the door, only to hear another comment from the woman.

"She's probably going to drug our noon meal and rob us blind."

Mira struggled to hold her tongue as she headed toward the mud room. She hadn't been this angry or hurt since dealing with Harley's relatives last spring. As she passed by the open kitchen door, Charlotte looked up from her post at the counter.

"Mira, honey, what's wrong?"

Mira stepped into the kitchen, moisture blurring her vision at the cook's compassionate tone. "Brenda Zivney has decided that I am some kind of thief who will drug everyone at lunch, and then steal everything that isn't nailed down."

Charlotte dusted off her hands and wrapped her in a hug. "Oh, honey, everyone knows you wouldn't even *think* of such a thing! I can't believe she would say something so cruel."

"I can." She put her arms around the cook, taking care not to drop her crutches, and leaned into the comforting embrace. "She's not the first one to think I was a thief or some kind of terrorist."

"That's terrible!" Charlotte's arms tightened, holding her closer as she wept. "None of us here think that."

"I know." Mira drew in a shuddering breath and stepped back. "I need to get out of here."

"What about your lunch, honey?" She sounded worried, as though afraid Mira might not come back if she left. "You'll need to make your biscuits in just a little while."

Mira dried her eyes with the soft cuff of her sweater

and sighed. "I know, but I don't belong here. I just don't fit in, and Della's sister-in-law hates me. I don't want to make this an unhappy family gathering."

"You won't, honey. If anyone makes it unhappy, it'll be Brenda."

"I still need time away from everyone to think." Not that she could go as far as she wanted; crutches and no car or money had her pretty well stranded on this palatial estate.

"Why don't you go down to the stable? You were just telling me this morning how much you love to be around the horses," Charlotte said, her tone a tempting lilt. "I'll even call Lucas and have him leave Dan downstairs. I've heard that dog is a good listener."

Escape wasn't worth making her friend worry. "I guess that would be okay."

"You go put on your coat and head down there. I'll give Lucas a call."

"Thanks, Charlotte." She turned to leave the kitchen.

"If you want to talk later, I'll be here."

Mira didn't respond. What could she say? That she wished she'd stayed in West Virginia and begged and pleaded with everyone in the area until they loaned her the floor in a back room or the corner of a barn? No, better to remain silent until she figured out what to do.

In the mud room, she pulled on the spare coat hanging on the wall and went out into the chilly late November air. The sun reflected off the snow, making everything glitter like crystal. Mira ignored the beauty around her as she carefully swung her way down the path. Even the magnificence of God's creation couldn't help right now.

She paused at the stable door and considered continuing on into the woods. After a moment, she opened the door and went inside, knowing she couldn't just disappear...at least not on crutches. Dan greeted her cautiously, his tail wagging as he eyed the crutches with suspicion.

"Hey, Dan, my extra legs are only temporary." She sat on a nearby hay bale, and the large mutt propped his chin on her thigh. "I'm glad Charlotte had Lucas bring you down here. I need a friend right now."

She leaned her crutches against the wall and removed the borrowed coat before running her hand across the dog's head. Tears slid down her cheeks as she thought of all the hurtful things Brenda had said. They sounded so much like what Harley's family had said after his death.

Even before the funeral, they had come to the cabin and removed everything even remotely valuable. They claimed it was so Mira couldn't steal anything, but she'd always suspected they only wanted the money from selling the items. Still, they had said some terrible things and made it crystal clear she was not welcome.

Now, Brenda Zivney was doing the same thing. The only difference was that this time Mira had people who wanted her to stay, the most important being Bill and Della.

She looked down at the dog now sitting beside her and leaning against her in a way that felt like a hug. "Dan, as much as I would love to leave right now, I can't. I can't do that to the Montaignes. They have been so kind to me, taking me in and including me in their family. It would hurt them if I left now. I'll get a job and as soon as I have enough money, I'll leave. Bill and Della will understand that I want to be on my own, and that way I won't have to deal with Brenda Zivney again after this week."

Dan looked up at her with his big brown eyes.

"Unfortunately, I still have to survive this week with her." She sighed, suddenly regretting her decision to make lunch. Staying in the stable and far away from Brenda sounded much better. "I guess I better visit the horses for a few minutes and then go see about those biscuits."

The dog followed as she made her way down the aisle. She patted each horse and spoke to it for a moment before moving on to the next. Why couldn't people be as friendly and accepting as animals?

As she neared Maggie's stall, she paused and looked at her canine companion. "You better wait here. We don't want to spook poor Maggie. Stay, Dan."

The dog dropped to his haunches in the middle of the aisle. Mira continued on, and when she glanced back, she found Dan right where she'd left him, watching her.

Maggie stuck her head over the stall door and snorted when she saw Mira on crutches.

"Hey, sweetie, it's just me." Mira used the horse's favorite soothing Hebrew. "The crutches aren't going to hurt you. They're just helping me walk for the moment."

Maggie shifted her weight, but stayed where she

was. Mira slowly raised her hand to pet the horse, relieved when the mare relaxed a little. As she stroked the horse's soft cheek and neck, the stable door opened. Brenda wouldn't come out there to continue her insults, would she?

A quick glance down the aisle revealed Wayne walking toward her. She gave the horse one last pat then walked up the aisle to join him. They met near Dan, who still sat patiently.

Wayne smiled, apparently unaware of his mother's feelings toward her. Or maybe he didn't care. "So this is where you disappeared to."

"Yeah, I had some stuff to think about." She reached down and scratched Dan on the head. "Good boy. Okay, you can get up now."

The dog stood up and greeted Wayne, tail waving. Wayne reached down and petted the happy dog. "I wondered why he was sitting there."

"I didn't want to risk him spooking Maggie." Why did he have to show up now, when she wanted to be left alone?

Wayne straightened and studied her, a furrow forming on his brow. "Is everything okay?"

"Not exactly." She adjusted her hold on her crutches, hoping he wouldn't press her and knowing he would.

"What's wrong?"

"Your mother hates me."

Wayne's eyes widened. "What?"

"After spending less than twenty minutes with me, she decided I'm a thief and will probably try to drug everyone at lunch." A twinge of guilt struck for being so blunt. Brenda was his mother, after all. But she had to let him know why she would be spending as little time near the woman as possible, and she didn't feel like sugar-coating it.

"Mom said that?"

"Yes." She gentled her tone, hoping he wouldn't hate her too, not when they were just becoming friends. "I don't know why she said it. Maybe she's having a bad day."

"Maybe." He didn't sound convinced and glanced toward the stable door. "I think I better go talk to her."

Not what she'd expected. She'd assumed he would show indifference, maybe a little sympathy. She'd never imagined he would defend her to his mother. "Don't cause any trouble on my account. It's not worth it."

"Trust me, you're worth it." He met her gaze with a warm smile. "I'll see you at lunch."

She swung along beside him up the aisle. "I may eat in the kitchen."

Wayne stopped and stared at her. "Eat in the kitchen? Why?"

"It would be better that way." Now she understood how Ben had felt when she invited him into the house for coffee. Why hadn't she seen the prejudice before? "I'm not part of the family, and I'm in the same class as Charlotte. I don't belong in the dining room during a family meal."

"You're a guest. Guests eat with the family."

Some of the family saw her as guests, some saw her as family, Brenda and who knew how many others saw her as a villain—trying to figure out her place in this crowd was too confusing. Mira headed toward the door again. She paused long enough to pick up the borrowed coat and pull it on. "I need to go make biscuits."

Wayne didn't say anything, but she could feel his gaze on her back as she went outside.

Twenty-Six

Mira found Charlotte measuring flour into a large mixing bowl. The cook looked up with a relieved smile. How worried had she been that Mira wouldn't come back?

Charlotte set down the measuring cup. "Hi, honey, are you feeling better?"

"A little. I came back to make the biscuits."

"I was just starting them, but you go right ahead and make them, if you want."

"Just let me wash up."

Once the huge batch of biscuits was in the oven, Charlotte fixed cups of tea and joined Mira at the kitchen table. "While you were in the stable, Bill's sister, her husband, and their kids arrived."

More relatives? Just what she didn't need. "Are they anything like Mrs. Zivney?"

"Not really, although the girl is a bit uppity."

"How old is she?"

"Fourteen, and her brother is seven. Charlie is a sweet boy, curious about everything, and loves animals. Adrienne, on the other hand, needs a few lessons on manners, although she has perfect manners around people in her own social class."

"This should be interesting." She sensed dealing with Adrienne would rank up there with facing Brenda. "Chances are I won't be the right kind of person for her. I mean, I'm poor, after all, and I'm living in her uncle's house free of charge."

"Adrienne doesn't have to know that."

"No, she doesn't *have* to know, but I'm sure she'll find out." Didn't people like that always find out what would be better left unsaid?

"Mm, you're probably right." Charlotte sighed and sipped her tea. "That girl seems to know everything that goes on, whether it concerns her or not."

Mira gazed at the pot of stew, her mind taking the same wicked turn it had when she'd arranged the lesson for Tabby's friends at Omar's restaurant. "Since she wants to know everything that's going on, shall I tell her she's eating deer for lunch?"

"Not unless you want to listen to a lot of shrieking." The timer went off, and Charlotte headed for the oven. "Although it could be very entertaining to see how the others react to that information. They're used to things like filet mignon and lobster. I'm not sure any of them have had deer, other than the Montaignes."

Mira's mood lightened a little as she watched Charlotte place the trays of golden biscuits on cooling racks. "I wonder if they know that lobsters eat the garbage at the bottom of the ocean."

"I doubt it." She laughed as she lined a pair of baskets with cloth napkins. "I can just imagine the looks on their faces if they ever found out."

Mira smiled and joined Charlotte at the counter to help transfer the hot biscuits to the baskets. If she could spend most of her time in the kitchen until Brenda went home, she might survive the week after all.

Once the last biscuit had been arranged, Charlotte pulled a pair of serving bowls from the cabinet and moved to the stove. Mira scooped the thick, fragrant stew into the bowls. Charlotte added a colorful fruit salad to the meal waiting on the counter as Anita walked into the kitchen.

The maid gave the air a sniff and smiled. "It sure smells good in here."

"You have Mira to thank for that," Charlotte said. "She made everything except the fruit salad."

Mira glanced at her. "You helped me with everything."

"But we used your recipes." Charlotte turned to Anita. "Everything is ready to be served."

"I'll let the family know."

After the maid left, Mira bit her lip and looked at Charlotte. "Would it be all right if I eat in here with you and Anita?"

"I don't mind, but it's really up to Miss Della."

Her chances of eating in the kitchen dropped through the floor. "I was afraid you'd say that."

Charlotte gave her a sympathetic pat on the shoulder. "It doesn't hurt to ask her."

"No, I guess it doesn't." Mira took a fortifying breath and straightened her spine. She could survive whatever happened...she hoped. "If I don't come back, I'm eating with the family."

"Okay, honey."

Mira made her way into the hall leading to the dining room and discovered everyone else heading the same way. She caught Della's eye, and the older woman excused herself from the group.

"Della," Mira said when she joined her by the kitchen door. "Would it be all right if I eat in the kitchen? Charlotte said it was up to you."

A small furrow formed on her otherwise smooth forehead. "Why don't you want to eat in the dining room with the rest of us?"

"I'm afraid it would cause too much trouble if I'm there."

"Why would it cause trouble? This is a family meal, and you are now a part of this family."

Mira shook her head, her gaze on the floor. "Not everyone sees it that way."

"If you're referring to the things Brenda said, you needn't worry." Assurance filled Della's voice. "I had a long talk with her, and then Wayne came and talked to her. She realizes that she badly misjudged you. I think you'll find she's much more open to you now."

Tabby stepped out of the dining room and joined them. "Come on! Everyone is dying of starvation in there because the stew smells so good."

"We're coming, Tabby." Della turned to Mira and lifted both eyebrows. "Aren't we, dear?"

"Yes, Della." She sighed, aware she had no other choice.

"Good." She smiled as they followed Tabby into the dining room.

As soon as Mira entered, a pretty black-haired

woman gave her a perky smile. "Hello, you must be Mira. I'm Wendy, Bill's little sister." She touched the shoulder of the blond man seated beside her. "This is my husband, Stephen."

"Hello," Mira said and sent a cautious glance toward Brenda. The woman smiled, which eased her worries a bit.

She followed Tabby around the table to two empty seats beside each other. As Mira sat down and laid her crutches on the floor, Mira noticed a blond-haired boy watching her curiously across the table. Presumably, that was Wendy's son, Charlie. A little farther along the table sat a black-haired teenage girl who stared at Mira with suspicion. That had to be Adrienne. Her attitude fit Charlotte's description perfectly.

The stew received rave reviews for its rich flavor. The biscuits met with the same enthusiasm for their fluffiness and buttery flavor. Mira's mood lifted as she listened to the comments. Apparently, her simple cooking could please even the fanciest people.

Midway through the meal, Brenda turned to her sister-in-law. "Della, I must have your cook give me the recipe for this stew. My cook never seems to be able to make a stew this rich."

Della smiled. "You'll have to talk to Mira. She's the one who made it."

Everyone focused on Mira, and she tried not to shift under their surprised gazes. Would they suddenly hate the stew now that they knew she'd made it?

Tabby indicated her bowl. "You made this?"

"Yeah." Mira wished her friend didn't look so amazed. Didn't she realize cooking your own meals was a part of life? "That's why I was in the kitchen all morning."

"How did you get the gravy so rich?" Wendy asked and took another bite.

"It's the venison jerky." Did she really want to get into this discussion? If she had a choice, no. As it was...

"*Venison jerky?*" Brenda poked at her stew suspiciously. "What else is in this?"

So much for the woman's opinion of her improving. "Potatoes, peas, carrots, onions, rosemary, sage, and thyme. Plus some salt and pepper and a lot of water."

"Why a lot of water?" Aaron asked, not nearly as disturbed as his wife. "It doesn't seem like there's very much water in here at all."

"Most of it got absorbed when the ingredients rehydrated. The rest of it is what made the gravy." Did these people never step foot in a kitchen? Considering the Zivneys and the Montaignes had cooks, probably not.

Suddenly, Charlie looked at his parents. "Mom, what's venison?"

The adults exchanged glances, and Mira had a feeling this little boy was sensitive when it came to animals. As Wendy made a couple of false starts, Adrienne turned to her little brother with a superior expression.

"Venison is deer meat."

Charlie stared wide-eyed at his stew as Wendy glared at her daughter. After a moment, he looked up at Mira. "Is this really made from a deer?"

Why did everyone keep looking at her? "Yes, it is."

Charlie glanced at his stew then turned to his parents. "May I be excused?"

"Yes, you may," Stephen said.

The boy pushed his chair back and left the dining room. Wendy watched him go, and then turned a concerned gaze on her husband. "We should go talk to him."

Guilt washed over Mira; her recipe had run him off. Della should have let her eat in the kitchen and avoided this disaster completely. Since she hadn't, maybe Mira could fix it. "I'll go, if you want. I know what it's like to love animals and find out you're eating one of the prettiest."

Wendy shot a questioning look toward her big brother and Bill nodded. She returned her gaze to Mira with a grateful smile. "That would be fine. Charlie is probably in the conservatory. That's usually where he goes when he gets upset here."

"Okay."

In the conservatory, Charlie sat on a wicker bench and stared at a fern. Mira swung over and stopped in front of him. "Can I sit down?"

Charlie shrugged, keeping his gaze on the fern. "I guess."

She took the seat beside him and leaned her crutches against the end of the bench. "You want to talk about it?"

He shot her an accusing glare. "You cooked a deer."

"Yes, I did." She'd guessed right. He was a softy when it came to animals.

"Why? Deer are so pretty."

"They are, but they also provide meat for us to eat.

Just like cows and chickens." She remembered having a similar conversation with Harley the first time he'd brought home venison after she immigrated.

"You buy that meat at the store." Charlie scowled and crossed his arms over his chest. "You had to kill the deer."

"How do you think the meat at the store gets there?"

"I don't know."

"The farmer raises the animals and sells them to other people who have to kill them and butcher them." Mira hoped she wouldn't give the kid nightmares. "By the time you see the meat at the store, it doesn't look anything like the animal it came from, does it?"

He shook his head, lowering his arms. "It looks like meat."

"By the time you cook venison, it just looks like meat, too."

"Are you sure?"

He looked so doubtful she had to smile. "Positive. There's still some venison in the kitchen. It's the same as what I used in the stew, except it hasn't been cooked with vegetables. Would you like to see what it looks like?"

Charlie looked around the room and shrugged. "I guess so."

She stood and positioned her crutches under her arms. "Come with me."

He walked beside her to the kitchen. Charlotte and Anita rose from their seats at the table when they entered the room.

"Can I get something for you, Miss Mira?" Charlotte asked.

"Charlie would like to see what venison jerky looks like."

"I'll go get it for you." Charlotte went into the pantry and returned a moment later with the container of jerky. "Here you go."

She set the container on the counter and stepped back. Mira opened the container and held it where Charlie could see into it. He studied the thin, dried meat then looked up at Mira with big eyes.

"This is deer?"

She nodded, glad she was getting through to him. "Yes, it is."

"And you used meat just like this for the stew?" Charlie asked.

"Yes, I did." She could almost see the wheels turning in his mind.

He looked back at the jerky and nodded. "You're right. It is just like the meat at the store."

Mira smiled and set the container on the counter. "It tastes pretty good too, doesn't it?"

Charlie paused before answering with a grin. "Yeah. It's almost better than hamburgers, and they're my favorite."

"Shall we go finish our stew, then?"

"Yeah!"

Twenty-Seven

Later that afternoon, Mira sat in the library with Wayne working on learning to read. The sound of approaching footsteps caused them both to look up. Anita carried a cordless telephone into the room.

"Miss Mira, a Yasmina Nasr wishes to speak to you."

"Okay." She gave Wayne an apologetic look and hoped he wouldn't mind the interruption as she accepted the phone. "Hey, Yasmina."

"Hi! How's your leg? Zeina told me what happened."

"It's a little better. I think I'll be off the crutches by Friday, although I'll still have to be careful how I walk for a while."

"I'm glad you're doing okay." A hint of relief touched her voice. "The reason I called is to find out if you're busy this evening."

"I don't know." Had Della said anything about plans for tonight? "I don't think I am. Why?"

"Our church is holding a dinner tonight at six followed by the regular Wednesday evening service. Would you like to come?"

Escape from the discomfort that seemed to stalk

her in this house? Absolutely. "I'll have to ask, but that sounds fun. Can I call you back in a little while and let you know for sure?"

"Of course. And you don't need to worry about transportation. Sa'id and I will pick you up and take you home."

"I'll call you back in a little bit." She disconnected and caught Wayne watching her with a smile. "What?"

He indicated the phone. "You've been here less than a week and you already have friends calling you. You must make friends quickly wherever you go."

"Not really. I just got lucky this time," Mira said with a shrug and reached for her crutches. "I need to go find Della or Bill and ask them if I can go with Yasmina tonight."

"Where is she going?" Wayne asked as he stood with her.

"To church." Mira smiled, excited by the thought. She hadn't been to a church service in far too long.

She found both Bill and Della in the foyer. Della was giving an instruction to Anita but dismissed the maid when Mira approached.

Mira stopped and glanced from Bill to Della. "Is there anything going on this evening?"

"Just visiting with our relatives," Della said.

"Would it be all right if I went to church with Yasmina and her brother instead?" Oh, how she hoped they would say yes! She hadn't been to church in nearly a year and she missed it. "They'll give me a ride."

"I would like you to get to know our family, dear." Della turned to Bill, her features uncertain. "What do you think?"

He shifted his gaze to Mira. "Yasmina is the other young lady you met Sunday evening?"

"That's right. She and her brother Sa'id are good friends with Akram and Zeina."

"I think it would be all right if you went with them. You'll have plenty of time the rest of the week to get to know our family members."

"Thank you!" If she were more like Tabby, she would give him a hug. "I need to go call Yasmina and let her know."

The doorbell chimed, and Mira looked up from coloring with Charlie in the living room. A moment later, Sa'id appeared in the doorway. She smiled as she laid aside her crayon and stood.

"Hi, Mira," Sa'id said, glancing at the coloring book on the table beside her. He lifted his gaze to hers and raised his eyebrows. "Ready to go?"

"Just as soon as I put my coat on."

She pulled it on, but as she started to zip it, Charlie grabbed her arm. "You didn't finish your picture."

She gently removed her arm from his grasp. "I'll finish it later. Right now, I'm going with my friend Sa'id."

Charlie glanced him. "Is he your boyfriend?"

"No," Mira said, shaking her head. "Just a friend."

"Adrienne has lots of boyfriends."

"I'm sure she does." She picked up her crutches and joined Sa'id. "I'll see you later, Charlie."

Once they were outside, Sa'id chuckled. "That was a cute kid."

"He's one of Josh and Tabby's cousins. Charlie's seven. His sister, Adrienne—the one with all the boyfriends—is fourteen."

"I bet that keeps life interesting," Sa'id said as they reached the car.

"During lunch she decided to tell Charlie the venison he was eating was deer meat." Mira rolled her eyes. "After I talked to him about how meat gets to the store and showed him some venison before it was cooked, he decided to finish his lunch."

Sa'id laughed as he opened the car door for her. "That sounds like something I'd do to my little sisters."

Yasmina turned in her seat behind the steering wheel to meet Mira's gaze. "What would my brother do?"

Mira grinned as she climbed in the back seat. "Tell your little sisters that venison is deer meat to make them lose their appetites."

Yasmina laughed and turned back around. "That sounds like stuff he's already tried."

"Like you've never helped me," Sa'id said as he slid into the front seat and closed the door.

"How many sisters do you guys have?" Mira asked as they started down the drive.

"There are three of us girls and two boys," Yasmina said. "I'm the oldest. Sa'id is next. Then our brother Zaki, who's a senior in high school; Samirah, who's a freshman; and Amala, who's in sixth grade."

Sa'id glanced over the back of the seat. "Do you have any brothers or sisters?"

Mira shook her head. "I'm an only child. I always wished I had at least one brother or sister, though."

Yasmina grinned into the rearview mirror. "I always wanted to be an only child."

They talked a little about their childhoods as they headed downtown, and Mira learned that before her parents' deaths, her experiences weren't that different from kids who grew up in the US. Friends, school, family vacations... They had all done those things and more.

Yasmina pulled into a gravel parking lot beside a big brick church with stained glass windows and parked in an empty space near the walk leading to the door. Mira and Yasmina followed Sa'id up the walk and into the building. The warm scents of roast turkey and pumpkin pie drifted up the stairway in front of them, reminding Mira of past Thanksgivings. Sa'id stopped at the top of the stairs and turned to her.

"Do you want me to find someone with a key for the elevator?" he said, indicating the shiny metal doors on the wall to the left.

"No, I can take the stairs." She looked at the handrails on both sides of the steps. "If you'll carry my crutches, I can go down faster."

"Do I want to know what you mean?" Sa'id said as she moved to the top of the stairs and handed him the crutches.

Mira grinned and hopped down the stairs, using the handrails for support. Laughter followed her all the way down. At the bottom, she turned around to find Sa'id and Yasmina on the stairs behind her.

"You're right. You can go down pretty fast." Sa'id

stepped off the last step and returned her crutches.

Mira slipped the crutches under her arms again. "Unfortunately, it takes a lot longer to go back up."

They hung their coats on a rack in the hallway and entered a large room filled with tables, chairs, and people.

"Hi, guys." Zeina met them with a smile just inside the door. "Mira, I'm glad you came. How's your leg?"

"Much better."

"Hey, where's Akram?" Sa'id asked, scanning the room. "I thought you two were going to come together."

"We did," Zeina said. "Your little brother drafted him to help in the kitchen."

Sa'id chuckled. "I'll go see if I can rescue him."

Mira watched him head toward a door on the far side of the room, greeting people as he went. Zeina started to say something, but a middle school-aged girl who looked like a younger version of Yasmina bounded up.

"Hi, Yasmina!" the perky girl said. "Is this the friend you went to pick up?"

"Yes, this is Mira Hassan. Mira, this is my youngest sister, Amala."

"Hello, Amala." She gave the girl a smile. Would she outgrow the perkiness or grow up to be as enthusiastic as Tabby?

"Hi, Mira! Are you really from Palestine?" Awe filled her voice.

"Yes, I am."

Amala grinned, her dark eyes sparkling. "That is *so* cool!"

"Hey, Amala," Yasmina said. "Do you know where Mom and Dad are?"

She pointed to a small cluster of people near the center of the room. "They're over there talking with Zeina's parents."

"Okay," Yasmina said as someone called her sister's name. "I guess we'll see you later."

"Yeah, I have to go help with the entertainment. Bye!" Amala waved as she bounced away.

Yasmina turned to Mira. "You'll have to excuse Amala. She's a bit hyper."

Mira laughed. That was one way to put it. More energetic than a squirrel on a caffeine high was another. "I bet she's a lot of fun, though."

"She is. And if you can get her to slow down long enough, she's pretty smart, too."

They joined the group in the middle of the room, and Mira received curious yet friendly looks.

Yasmina laid a hand on her shoulder. "This is Mira Hassan."

"Hi, Mira, I'm glad you came." A middle-aged man resembling Sa'id smiled. "I'm Yasmina's father, Hamid Nasr, and this is my wife, Nadia."

Nadia looked like an older version of Yasmina. "It's so nice to meet you. Yasmina tells us you're from Palestine."

"That's right." Mira's hope of a comfortable, relaxing evening grew with each person she met.

"So am I," another man said, his English colored with a familiar accent, one Mira hadn't heard without a West Virginian flavor in a long time. "I'm Rashid Talhami, Zeina's father. My wife is Kamila."

"Our children tell us you know their grandmother," Kamila added.

Mira smiled and nodded. "Yes, I lived a few houses away from her. Teta Nida treated me like one of her grandchildren."

Kamila's eyes lit up. "Ah, so you're the one she talked about. Whenever I talked to Nida on the phone, she would tell me about the family, and then tell me about a girl in the village who was just a little younger than Akram and Zeina."

"Teta Nida told me about her American grandchildren. I always thought it would be cool to meet them, but I never expected it to happen."

The group laughed. A moment later two teenagers joined them. Hamid turned to Mira.

"These are two more of our children. Zaki, Samirah, this is Mira Hassan."

"Nice to meet you." She offered the teens a friendly smile.

Samirah returned the gesture. "It's nice to meet you, too."

"Yeah," Zaki said. "Unfortunately, we don't have time to talk right now, but Amala insisted we had to come meet you."

"And now we have to get back to work," Samirah added with an apologetic note in her voice.

"I'll see you later then," Mira said as they turned to leave.

"Hey, Zaki," Zeina said. "What did you do with Akram and Sa'id?"

"They're filling water glasses." He pointed to the front of the room before he headed back to the kitchen with his sister.

Nadia gave Mira a questioning look. "Have you already met our youngest?"

"Yes, she found us right after we arrived. She disappeared after saying something about helping with the entertainment for tonight."

"She's in the youth choir. They're going to sing a few songs as everyone is seated."

Rashid looked toward the stage at the front of the room. "It looks like they are about to begin."

Mira followed his gaze, impressed with the number of middle and high school students on the stage. Fifteen to twenty kids of every imaginable size, shape, and color were lining up in three rows.

Kamila turned to her daughter. "Are you girls sitting with us or your friends?"

"We were planning on sitting with our Sunday School class," Zeina said. "If you guys don't mind."

Rashid smiled. "That's fine. Are your brother and Sa'id sitting with you?"

"As far as I know."

He nodded. "We'll see you later, then."

Twenty-Eight

The youth choir sang with an impressive amount of talent as Mira followed Zeina and Yasmina to a table at the back of the room. Several young adults had already gathered at it and a few more were drifting back. She gripped her crutches tighter, hoping the people closer to her age would be as welcoming as Yasmina's and Zeina's parents had been. Unfortunately, she hadn't had the best experience with groups of people her own age back in West Virginia.

"This is the College and Career class," Yasmina said as they reached the table. "Everyone in it is between the ages of eighteen and thirty."

"Except for our teacher, Pastor Jeff," Zeina said. "He's the senior pastor here and sixty."

A blond man at the other end of the table spoke up. "Everyone at the table tonight is between eighteen and thirty. Pastor Jeff is sitting with his wife close to the stage."

Yasmina smiled and turned to Mira. "That's Tony. He fits into the career category."

Tony laughed. "Yeah, I work as a mechanic at Al's

Garage over on Hearst Boulevard."

"Everyone, this is Mira Hassan." Yasmina pointed out the people standing by the table. "Mira, that's Andy, Lucy, Carol, Duane, Michael, Hannah, Phil, Tamara, Ana, Stacey, and Tyrone."

"Hi." Mira prayed they didn't expect her to remember everyone's name.

"Hi, Mira," Carol said. "So, are you college or career?"

"Neither one right at the moment." Despite her initial worry, she doubted this group would mind. "But I'm hoping to find a job soon."

"You should talk to Pastor Jeff," Duane said. "He always seems to know who's hiring."

"I'll do that." Maybe she could get out on her own sooner than she'd hoped.

Minutes after they sat down, Akram and Sa'id joined them. The friendly greetings everyone gave them were so similar to the ones Mira had received that she felt as if she belonged. Her spirits rose, even as she questioned decisions she'd made.

Why had she struggled on her own for so long rather than seeking out people who would accept her? Maybe instead of hiding in the woods after Harley and Marnie died, she should have gone to a city and sought help from a church like this.

She pulled her thoughts away from what she could have done and focused on the moment. The past was over, finished, and no amount of dwelling on it now would change a thing, except maybe to keep her from enjoying time with friends.

When the choir finished its short set, a gray-haired

man in a sport coat and tie walked onto the stage and said the blessing. One of the guys—she couldn't remember if he was Phil or Tyrone—told Mira the man was Pastor Jeff.

As the youth group pushed out carts of steaming serving bowls and platters, Ben Petros came in and headed for the table in the back. He pulled out the only empty chair at the table and sat down beside Mira. If the look on his face meant anything, he was just as surprised to see her as she was to see him.

"Sorry I'm late," Ben told the group, and then he turned to Mira with a warm smile. "Hey, Mira. I didn't know you were coming tonight."

Her heart did a little dabke under his chocolate brown gaze. "Yasmina invited me this afternoon."

His eyebrows rose. "You know Yasmina?"

"Yeah, I met her, Zeina, Sa'id, and Akram a few days ago."

"That's cool." He glanced toward them. They stared back. "What?"

Akram shrugged, an apparent attempt to hide his curiosity. "I didn't realize you knew Mira."

"I met her in the stable where I work." He turned to Mira again. "That reminds me, how's your leg?"

She smiled at his concern. Had he missed seeing her that morning for their daily conversation? "It's doing okay. I should be off the crutches in the next couple of days."

"I'm glad to hear it," Ben said as their table's food cart arrived.

The group passed around turkey, mashed potatoes, green beans, rolls, and a few other foods. While they ate, Mira learned that the youth group had prepared the meal as a service project. After tasting everything, she decided either the kids were talented cooks or they had been supervised by one. The youth group served pumpkin pie, and the choir returned to the stage to provide more music, both vocal and instrumental.

When the dinner ended, everyone headed upstairs for the worship service. At the insistence of Akram, Ben, and a little old lady with a walker, Mira rode in the small elevator.

As the old woman pressed the button to take them up a level, she smiled. "You seem to have impressed several of our young men."

Whatever small talk Mira had expected, that certainly hadn't been it. "What?"

"I've been watching people for a long time, and several of the young men here tonight noticed how pretty you are." She gave Mira a sly look. "That Ben Petros is a nice young man."

"Yeah, I know." Why was she having this conversation? She didn't know this old lady from Eve. "He and I have talked a few times."

"I'm sure he'd like to talk a few more times," the old woman said with a knowing smile as the elevator stopped and the doors slid open. "Enjoy the service."

Mira followed her off the elevator and found Zeina, Yasmina, and Carol waiting for her. Akram, Ben, and Sa'id were volunteering as ushers. Mira let the old woman get out of hearing range before turning to her companions. "Who was that lady with the walker?"

"That's Lydia Petros," Zeina said. "She's Ben's grandmother."

"Oh." She should have known. "Now I understand."

"Understand what?"

Carol laughed. "Did Lydia try to fix you up with Ben?"

Mira stared at her. "How did you know?"

"Lydia is always trying to find the future Mrs. Ben Petros," Carol said, her expression amused. "She's convinced he'll never find anyone on his own. If she saw you talking to Ben, she'll decide you could be the one."

"She's sure Ben would like to get to know me better." The words slipped out before she could consider the consequences.

"That sounds like Lydia," Yasmina said with a laugh, and then gave Mira an appraising look. "Of course, the way Ben looked at you during dinner... She could be right."

Mira's cheeks warmed. "He didn't look at me any differently than he looked at you guys."

"That's not how it looked from my seat." Zeina flashed her a teasing grin.

Carol and Yasmina laughed, and after a second, Mira did as well. She had noticed that Ben seemed awful interested whenever she made a comment during dinner, but there was no way she would admit it to her new friends. They seemed a little too determined to follow in Lydia's footsteps.

They went into the sanctuary, and several people introduced themselves to Mira. She loved the friendliness of the church. If she could get a ride or borrow a car from the Montaignes, she'd start coming regularly.

Pastor Jeff joined them as they settled into a pew

near the back.

"Welcome to Colton Avenue Church." He shook her hand. "I'm Jeff Burchard, the senior pastor. Everyone calls me Pastor Jeff. What's your name?"

"Mira Hassan."

Pastor Jeff nodded, recognition flashing across his face. "Sa'id mentioned that you're looking for work."

"That's right." How had Sa'id found out?

"Find me after the service, and we can talk about what kind of employment you're interested in. Right now, I'd better get up front before they start without me."

Mira watched him walk to the front of the sanctuary and take his seat on the platform as the song leader stepped up to the microphone. The words for the hymn were projected onto a large screen above the platform. She didn't know the song, so she listened to the congregation sing and discreetly scanned at the people around her. When she glanced to her right, she spotted Ben standing next to the wall, watching her. She ducked her head and quickly faced the front again.

Was Lydia right? Did he want to get to know her better? She wouldn't mind if he did. He was much more her type than Ryan or Wayne.

It was no surprise when Pastor Jeff preached on thankfulness. As Mira listened to the sermon, she realized she had a lot to be thankful for despite all the difficulties in her life. She had a beautiful place to live, people who cared about her, new friends, and she could walk. That was something she was always thankful for, at least since the bombing in Jerusalem.

After the service ended, Yasmina, Carol, and Zeina

went to collect as many people as they could to go out for coffee. Mira headed to where Pastor Jeff stood at the back of the sanctuary and waited patiently while he wished several people a happy Thanksgiving and said he would see them on Sunday.

Finally, he was able to slip away, leaving the associate pastor to greet the rest of the congregation. Mira followed him to a quiet corner of the large room so they could talk without interruption.

"So, Mira, have you ever had a job before?" Pastor Jeff asked.

"Not really. I've done a little babysitting. I lived on a farm for a little over six years and helped with the work there. I know how to cook simple farm-style meals, and I know a lot about the forest."

"Hm. Those are all useful skills, but I can't think of a job in the city where they would help." Pastor Jeff tapped a finger against his chin. "Do you have a degree in anything?"

She shook her head. Maybe she wasn't as employable as she'd hoped. "No, I've never been to college."

"Okay...What are you interested in?"

"I love music and animals." But could that help her find a job?

Pastor Jeff brightened. "I know of a veterinary clinic that's looking for a receptionist. How are your typing skills?"

Heat crept into her cheeks. "Unless everything is written in Hebrew or Arabic, I'm going to have some trouble with the files."

"Never learned to read English, huh?" The pastor gave her an understanding look.

"No, I had too many other things to learn after I moved to the United States." She breathed a sigh of relief when his opinion of her didn't seem to change.

"We have a literacy program that can help you learn to read. My wife, Norma, is one of the tutors. I happen to know she has a slot free Tuesday afternoon, if you want to come by."

"That would be great!" As nice as it had been having Wayne help her, working with an actual tutor was a dream come true.

"Okay, I'll let her know to expect you about two. Just come in the main door of the church, and she'll be in the last room on the right." He gave her a thoughtful look. "You mentioned that you love music. Do you play an instrument?"

"I play the violin. Although, my technique is more Appalachian fiddle than classical violin."

"The Mercer Center for the Arts might be willing to hire you as a folk fiddle instructor. They wouldn't be able to pay you much more than minimum wage, but it would be better than nothing."

"It sounds perfect." Getting paid to help others who shared her love of fiddling would be nothing short of amazing. "When I lived in West Virginia, I helped a friend's son learn the basics of fiddling and had a lot of fun."

"Okay, I'll call the Mercer Center Monday and see if they're interested," Pastor Jeff said as he pulled a small notebook and a pen from his suit coat. "Let me have your phone number and I'll call you after I know what they say."

She recited the Montaignes' number. "Thank you so

much for your help."

Pastor Jeff smiled and tucked the notebook back in his pocket. "That's what I'm here for. I do have one more question, though."

"What's that?"

"Do you have a high school diploma?"

Mira shook her head. "No, I haven't been to school since I was thirteen."

"I bet there's a fascinating story behind that."

Fascinating, terrifying, and well on its way to a happier chapter...she hoped. "It's kind of a long story."

Pastor Jeff nodded. "I guess it will have to wait for another day, then. In the meantime, we have another program you might be interested in. It helps people earn a high school diploma."

"I would love to earn my diploma." Why hadn't Harley and Marnie's pastor back in Selma been this helpful? Then again, he'd been on the school board that thought it would be best if she didn't attend the public school.

"I'll give the information to Norma, and she can go over it with you Tuesday. Now, you have a happy Thanksgiving, and I hope to see you Sunday."

"I'll try to be here."

She scanned the nearly empty sanctuary for her friends so they could leave.

They were nowhere in sight.

Twenty-Nine

Surely Yasmina, Sa'id, and Zeina wouldn't have abandoned her. They had to be somewhere in the church, but where?

Before Mira could decide where to start looking, Ben walked into the sanctuary carrying her coat and wearing his own. He headed toward her, and she met him halfway.

"I brought your coat for you," he said, holding it for her.

"Thanks." She leaned her crutches against the end of a pew and slipped her arms into the sleeves. "Where did everyone go?"

"To the coffee shop." He watched her adjust her hold on her crutches. "I had to help put the microphones away, so I volunteered to give you a ride over there when you finished talking to Pastor Jeff."

No way could she hold her friends leaving against them now, despite her certainty that they'd set her up. "Are you ready to go?"

"I was just waiting for you." He led the way to a side door. "I'm parked out kind of far. Do you want me to bring my truck up to the door?"

She smiled and shook her head. "No, I like to walk, even if it is on crutches."

"In that case, allow me," Ben said with a smile of his own as he opened the door for her.

They stepped out into the cold night air and crossed the street. Ben shortened his normally long stride to match Mira's cautious pace as they walked down the mostly clear sidewalk.

"Did you enjoy the service?" he asked.

"Yeah, I did," she said, thinking back over the evening. "It felt so normal and comfortable after all the changes in my life recently. And everyone was so friendly."

"I'm glad you liked it. Are you going to come Sunday?"

"I'm going to try. What time should I get here?"

Ben unlocked the passenger door of an old, dark brown pickup truck as he answered. "Well, Sunday School is at nine-thirty, and then there's half an hour of fellowship at ten-thirty. The morning service starts at eleven, and there's an evening service at seven."

"Sounds like I have a lot of options," Mira said with a laugh as he opened the door for her. She climbed in and waited until he had settled into the driver's seat before continuing. "When do *you* think I should arrive?"

He started the engine and glanced at her. "I think you'd enjoy the College and Career class. Pastor Jeff does a great job of applying the Bible to real life."

"I guess I'll plan on nine-thirty, then." And sitting next to Ben, if the way he looked at her meant anything. "Now all I have to do is find a way to the church."

"I could give you a ride, if you want," he said as he pulled away from the curb.

Mira hesitated. As much as she might enjoy it, she didn't want to inconvenience him. "I'd hate for you to have to go out of your way. I'm sure I can get someone at the Montaignes to drive me."

"I don't mind going out of my way for you."

Her heart melted. "Well, if you're sure."

"I'll pick you up between nine and nine-fifteen Sunday morning."

A few minutes later, Ben turned into the parking lot of a shopping center. As he drove to the opposite end, Mira recognized the store in the middle of the long building.

"I was out here a few days ago," she said as they passed Stuart's.

"Really? Did you stop at the coffee shop, by any chance?"

"No, we were at Stuart's. Della insisted I needed a riding helmet."

"Yeah, that's one of the big rules in the stable," Ben said as he pulled into a parking space. "Everyone who rides has to wear a helmet. Unless, of course, they have a bad leg act up while out in the woods and need a ride back to the stable."

Mira laughed at the reminder and looked at the coffee shop. Brightly lit and filled with people, it exuded a welcoming, relaxed atmosphere.

"You ready to go in?"

She turned to find him watching her in the light

from a nearby lamppost. "Yeah."

They climbed out of the truck and walked side by side to the building. Ben opened the door and followed her inside. She spotted their friends at a group of tables in the back.

As they made their way back, the man behind the counter grinned at them. "Hey, Ben, how's it going?"

"Just fine, Harry." He led Mira over. "I'd like you to meet a friend of mine. This is Mira Hassan."

"Hey, Mira," Harry said cheerfully. He looked at her crutches. "You slip on some ice?"

She shook her head. "No, I got kicked by a horse. Thankfully, it's just a bruise."

"Well, I hope it heals soon. You guys want to go ahead and order?"

"We'll have regular coffee." Ben glanced at Mira. "That okay with you?"

"That's fine," she said with a smile.

"Okay, I'll bring it to you in a couple of minutes." Harry swiped a rag across the counter. "I have a fresh pot brewing."

"Thanks, Harry," Ben said.

He and Mira continued on, and their friends greeted them warmly as they removed their coats and sat down. Mira noticed that the only chairs left were right next to each other. When she saw the grins Zeina, Carol, and Yasmina gave her, she figured they had arranged it on purpose. Not that she minded; Ben *was* handsome, after all, and he had turned into a good friend.

"Did Pastor Jeff have any job information?" Sa'id asked.

Her heart lifted just thinking about it. "He's going to call the Mercer Center Monday and see if they're interested in a folk fiddle instructor."

"You play the fiddle?" Akram said.

"Yeah. My mom taught me some, and then a cousin taught me more."

"What type of songs do you know?"

Why was he so interested? Unless it was because he was a musician himself. "Mostly Appalachian folk songs, but I know several from the Levant and a few classical violin pieces."

"That's an interesting assortment," Carol said.

Zeina looked at her brother. "Didn't you tell me your band is looking for a fiddle player?"

"Yes, I did." Akram focused on Mira again. "If the others agree, are you interested in joining a band?"

That's why he was so interested in her musical ability? "I never thought about it before."

"Have you ever played in public?" Zeina asked.

"When I lived in West Virginia I played at a couple of dances and competed at the county fair."

Sa'id leaned forward, his expression interested. "Did you win?"

"Once, and I came in second and third a couple of times."

"Let me talk to the other guys and see what they have to say," Akram said. "Don't take this the wrong way, but I don't know how some of them would feel about a single woman in the band."

"That's okay. I understand." She remembered her life in Palestine and some of the cultural rules. If the other band members had been raised the same way, it made sense that it would influence them even in a more permissive society like America.

Ben shifted his gaze back and forth between them. "I think I missed something."

"When I still lived in Palestine, it was frowned upon for a single woman to spend as much time alone with men, especially single men, as I would rehearsing with the band," Mira said. "It's not that they don't like women, it's more that they want to protect her reputation. Apparently, some of that thinking came to America."

"There are a couple of men in the band who are resistant to the American way, but if they think about it for a while, they usually relax and accept that we do things differently here." Akram met Mira's gaze. "If I manage to talk them into it, you'll have to audition."

"That's fine. Just let me know when and where." Nerves fluttered their way through her stomach, but she smiled anyway. She'd expected the need to audition. The Mercer Center would likely require an audition as well.

Harry delivered the coffee, and the conversation moved to other things. About nine thirty, the group decided to call it a night. When they arrived the counter to pay, Mira reached into her pocket for the money Bill had given her in case they went somewhere after church. Ben stopped her and paid for her coffee.

"In exchange for the coffee you gave me the other day," he said with a smile as they went out into the parking lot with the others. "I'll see you later."

"Thanks, Ben," Mira called after him as he headed for his truck.

The rest of the group split up, and Mira followed Yasmina to her car. Zeina went with them. As they pulled out of the parking lot, Mira studied her companions. Maybe now she could find out if her suspicions were correct.

"Why do I get the feeling you guys set me up tonight?"

Yasmina and Zeina exchanged glances in the front seat.

"What do you mean?" Zeina asked.

"You abandoned me after church so Ben had to give me a ride." Mira didn't believe their innocent act for a second. "Then you arranged it so he and I had to sit next to each other at the coffee shop."

"Yeah, okay." Yasmina laughed. "We set you up, but Carol helped."

"And you didn't look like you minded," Zeina said. "Neither did Ben."

Never had Mira been more thankful for a dark car. With the low light, her friends probably wouldn't notice if her face was bright red. "No, I didn't mind. Not too much anyway. As for Ben, he offered me a ride to church on Sunday."

"Which you accepted," Yasmina said, glancing at her in the rearview mirror.

"Which I accepted." Mira smiled, feeling a little shy. Receiving interest from a guy she liked was still new.

"Lydia will be so pleased," Zeina said, flashing a grin over the back of the seat.

"How will she know? Unless Ben tells her, I mean."

"There is no such thing as a secret in that church. Someone will see the two of you arrive together and tell Lydia."

"And she'll start hearing wedding bells," Yasmina said with a laugh.

"Y'all are getting ahead of yourselves." But she could imagine Lydia measuring Ben for a tux.

"Are we?" Zeina turned to look at her with raised eyebrows.

"Yes. He hasn't even asked me out."

"Give it time," Yasmina said. "Just out of curiosity, do you have plans Saturday in case Ben calls?"

"Believe it or not, I have a date." Why did the admission embarrass her?

"Really?" Zeina said, the teasing tone absent from her voice. "With who?"

"One of Tabby's cousins. He did a big favor for me, and when I asked how I could thank him, he asked me out."

"Wow. He must really like you," Yasmina said. "Either that or he's a player."

"Is it one of the cousins I met yesterday?" Zeina asked.

"Yes, amazingly enough, it's Wayne." Mira didn't have to wait long for her reaction.

"Wayne!" Zeina's eyes widened and her jaw dropped. "He's the one who got you kicked!"

"I know, but then he became a decent human being." She still didn't understand it, but she wasn't going to complain. "He sent me flowers to apologize for acting stupid and spooking the horse."

"Yeah, he likes you," Yasmina said with a decisive nod. "No player would cause a horse to kick you and still think you'd go out with him."

Thirty

Thursday morning, Mira awoke with a start when something heavy landed on her. She'd barely opened her eyes when Frank jumped off again.

"Ugh, you're heavy." She groaned and rubbed her eyes. "I think I prefer whiskers in the face."

The cat sprawled on the foot of the bed, playing with a soft green ball that had a bright purple feather sticking out of it. He looked at her and meowed loudly. Then he grabbed the ball with his teeth and ran out of the room.

"I didn't think it was possible for that cat to be hyper," Mira muttered as she climbed out of bed.

After a quick shower, she put on a long skirt and a tunic-style sweater that came to mid-thigh. Even though she'd been shocked at the price of the outfit, she was thankful Della had insisted on buying it. No matter how the day went, at least she would look as if she belonged.

She braided her hair, leaving a few shorter strands framing her face, and headed down to the kitchen. Charlotte was stirring something on the stove, and

Mira watched for a moment.

"Morning, Charlotte. Is anyone else awake?"

"They're in the little dining room," she said, moving to another pan.

"Is there anything I can do to help?"

"No, honey, I have it under control." Charlotte paused long enough to give her a smile. "You go sit down, and I'll fix your breakfast."

When Mira arrived in the dining room, she found Bill, Charlie, and Wendy already eating.

"Good morning, Mira," Bill greeted her.

"Morning," she said as she sat down.

"Did you have fun with your friend last night?" Charlie's wide-eyed curiosity made her smile.

"Yes, I did." At least he'd quit thinking Sa'id was her boyfriend. "We went to church, and I saw some of my other friends."

"What church was it?" Wendy asked.

"Colton Avenue Church."

"They do a lot of work in the community," Bill said. "The head pastor there is a good man who really cares about people."

Mira nodded; she'd noticed that about him. "I talked to him for a little while last night. He's going to see if the Mercer Center for the Arts will hire me as a folk fiddle instructor."

"There's a fundraiser Saturday night for the Mercer Center," Wendy said. "They're going to have a string quartet from the center."

"Della and I had considered attending," Bill said, "but we decided this week was busy enough already."

Wendy nodded, her features understanding. "Stephen

and I will be there, since we're in town anyway. The Mercer Center is so important to the community. There are many talented children who would never have the opportunity to learn an instrument without it."

"Don't forget the art, dance, and drama instruction they offer," Bill said.

Charlotte brought in Mira's breakfast, refilled coffee cups, and left the room. Mira was about halfway through her meal when Wayne came in. As he passed her, he handed her a square of embossed, cream-colored card stock with something printed on the front in a fancy script. She had no chance of reading it with her limited knowledge of written English.

She met his gaze. "What is this?"

"Information about a formal fundraiser Saturday night," Wayne said as he settled into a chair across the table from her. "What do you think?"

A little more information about what a formal fundraiser entailed would be nice, but she didn't want to go that in-depth with an audience. "Um, okay, I guess."

"I can always find something else, if you'd prefer."

"Oh, no, this is fine." She wished he would let it drop until they were alone. "I've just never been to a formal fundraiser."

Bill looked from Mira to his nephew and back. "Have I missed something?"

She glanced at Wayne. "Uh..."

He turned to Bill. "I told Mira I'd find something for us to do Saturday night. I talked to some friends and arranged tickets to this fundraiser."

"I see." Bill looked a little confused, but he didn't seem to mind.

Wendy just looked curious. "What is the fundraiser for?"

"The Mercer Center for the Arts," Wayne said.

"Oh, Stephen and I are attending that," Wendy said with a smile. "Perhaps the four of us could go together."

"That's fine with me."

"I'll talk to Stephen and see what he thinks."

Mira set the card on the table and resumed eating her breakfast. Maybe Wendy would help her know what to expect and how to act. If not, she would have to rely on Wayne and hope he didn't think she was a backwoods hick.

Della stepped into the room as Wendy and Charlie headed out. As she took her place at the table, she glanced at the card beside Mira's plate. "What do you have there, dear?"

"Information about the Mercer Center fundraiser." How would Della react when she heard Wayne was taking her?

"Oh?" Della sent a questioning glance toward her husband.

"Wayne has offered to take Mira," Bill said.

Della turned a surprised gaze on her nephew. "That's very kind of you, Wayne."

"It was very kind of Mira to accept." He sent her a charming smile.

"Yes, it was," Della said with another glance at her husband. "May I ask how all this came about?"

Wayne and Mira looked at each other. She had no

clue how to explain that one.

"It's kind of funny, actually," he said, shifting his attention back to his aunt. "I was helping Mira with something, and she asked how she could thank me. I suggested a date and, to my surprise, she agreed."

Della lifted her eyebrows. "May I ask what you were helping her with?"

Wayne turned to Mira. So much for letting him explain everything.

Heat crept into her face as she faced Della. "You might as well know. I can't read English. Wayne was helping me learn a few words."

The woman's eyes widened. "I had no idea."

"That's because I didn't want you to know. I have an appointment Tuesday with a literacy tutor at the church I went to last night."

"That's wonderful, dear." Della smiled. "If you would like my help in learning to read, just ask."

"Thank you." Mira breathed a little easier. Della didn't seem to mind that she had been kept in the dark.

Mira finished her breakfast and excused herself. As she headed toward the music room, small feet came running up behind her.

"Mira!" Charlie exclaimed.

"Charlie!" she said with identical enthusiasm as she turned around. "What's up?"

"Are you and Wayne really going to the same party as Mommy and Daddy?"

"We sure are."

"Do you have a really fancy dress like Mommy?"

"Not yet, but I'll get one." Della would likely insist

on buying it.

"Mommy's going to get her hair done for the party. Are you?"

"I suppose I will." Fancy dress, getting her hair done... What had she agreed to?

Charlie stared up at her, his eyes wide. "Is Wayne your boyfriend?"

The boy never gave up. "No, Charlie, he's not."

"Then why are you going to a fancy party with him?"

She wondered that herself, but no way would she admit it to a seven-year-old—or anyone else. "Because he's my friend and he asked me to go. You've been to a party with your friends, right?"

"Yeah, I went to Tommy's birthday party. There were girls there, too."

He'd given her a perfect example. "And were any of them your girlfriend?"

"Yuck! No!" Charlie gave an emphatic shake of his head.

"But you were at the party with them anyway."

"Yeah, okay," he said, and Mira knew she had made her point. "What are you doing now?"

She would never tire of his insatiable curiosity. "I'm going to go play the violin for a while."

"Can I listen?" He gave her a sweet, hopeful smile.

"Sure." What was it with this family and wanting to hear her play?

She played for about an hour while Charlie listened with rapt attention. The music helped her relax enough to face Bill and Della's relatives, who started arriving shortly after she put the violin away. Charlie told everyone he could find that she played the violin "as good as Aunt Della," but Mira didn't mind too much. It put her on a more equal level with everyone else if they thought she was a great violinist.

As she stood by a tall narrow table along the back of one of the sofas in the living room, taking a break from mindless chitchat with people she didn't know, three of the cousins around her age joined her.

"Someone mentioned that you made venison stew," Cheryl said.

"Yes, I did." She smiled, pleased someone had enjoyed the meal enough to mention it. "Everyone seemed to like it."

"Oh, I'm sure they did. I was just wondering where you found the venison. I don't believe I've ever seen any for sale around here."

"I brought it with me from West Virginia."

Amber tilted her head. "Do they sell venison there?"

"Not that I know of. We always hunted for it."

"You hunted for it?" Shane raised his eyebrows. "Does that mean you also butchered it yourselves?"

"Yes." What was with their extreme interest in deer?

"Did you cure the hide as well?"

"Of course." She had no doubt they were up to something, but she couldn't figure out what.

"Wherever did you learn how?" Cheryl asked with innocence that stunk of insincerity.

"My cousin taught me."

Their snickers confirmed they saw her as a joke.

Josh, Wayne, and Brandon joined her, giving her hope she might survive this encounter with a minimum of embarrassment.

Shane looked annoyed by their presence. "What do you want?"

"Some respect for our friend," Josh said.

Amber's expression turned pouty. "We were just talking."

"Right." Wayne's sarcastic tone made Mira wonder how much of the conversation he'd heard.

Brandon turned to her. "You'll have to excuse our cousins. They suffer under the misguided delusion that everyone in West Virginia is related and uneducated."

She smiled sweetly, realizing she could turn the joke back on them. "Then they'll be pleased to know I'm related to very few people in West Virginia and speak three languages fluently."

Cheryl's jaw dropped. "You speak *three* languages?"

"Of course." Mira could fake innocence as well as Cheryl, and maybe better. "Did I forget to mention that I lived in Israel until I was thirteen?"

She smothered a laugh at their stunned expressions. They must have somehow missed the biggest clue she was from another country—her accent. After another moment of awkward silence, Cheryl, Amber, and Shane walked away. Before Mira could thank the guys for coming to her rescue, a gray-haired woman who appeared to be in her late seventies joined them.

"You handled yourself well, dear," she said, gracing Mira with a smile. "I'm Trudy Montaigne, Bill and Wendy's mother."

"It's nice to meet you, Mrs. Montaigne." She liked this woman who reminded her of an American Teta Nida. "I'm Mira Hassan."

"Please, call me Grandma Trudy. Everyone else

does." She turned to Josh, Brandon, and Wayne. "Will you boys forgive me if I steal Mira away for a little while?"

"Of course, Grandma Trudy," Josh answered for all of them.

"Good." She returned her gaze to Mira. "Shall we find someplace quiet to sit?"

Mira followed her out of the living room. What did she want to talk about? The way she'd handled herself with the cousins? Her date with Wayne?

Trudy led her to the conservatory, which was empty of people. They sat down on a wicker bench, and Mira leaned her crutches beside her.

"My son has told me quite a bit about you, Mira," Trudy said. "I was sorry to hear that you've had so difficult a life at such a young age, although I must say your story sounds familiar."

Not what she'd expected the woman to say. "It does?"

"Yes, I once knew a young violinist who traveled to Israel. She fell in love with a Palestinian man, and despite her family's wishes, she married him."

Mira gasped, her heart thumping against her ribcage. "You knew my mother?"

Thirty-One

"I believe I may have. Was your mother Louise Potter?"

"Yes, she was." Tears stung Mira's eyes.

Trudy patted her arm. "Your mother was a wonderful person. From what Bill has told me, you are very much like her."

"Thank you." Mira drew in a shaky breath. Who else in her family had this woman met? "Did you...did you know my grandparents?"

"I still do, although I don't see them nearly as often anymore."

She struggled to absorb the fact that the people who had disowned their daughter, shown no concern for her death or their own granddaughter, were still alive. "What are they like?"

"Well, your grandfather is stubborn and bullheaded, and he's gotten rather cranky in his old age. Your grandmother is a sweet woman, but too timid for her own good."

"What do you mean?" Did she really want to know? But after a lifetime of knowing almost nothing about her relatives, she craved any information she could get.

"Although she didn't approve of her daughter's choice in husbands, she didn't want to cut off all contact with her. Unfortunately, she wasn't willing to stand up to her husband when he decided to disown your mother."

"Why not?" The conversation opened old wounds caused by the actions of people she'd never met, but she sensed it would be as healing as cleaning out an abscess.

"To be honest, I think she's a little afraid of him. But she did do something later on that showed she didn't agree with him."

"What did she do?"

"You created quite a stir in your mother's family when you were born." Trudy chuckled softly. "Your grandmother and your great-grandparents wanted to see you, but your grandfather forbade his wife to have any contact, and your great-grandparents' health prevented them from traveling."

Mira wanted to ask about her great-grandparents, but she held her tongue. There would be time to learn about them later, after she found out what her grandmother had done.

"So, your grandmother contacted their attorney and their accountant and set up a trust fund for you. Your grandfather threw a fit, but there was nothing he could do about it. What she had done was perfectly legal, since early in their marriage your grandfather had given her equal control over their finances."

She'd always thought both of her maternal grandparents were angry about her mother's marriage and her birth. Hearing that the truth was so different from what she'd believed left her struggling to adjust. "I have a trust fund set up by my grandmother?"

"Yes, and if I remember correctly, you gain full control of it at the age of twenty-one." Trudy studied her. "How old are you?"

"Twenty, but my birthday is in a couple of weeks." This had to be a dream. Nothing like this ever happened in the life of a poor orphaned immigrant. Not outside of fairy tales, anyway.

"Well, then, you will be very well off in a couple of weeks," Trudy said with a smile. "Of course, there are also your great-grandparents' wills to consider."

"Their wills?" Wasn't a trust fund enough?

"Yes. I'm not sure what they did, but both sets of your great-grandparents did something that involved you and made your grandfather very angry."

Mira stared at the fern in front of her, trying to reconcile everything this old woman said with the lack of contact from her mother's family. She hadn't received so much as a postcard. "I never knew about any of this."

"I'm sure Bill can have his lawyer find out all the details."

"Can you explain all of this to Bill so he can talk to his lawyer?" Mira glanced at her. "I don't think I understand it well enough."

"Of course, dear," she said, giving Mira a reassuring pat on the knee. "This probably wasn't the best time to tell you all of this, but I wanted you to know that, at least in terms of money, you're just like everyone in this family. There is no need for you to feel like you're out of place."

"Thanks, Grandma Trudy."

That evening after the big Thanksgiving dinner, Della and Wendy found Mira speaking with Grandma Trudy in the conservatory again.

"Mira, we need to talk about Saturday," Della said.

That didn't sound good. "It's okay if I go, isn't it?"

Della's warm smile relieved some of Mira's worry. "Of course it is, dear. That wasn't what I meant at all. We need to talk about what you're going to wear."

Curiosity sparked in Trudy's faded green eyes as she turned to Mira. "Where are you going?"

"To a formal fundraiser for the Mercer Center for the Arts. Wayne is taking me." Saying it without feeling bashful got easier all the time.

"He's such a nice young man," Trudy said. "What does your dress look like?"

"That's what we need to talk about." Della met her mother-in-law's gaze. "Mira doesn't have a dress yet."

"Oh, dear." Trudy made a *tsk-tsk* sound. "That is a problem."

"We'll have to buy one tomorrow," Della said. "We'll also have to set up a hair appointment for you on Saturday."

"Why?" This was turning into a more complex date than she'd expected.

"Because you always get your hair done when you attend a formal function."

"That seems like an awful lot of trouble." Thoughts of dress shopping floated through her mind, bringing up memories of the afternoon at the department store with Della and Tabby. "Maybe I should tell Wayne the fundraiser isn't such a good idea after all."

"Oh, no, don't do that." Wendy sounded appalled at the mere suggestion. "I'll make an appointment with the hairdresser I'm going to. That way we can go together."

"That wasn't what I was talking about." Mira wished she could go back in time and tell Wayne a simple dinner-and-a-movie date would be better. "I meant shopping for a dress. I just went clothes shopping last weekend. I don't like it enough to want to go again this soon."

The other women laughed.

"It's a part of life, dear," Trudy said. "And it's one you'll have to get used to. I have a feeling you'll be attending a lot of functions like this soon."

"Not too many, I hope." She would rather muck out stalls than go through the hassle of shopping for formal dresses and getting her hair done. "So much has changed. It's going to take a while to get used to it."

"I know, dear." Trudy patted her knee, her gaze full of understanding. "But formal functions are a part of your life now."

"I know." Mira sighed.

In a way, she almost wished Trudy had never said anything about her mother's parents and grandparents. At least when she thought she didn't have a penny to her name, she knew who she was. Now, she felt as if she'd been reinvented without her consent and they forgot to tell her about her new identity.

"Is there something I should know?" Della's gaze

shifted back and forth between them.

Mira exchanged a glance with Trudy. It would all come out sooner or later anyway. "It seems that in a couple of weeks, I'll gain control of a substantial trust fund and who knows what else."

"I'm afraid I don't understand." Della's eyebrows drew together.

"Why don't you ladies sit down?" Trudy lifted her hand toward a wicker bench near them.

Della followed her advice, but Wendy hesitated. "Maybe I should leave you alone to talk."

"Sit down, Wendy," Trudy said. "I'm sure this will be in the society pages soon anyway."

"Okay, Mom." Wendy took the seat beside Della.

Mira sat quietly as Trudy explained the trust fund and Mira's mystery inheritance from her great-grandparents. When she finished, Della and Wendy sat unspeaking for a moment.

"Well, that certainly is an interesting turn of events," Della finally said. "We'll have to introduce you into society, dear."

"What does that mean?" And did she want to go through it?

"Fancy parties, formal dinners, and—given your age—many eligible suitors," Trudy said with a smile. "You'll be expected to move in certain circles and attend certain functions."

And live in a world where discomfort was a constant companion. Mira heaved a sigh. "I think I preferred being poor. At least then nobody cares what I do as long as I don't bother them."

"Depending on what those wills say, you're probably

wealthy enough to do whatever you want." Trudy's smile took on a teasing quality. "They'll just say you're eccentric."

Mira considered her new friends, including Ben. "So, I could break some of the rules of high society and no one will care?"

"If they do, they won't say anything," Trudy said with a chuckle. "They'll want to stay on your good side."

"Who are your grandparents and great-grandparents?" Della asked.

Before coming to Dayton, she wouldn't have thought it would matter. Around here, however, who your family was appeared to be as important as who you were. "Well, my mother was a Potter, but I don't know about anyone else."

"Your grandmother was a Doyle before she married into the Potter family," Trudy said.

"Potter and Doyle?" Della's eyes widened. "As in Potter Porcelain and Doyle Manufacturing?"

Trudy nodded. "That's right."

So, Della had heard of her relatives. Mira wasn't sure what to do with that knowledge, so she focused on something else. "What are Potter Porcelain and Doyle Manufacturing?"

"The businesses your great-grandfathers started that have since grown into multibillion-dollar companies," Trudy said.

Mira slumped against the back of her seat and tried to remember how to breathe. She was descended from billionaires? No wonder Trudy had assured her she fit in with the Montaignes' circle. "Oh, wow."

"Oh, wow is right," Wendy said. "Remember your question about people caring what you do? The answer is no. You could go to that fundraiser Saturday wearing sweats, and when people hear who your family is, no one would say a word."

Mira glanced at her with a faint smile. "Given who my family is, I think I better wear something a lot fancier than sweats."

Thirty-Two

Friday morning, Mira left her crutches in her room when she went down for breakfast. Her leg was still sore, but she could walk with little discomfort.

The moment she stepped into the dining room, Tabby squealed. "You're off the crutches!"

"Yeah." She took a seat beside Tabby. "It didn't hurt to walk around my room, so I decided to try going without them."

"It looks like the experiment is a success."

"So far, anyway." She hoped she could continue to walk unaided. Having to use crutches wasn't on her list of favorite things.

"We'll hope it continues to be successful," Della said. "I'm sure selecting a dress will be much easier if you can walk without crutches."

"Oh, that's right!" Tabby grabbed Mira's arm. "Please tell me I can help you pick your dress."

She remembered how helpful Tabby had been the last time they'd gone clothes shopping. "Sure. You know more about what I need than I do."

Tabby bounced in her seat and turned to her

mother. "We should start at Angela's."

Della nodded. "They do have lovely gowns."

Mira quietly ate her breakfast while Tabby and Della discussed shops and dress styles. Wendy added a few comments here and there, and Mira once again wondered if this date was truly worth all the fuss everyone was making. After all, it was only to thank Wayne for showing her a few words in English. Surely something less involved would work—like baking him a pie.

The Montaigne women wouldn't let her back out of the shopping trip. Despite her best efforts to convince Tabby she'd just talk Wayne into doing something less fancy, Mira found herself in the back seat of Della's car on the way into Dayton.

Three boutiques and way too many dresses later, she studied herself in the full-length mirror and smiled. "I think this is the dress."

She turned around to see what the others thought.

"It's perfect!" Tabby clasped her hands and held them to her chest.

"You look beautiful, dear." Della's proud smile resembled that of a mother helping her daughter pick out her first prom dress.

"You'll turn everyone's head when you walk into the room." Wendy gave a small chuckle. "I think I should be jealous."

Della laughed. "I know I am."

Mira faced the mirror again and gazed at the floor-length, dark blue gown that fit like it had been made for her. The sleeveless bodice shimmered when she moved and had a modestly scooped neckline. A silky, dark blue shawl draped across her shoulders, and she wore a pair of low-heeled shoes in the same shade. She certainly looked like the granddaughter and great-granddaughter of billionaires, if she ignored the split ends in her hair. "So, this will work?"

Wendy nodded. "Definitely."

"Go ahead and change back into your clothes, dear," Della said.

Mira headed for the dressing room. She loved the way the skirt flowed when she moved, and the soft fabric against her skin made her feel like the princess Tabby had once said she was pretty enough to be.

As she changed back into her jeans and the hoodie Josh had let her keep, she realized she would soon be able to pay Della back for this dress and the other clothes she had bought. Once she turned twenty-one and gained control of the trust fund Trudy had told her about, the first thing she planned to do was give Della enough to cover everything she had purchased for her.

Knowing she would be financially independent before Christmas brought a smile to Mira's lips as she carried the dress and shoes into the main part of the boutique.

At the hairdresser's the next afternoon, Mira sat in one of the chairs and tried not to feel out of place. Any time she'd wanted her hair trimmed throughout childhood, her mother had plopped her in a chair in the backyard and taken a pair of scissors to it. After moving to the United States, Marnie had taken over the task of hair cutting whenever Mira asked. How was she supposed to explain to these people that professional styling was as foreign to her now as English had been seven years ago?

Thankfully, Wendy occupied the chair beside her and helped her discuss hairstyles with the stylist. In the end, they all agreed Mira should cut her hair into long layers before getting it styled in an upsweep of curls for the evening.

After three hours at the salon, both women were deemed ready for any formal occasion, and they headed back to the Montaigne estate to dress. As Mira did her makeup with more care than the last time she'd applied it, Della, Wendy, and Tabby gave her a fast lesson on proper etiquette for the occasion. Trying to keep all the rules straight was enough to give anyone anxiety, but Mira did her best to appear calm. If she let them know about the worry attacking every thought, she would undoubtedly receive enough sympathy and reassurance to make her scream.

By the time she headed downstairs to meet Wayne, Mira had decided she was insane. What else could have made her think she would be able to fit in with the other fundraiser attendees? There were so many things she didn't know. Even though Trudy had assured her she was as wealthy as anyone who would be there—and wealthier than many—she still felt like the poor girl from West Virginia she had been for years.

Della stepped close when they reached the first floor and patted her arm. "You're going to be fine, dear. You look lovely, and you know how to behave properly."

Wendy moved to her other side and smiled. "Besides, you're a member of the Potter and Doyle families. If you make a mistake, just mention that fact and people will be so impressed they won't remember what you did."

"That removes a lot of pressure." Mira welcomed her new friend's humor.

Wendy laughed as they entered the living room where the men waited. Bill, Stephen, and Wayne rose from their seats to greet them.

Bill ran his gaze over them with a smile. "You ladies look stunning."

"Stephen and Wayne look pretty good, too," Wendy said with a glance at their black tuxedos and crisp white shirts.

"Wayne, we'll be the envy of every man there." Stephen walked over to his wife. "You're beautiful, darling."

"Thank you, dear." She rewarded him with a pleased smile.

Wayne joined Mira with an appreciative gleam in his eyes. "You know, Stephen, I do believe you're right."

A swarm of butterflies took flight in Mira's stomach as she smiled shyly at her date for the evening. She hoped she could live up to his expectations or at least avoid embarrassing either of them. As they went out to Stephen's waiting car, she adjusted the warm wrap Wendy had loaned her. Even if everything else about the evening turned into a disaster, no one could ridicule her clothing.

Wayne and Mira rode in the back as Stephen drove

to the Mercer Center. She tried to appear completely calm and relaxed even though she was a nervous wreck inside. She knew she had failed when Wayne turned to her.

"Nervous?"

"A little." Her cheeks heated. Why did he have to see through her act?

He patted her knee with a smile. "Don't worry, this will be fun."

"I'm sure it will also be different from anything I've ever been to."

"Most likely, but you look the part, even if you don't feel it. And after the way you handled yourself Thursday with my cousins, I know you'll do great tonight."

"Thanks, Wayne." His confidence in her bolstered her faith in herself.

The Mercer Center was housed inside an old redbrick school building. Mira found it a little strange to leave the car in the care of a valet outside such a modest building, but the others took it in stride. Inside, they checked their coats and wraps with a cheerful young woman. Mira adjusted her shawl and allowed Wayne to lightly rest his hand on her back as he guided her toward a beautifully decorated room.

The moment she entered, several sets of eyes focused on her. Wayne offered his arm, and she took it the way Della had shown her. Maybe if she played the part of a rich young woman, people would quit staring at her.

"Shall we go introduce you to some people?" Wayne lifted an eyebrow.

Did they have to? She already knew the answer and managed a smile. "I suppose we should."

They strolled among the formally dressed men and women, and she started to relax. With her current attire, she blended in with them. Each person Wayne introduced her to expressed polite interest, but she soon realized all the looks she'd been receiving since she walked in were simply curiosity because of who she was with. Thanks to a brief interview by a reporter from the *Dayton Post*, Mira learned Wayne was considered one of Ohio's most eligible bachelors.

Wayne introduced her to several more of Dayton's elite, and Mira began to believe she would make it through the evening without incident after all.

Then she saw Paul Washburn and Shannon Crosse heading straight for them. She groaned softly, and Wayne glanced at her.

"What's wrong?"

She kept her focus on the approaching couple. "This is going to be interesting."

He followed her gaze. "You know Paul and Shannon?"

"Well enough," she said and pasted a smile on her face as they arrived.

Shannon scanned Mira from head to toe and back, her features twisted by a look of disgust. "How did *you* get in here?"

"Hello, Shannon, Paul," Mira said, faking a friendly tone. "Do you know Wayne Zivney?"

The disgust vanished in an instant, replaced with a smile as Shannon stopped just short of batting her eyelashes at him. "Of course I do."

"Good evening, Wayne." Paul offered his hand.

Wayne gave it a hearty shake and released it. "Good evening. I see you already know my date."

"Your *date*?" Shannon stared at him as if he was an alien species.

"Yes, she did me the great honor of agreeing to accompany me tonight," Wayne said in the pompous tone Mira was beginning to appreciate.

She had to struggle to keep from laughing at the bewildered expressions on Shannon's and Paul's faces. Apparently they found it mind-boggling that someone of Wayne's standing could possibly be interested in who they thought was a poor immigrant from rural West Virginia.

After a moment, Shannon gave Wayne an innocent look. "You do realize she doesn't have a penny to her name or any sense of class."

Wayne faced Mira and cocked his head to the side as if studying her. Then he winked and turned back to Shannon, his expression now puzzled. "Are you sure? Mira looks very classy and just as wealthy as you."

Shannon gasped, but before she or Paul could respond, the reporter from the *Dayton Post* joined the group.

"Excuse me, Miss Hassan." She sounded unduly apologetic and a little awed. "May I speak with you for a moment?"

"Sure." Mira gracefully turned toward her and prayed that whatever the reporter wanted wouldn't give Shannon more ammunition against her.

After a couple of false starts, the reporter said, "Miss Hassan, why didn't you mention before that you are the mystery heiress to the Doyle and Potter fortunes?"

Shannon gasped again, swaying this time, and a wide-eyed Paul reached out to steady her. Wayne looked as stunned as Paul as he waited to hear Mira's answer.

So much for avoiding an awkward situation. "Well, I didn't know it was a mystery."

"I've spent the last ten years trying to find out who inherited the bulk of those estates," the reporter said. "I just found out a few minutes ago that it's you."

"I'm not sure what to say." How much had she inherited?

"Will you let me interview you for a feature article?"

"I suppose." What did the bulk of the Doyle and Potter estates constitute to receive such interest from a reporter? "I'll need to check my schedule before I set a time."

"That's fine," the reporter said, regaining her former finesse. She handed Mira a business card. "If you could call me as soon as possible, I would be grateful."

What would Della do in this situation? Mira graced the woman with a blasé smile. "Of course."

The reporter excused herself, and Paul and Shannon mutely drifted away. Wayne guided Mira over to the dance floor set up near the string quartet.

"Would you care to dance?"

She watched the couples gliding by, and her nerves gave a renewed flutter. "I don't know how."

"Just follow my lead." He led her onto the floor.

A moment later, they slowly danced to the beautiful classical music played by the quartet. Wayne moved them to a fairly empty corner of the floor.

"What was that reporter talking about?" he asked, his voice low enough that it wouldn't carry.

She had so hoped she could wait a little longer to admit who her family was, but that was no longer an option. "According to Grandma Trudy, the Potters and the Doyles were my great-grandparents. Apparently, they did something to their wills that involved me and created quite a stir in both families." She looked at him, praying he would see her honesty. "I didn't want to tell that reporter, but I have no idea what I inherited. Until Thursday, I didn't even know I had been named in any wills."

Wayne was quiet for a moment. "How long have you known you were descended from the Potters and the Doyles?"

"Since Thursday when Grandma Trudy told me. I knew my mother's maiden name was Potter, but it didn't mean anything to me."

The quartet finished the piece, and Mira and Wayne applauded politely with the others on the dance floor. Then they headed to one of the small tables set up around the perimeter. Wendy and Stephen joined them a moment later.

"Well, Mira, it looks like the secret's out," Wendy said.

She nodded, her mind racing. "I just can't figure out how."

"I called Della to see if she had spoken to anyone about it." Wendy gave her an apologetic look. "She hadn't, but it appears Adrienne was eavesdropping when Mom told us about your family. My daughter will apologize to you for calling the newspaper."

"She doesn't have to. Grandma Trudy warned me it would be in the papers soon anyway. I was just hoping to know what I inherited before getting interviewed about it."

"From that reporter's comments," Wayne said, "I'd say you inherited quite a bit."

Thirty-Three

The tone of the evening changed after the reporter left. No longer did Wayne have to take Mira over to people to introduce her. They came to her to introduce themselves. Rather than being the nobody Wayne Zivney brought to the fundraiser, she became the heiress who accompanied him.

Everyone seemed to have some idea of what she had inherited except her. Trying to pretend she didn't feel like a fraud was exhausting, but she had to do it. No one cared that she'd grown up poor. She was the heiress to the Potter and Doyle fortunes, and people expected her to be as comfortable with that as they were with their own wealth.

As much as she tried not to care what people thought of her, finding out she was rich changed things in ways she was still trying to understand. She no longer had the freedom to do as she pleased and completely ignore the rules of high society. Thanks to her great-grandparents, she now risked a public scandal if she stepped too far outside the expectations for a young lady of means.

By the time the evening ended, Mira was ready to go find a nice cabin deep in the woods of West Virginia and stay there until everyone forgot who she was. Instead, she climbed into the car with Wayne and rode quietly back to the Montaignes'. After telling Wayne good night, she talked to Bill and Della for a few minutes about the evening before excusing herself to go to bed. Bill promised to call Richard Halliday and have him look into Mira's trust fund and inheritance.

Tabby joined Mira in the upstairs hallway and followed her into her room.

"Wayne told me you ran into Paul and Shannon."

"Yeah, that was interesting." Mira walked over to her bed and sat down on the edge. Even though her leg had healed enough that she didn't need crutches, it still ached after the long evening.

"How did they act?"

"Shocked that I'm rich." She started pulling out hairpins to let her hair down. "I thought Shannon was going to faint when that reporter mentioned my great-grandparents."

Tabby giggled. "I wish I could have seen that. Nothing ever fazes her."

"That did." Mira grinned at the memory.

"So, did you have fun?" Tabby began helping her remove the hairpins.

"It was kind of fun, although it was a bit strange after people found out about the Potters and the Doyles."

"What do you mean?" Tabby removed the last pin, sending Mira's hair cascading down. "Oh, you got your hair layered! I love it!"

"Thanks." She kicked her shoes off as Tabby sat down beside her. "All these people that didn't seem to care one way or the other if I was there at the beginning of the evening suddenly started going out of their way to talk to me."

"That would be strange. What did you think about the rest of the evening?"

"It was nice, but it's not really my thing. Give me a good ol' barn dance any day."

"You'll get used to these functions." Tabby gave her shoulder a sympathetic pat. "I'm sure you'll be getting a lot of invitations soon."

"Maybe." Everyone seemed to think it was inevitable, but Mira hoped people would forget about her quickly once the novelty of discovering the identity of the mystery heiress wore off.

"So, are you and Wayne going to go out again?"

"I doubt it. He's a nice guy, but we both agreed that this was a one-time deal."

"What about Ben?" Tabby asked with a grin. "I know you talked to him this morning and you're going to church with him tomorrow."

Warmth settled in Mira's chest at the thought of the handsome stable boy. "That has definite possibilities."

"I wonder what Mom will say," Tabby said with a laugh.

"Not much, I'm sure. I'm a Potter and a Doyle, remember?"

The next morning, Mira dressed in a long skirt and a

sweater. She couldn't help comparing her anticipation of going to church with Ben to her nerves about going out with Wayne the previous evening. Based on that alone, she had no doubt she'd made the right choice by telling Wayne their date was a one-time thing.

She was waiting in the living room when the doorbell chimed. Della stepped into the entryway as Mira opened the front door. Ben stood on the other side and smiled.

"Good morning, Mira."

"Morning, Ben." She loved seeing him to start her day.

"You ready?"

"I just need to get my coat." Mira opened the door a little wider and stepped back. "Come on in."

He stopped just inside the door and gave Della a friendly, if uncomfortable, smile as Mira headed for the living room. "Good morning, Miss Della."

"Good morning, Ben. It was kind of you to offer to drive Mira to church."

"It's my pleasure," he said as Mira returned wearing her coat.

"I'll see you later, Della," Mira said as Ben opened the door.

"All right, dear. Have fun."

Once they were in his truck, Ben sighed and visibly relaxed.

"That was a bit awkward," he said as he steered the truck down the drive.

Mira smiled. "But not too bad."

"No, not too bad." He glanced at her before turning onto the road. "Did you see the paper this morning?"

"No, I haven't. Why?"

He opened the glove compartment and pulled out a folded newspaper. "Take a look."

Mira accepted the paper and studied it as Ben drove down the road. A large picture of her and Wayne from the previous night stared back at her. Below the photo was a headline in large black letters. The only words she recognized were her first and last names.

She glanced at Ben, uncertain of his reaction. "I don't know what to say."

"I was a bit surprised to see that, although you look beautiful in that picture." His voice and expression gave her no clues to his thoughts.

"Thank you." She dropped her gaze to the paper again. How had she forgotten about the photograph the reporter had insisted on taking?

After a moment, Ben spoke. "I know it's probably none of my business, and feel free to tell me if it isn't, but are you and Wayne Zivney seeing each other?"

"No, we're not." Mira shifted in her seat to face him. "Last night was a one-time thing. He did a favor for me, so I agreed to go to the fundraiser."

Ben glanced at her. "That's it?"

She smiled and nodded. "He and I are from different worlds, and that became obvious to both of us last night."

"According to that article, you're from very similar families."

"Not really." She laid the paper on the seat between them. "I never knew my grandparents or my great-grandparents. I didn't even know anything about them until a couple of days ago."

Ben glanced at her again. "Really?"

"Really. The only family members I've ever known were my parents and Harley and Marnie. All I knew about my grandparents on either side is that they disapproved of my parents' marriage. My mom and dad were disowned by both families. The only life I've ever known is one of hard work and not a lot of money. There was also plenty of love to make up for anything we didn't have."

Ben was quiet for a few minutes. When they stopped at a red light, he turned toward Mira. "I'm glad your great-grandparents and your grandmother found a way to give you the life you deserve."

Relief washed through her. He was still going to treat her the same way he always had. "I wish I could have met my great-grandparents. I'm hoping I'll have the chance to meet my grandparents someday soon."

"I hope you get that chance, too." He hesitated before continuing. "If you need a friend to go with you, I'll gladly be that friend."

"Thanks, Ben." Her heart melted at the sweet offer.

The light changed, and they continued on to the church.

It was an interesting morning. Everyone there had seen the picture and the article in the paper or heard about it. They asked Mira all kinds of questions about her family, her inheritance, and her plans for the future. Most people wanted to know things she couldn't answer because she didn't know herself. One question she could answer, however, came from Pastor Jeff.

"Do I still need to call the Mercer Center tomorrow?"

"I'd still like to teach people to play the fiddle, but now I can do it for free," Mira said. "They can put the money to use somewhere else."

"They'll be glad to hear it." Pastor Jeff smiled. "They usually have a hard time finding instructors who will work for free."

"Well, they can have a fiddle instructor for nothing if they want one," Mira said with a laugh.

"I'll call in the morning and see what they say."

After the church service, Lydia Petros shuffled rapidly up to Mira and Ben. He leaned down to give her a kiss on the cheek.

"Good morning, Grandmother."

"Good morning, Ben." Lydia smiled sweetly. "Are you bringing Mira to dinner?"

"I haven't asked her yet." He turned to Mira. "Our family gets together for dinner at my aunt and uncle's farm after church every Sunday. Would you like to come?"

"That sounds like fun, if you don't think anyone will mind."

"People are always bringing friends with them," Lydia assured her. "They'll be glad to meet a friend of Ben's."

He rolled his eyes. "My family thinks I work too hard. They always complain that I never bring anyone to the family dinner."

Mira laughed. "Now they won't be able to complain, but you're on your own with the working too hard thing."

"That's okay, they'll understand why I work so hard when I graduate in August instead of having another year to go," Ben said, giving his grandmother a pointed look.

"I know, you work hard so you can graduate early," Lydia said with a smile that gave Mira the impression that they'd had this discussion many times before. "But at least you have a very pretty friend to bring to dinner."

Ben shifted his attention Mira with a smile. "Yes, I do."

Lydia shuffled off, and Mira tried to ignore the way her face warmed under Ben's gaze.

"This probably sounds strange," she said, "but how does your grandmother get to church?"

"She lives with my Uncle George and Aunt Sandy, so they bring her on the way to their church and pick her up on the way home. Uncle George and Aunt Sandy are the ones with the farm."

"Do you have a big family?"

"Pretty big," Ben said as they drifted toward the door. "I have an older brother who's married and has two kids. Uncle George and Aunt Sandy have two children, both of whom are married and have three kids between them. Then there's Aunt Helen and Uncle Dave. They have three kids, all married and with kids of their own."

"That is a big family." A pang of envy hit. What would it have been like to grow up with such a large family instead of only her parents followed by only Harley and Marnie?

"You'll get to meet most of them. Maybe all of them."

Mira's pulse picked up speed. "They'll all be there?"

"Yeah, there may be a lot of us, but we're pretty

close." He looked a little embarrassed. "I should warn you. They'll probably drop some hints about marriage or dating."

"Dare I ask why?" She didn't bother to tell him that Lydia had already dropped some hints.

"I'm the only one old enough to be married who isn't. Of course, my family tends to forget that I want to be out of school before I consider marriage."

"That makes sense," Mira said. "As for dropping hints, you wouldn't believe how many of the women at that fundraiser last night have eligible sons, grandsons, and nephews."

"That's what you get for inheriting who knows what."

"Oh, the things I put up with." She heaved a melodramatic sigh.

Ben laughed but then sobered as a couple came in and joined Lydia. "My aunt and uncle just arrived to pick up Grandmother. Would you like to meet them?"

Mira glanced toward them and found the couple studying her. "I think I better. They might die of curiosity if they have to wait much longer."

He chuckled and led her over to his relatives. "Uncle George, Aunt Sandy, I'd like you to meet my friend Mira Hassan."

She had to try hard not to laugh at their huge smiles.

"Mira, I'm so happy to meet you!" Sandy said. "Mom was just telling us that Ben invited you to dinner."

"Yes, he did," she said. "I'm happy to come, if that's okay with you."

"Oh, absolutely! With a family as large as ours, what's one more?"

"I have some friends who used to tell me that all the time."

"So, we'll see you in a little bit." George's eyebrows rose in inquiry.

"Of course, Uncle George," Ben said with an amused glance at Mira.

Thirty-Four

The bright sunlight did nothing to warm the chilly air as Mira and Ben left the church. They strolled toward his truck, stopping several times along the way to exchange small talk with other churchgoers. Finally, they reached the quiet confines of his brown pickup.

Mira caught Ben watching her as he let the engine warm up, and self-consciousness hit. "What?"

"I was just thinking about the way people seem to be drawn to you."

"I can think of plenty of people that seem to be repelled by me."

"That attitude right there is one reason people are drawn to you," Ben said. "You're so unaware of how wonderful a person you really are. You're beautiful and talented, yet you seem surprised that anyone thinks so."

She resisted the urge to tell him it was because of experience with too many people who thought the opposite. Heat crept into her cheeks, and she looked down at her hands clasped in her lap. "Ben, you're embarrassing me."

"You asked what I was thinking," he said and put the truck in gear.

She lifted her gaze to find him smiling. "I know, but I wasn't expecting you to be thinking about me."

"That just proves my point." He glanced at her with twinkling eyes.

"I hate it when people say that to me."

"Does it happen often?"

"No, but I just decided that I hate it," Mira said with a laugh.

A few minutes later, they were heading back the same way they had come earlier in the morning. Mira watched out the window for a while, noticing everything they passed was rather familiar. She turned to Ben.

"Where do your aunt and uncle live?"

He grinned. "Just down the road from the Montaignes."

"They're Bill and Della's neighbors?" Her eyebrows rose. She couldn't imagine the couple she'd met at the church living in such a wealthy neighborhood.

"If you count living about three miles away as neighbors."

"What kind of farm do they have?"

"Just a regular farm. Uncle George harvested his corn a few weeks ago, and he's got some winter wheat planted in another field. They have a couple of dairy cows, some horses, and chickens. There was a turkey, but we ate him for Thanksgiving."

"That sounds about like Harley and Marnie's farm," Mira said. "Except they had barn cats and a dog."

"Uncle George and Aunt Sandy have barn cats, too."

Ben turned into a long drive. "They're between dogs right now."

He parked next to the barn, and Mira marveled at the number of cars already parked between the barn and the house. As they climbed out of the truck, another car came down the drive.

"That's my brother and his family," Ben said as the car parked near them. "They'll be ecstatic to know I really do have friends."

A man similar in appearance to Ben, but a few years older, stepped out of the car with a grin.

"Hey, little brother, who's your friend?"

"This is Mira Hassan," Ben said a pretty woman climbed out of the car and opened the back door. "Mira, this is Peter and his wife Tara."

Before any more could be said, two small children came running toward Ben. He knelt to greet them.

"Hi, Uncle Ben!" the little boy said happily.

"Hi, Joey, and how are you?"

"Great! I made a sheep in Sunday School."

"Did you really?" Ben gave his nephew an impressed look.

"Uh-huh," Joey assured him with a nod, and then looked over his shoulder at Tara. "Mommy, can I show Uncle Ben my sheep?"

"Sure." She smiled and held out her hand. "Let's go get it out of the car."

As Joey ran back to the car, Ben turned to his niece.

"Hi, Grace, do you have a hug for your uncle?"

She gave him a sweet smile and wrapped her little arms around his neck. After a moment, it became obvious that she wasn't going to let go anytime soon.

315

He picked her up as he stood.

"This is my favorite little leech," Ben said, turning to Mira. "Hey, Grace, are you going to say hi to my friend Mira?"

The dark-haired girl smiled shyly at her then buried her face in her uncle's shoulder.

Peter laughed. "Apparently not. Grace isn't much of a talker, but Joey more than makes up for it."

"How old are they?" Mira asked.

"Grace is almost three and Joey's four," Peter answered.

Joey ran up carrying a piece of construction paper with cotton balls glued to it. "Here's my sheep!"

Ben surveyed the picture and nodded. "That's an awesome sheep."

"Why don't we go inside where it's warm and show your sheep to Grandma and Grandpa?" Tara said.

"Okay!" Joey ran toward the house.

"Oh, to have that much energy." Tara laughed and turned to Mira. "Hi, Mira, how are you?"

"Good. You have adorable children."

"Thank you," Tara said as they followed Joey to the house. "It's nice to see proof that Ben has a life outside of work and school."

Ben chuckled. "Nice try, Tara. I met Mira at work."

"But you're not at work now, are you?" Peter said.

Cheerful voices and laughter surrounded Mira the moment she stepped inside. The women in the kitchen welcomed her like she was a part of the family. Ben introduced everyone as he guided her out of the kitchen and into the living room. She had no hope of remembering all the names, but she would never forget the faces. Each one of them smiled and made it clear she belonged there, even if only for the day. Ben's parents, Dimitri and Ellen, greeted her with more warmth than the others.

Mira remembered Ben's warning about how his relatives might drop hints about dating. From the welcome she received, she had a feeling they'd skipped hinting and gone straight for assuming. Not that she minded. If Ben ever asked her out on a date, she wouldn't even have to think about it before saying yes.

The buffet-style meal was set up in a huge room with two long tables that had enough room to seat everyone there, plus a few more. A mismatched collection of serving dishes covered another table off to one side. Either Sandy and George shopped at garage sales and thrift stores or those dishes belonged to more than one family.

Before Mira could go ask Ben about it, Ellen stepped up beside her. "It's quite a meal, isn't it?"

"It looks wonderful." She wasn't sure what all of the dishes were, but mouthwatering scents filled the room. "I assume Sandy had a lot of help preparing this."

Ellen laughed. "Every family here donated something to the meal. We turned the weekly family dinner into a potluck years ago. The family got so large that it just wasn't fair to put all the cooking on one family. So, now every one brings a dish or two."

"That's wonderful." It reminded Mira of the days when Harley and Marnie had taken her to church potlucks. The variety of foods had been an amazing way for a Palestinian girl to learn about American cuisine without getting judged for her ignorance. She'd just taken a little of whatever looked good, and then Marnie explained what she'd selected once they were seated.

The rest of the family gathered in the dining room, and George said a prayer for the meal and the people about to enjoy it. Ben guided Mira through the serving line, pointing out the dishes he considered best, and then he led her to seats at the end of one of the tables. His brother's family surrounded them. Mira stayed quiet through much of the meal, absorbing the friendly conversation and laughter around her as she ate both American and Greek foods.

After lunch, she offered to help clean up and received the job of wiping down the tables once others had cleared them. As she finished the last table, she realized she had company.

"Hi, Grace," Mira said with a smile.

The little girl smiled and held out a piece of paper. "I made you a picture."

"Why, thank you, Grace!" She accepted the crayon drawing.

"It's you and Uncle Ben," she said, pointing to the two multi-colored scribbles.

"It's very pretty. I'll have to hang it up when I get home."

Grace smiled shyly and wandered off. Mira looked at the picture again and shook her head. Even a little girl who wasn't quite three yet was trying to set her up with Ben.

After returning the dishcloth to the kitchen, Mira went into the large living room where most of the family had gathered to talk. Ben joined her and tapped the paper in her hand.

"What's this?"

"A picture Grace drew for me." She pointed to the scribbles. "According to her, that's me and that's her Uncle Ben."

"You should feel special. Grace doesn't draw pictures for just anyone. She must really like you."

"She's a sweet little girl."

"She also has good taste in people." Ben smiled and gazed into her eyes.

Mira blushed and looked away. She found several of Ben's family members watching her with smiles. Knowing they approved of her was great, but she didn't know how to handle the way they all seemed to think she was dating Ben. Should she tell them the truth? That they were good friends and nothing more? Or were their reactions an indication that Ben had told them there was a romantic relationship?

She shook off her confusing thoughts. There would be plenty of time later to figure it all out. For now, she planned to enjoy spending time with Ben and a family that welcomed her as warmly as the village she'd grown up in.

About the middle of the afternoon, people began putting on their coats and preparing to leave. After receiving an invitation to join the family dinner anytime, Mira headed out the door with Ben. They strolled toward his truck, saying goodbye to the family members climbing into their cars.

She hated the thought of leaving this wonderful family, but it was inevitable. No matter how much she had enjoyed getting to know them, no matter how warmly they'd accepted her into their midst, they weren't her family.

Ben paused by the barn door. "Would you like to see some of my uncle's animals?"

Mira nodded and followed him into the barn. He introduced each animal by name, and she petted the velvety noses that greeted her over the stall doors. When they reached the back of the barn, they turned around and walked slowly toward the door.

"You're awful quiet," Ben said.

Mira gave him a sheepish smile. "Sorry."

He stopped in the middle of the aisle and studied her. "Is something wrong?"

"Oh, no, today has been perfect!" Her gaze drifted to one of the barn cats taking a bath. "It's just that..."

"What is it, Mira?" Ben's gentle tone made her want to cry.

"Today is the first time since I moved to America that I've felt like I belonged," she answered softly, bringing her gaze back to him. "I mean, I felt wanted by Harley and Marnie, but their family treated me like I was contagious. I had a couple of close friends who included me, but I still felt like an outsider. It's the same way with the Montaignes. They include me in everything, but I know I don't belong. Here, I felt like I was with my own family."

"I'm glad you feel welcome here. Everyone likes you, and when they invited you to come again, they meant it."

"I'd like to come again." More than anything, she wanted a family of her own.

"Good. I'd like for you to get to know my family

better." His smile added to the sincerity in his voice and eyes.

She dropped her gaze as she weighed what she was about to say, but then lifted her eyes to his as she spoke. "I want to meet my grandparents. They may refuse, but if they agree, will you go with me?"

"Of course, I will," he said without hesitation. "If you want me to go with you to talk to anyone else, all you have to do is ask."

"Thanks, Ben."

They started walking toward the door again. Ben reached for her hand, grasping it gently.

"Mira, I want you to know that you can talk to me about anything. You're my friend, and I care about what's on your mind."

She glanced at him as one of her biggest insecurities flashed to mind. "In that case, I'll tell you something I haven't told another living soul."

"What's that?"

"I'm scared to death of being rich." Her eyes misted over as she waited for his reaction.

He wrapped her in a comforting hug. "It'll be okay."

"I don't want people to treat me differently just because I have money." Her words were muffled by his coat as she slipped her arms around him. "I've already had that start happening. People who ignored me when they thought I was poor want to be my best friend now that they know about my inheritance."

"You don't have to worry about me treating you differently," Ben said, holding her a little tighter. "To me, you're still the same girl who walked into the Montaignes' stable last week. I liked you before you found out you had inherited anything."

"Really?" Mira took a step back and searched his face for any sign he was telling her less than the truth. She didn't find it.

"Really." He reached out and brushed away her tears. "I love my job in the stable, but I look forward to seeing you every morning even more."

Her heart picked up speed. "I look forward to getting to talk to you, even if it's just for a few minutes."

They stared at each other in silence just long enough for Mira to wonder if he would kiss her. Then Ben cleared his throat and stepped back.

"I should probably get you home."

"Yeah, Bill and Della are probably wondering where I am."

She was a little disappointed, but also relieved. A lot of confusing feelings swirled through her. She needed time to sort through them before adding more, even the good feelings getting kissed by Ben would undoubtedly bring.

When he stopped his truck in front of the Montaigne house, Ben turned to her. "Do you want a ride to church this evening?"

"I don't know. I need to talk to Bill about this whole inheritance thing, and I don't know if the Montaignes have anything planned for this evening."

He pulled a pen and a scrap of paper out of the glove box. "If you decide you want a ride, give me a call. For that matter, feel free to call if all you want to do is talk."

"I will." Mira accepted his number and opened her door. "Thanks for a great day, and thanks for listening."

"Any time. See you later, Mira."

She smiled and climbed out of the truck. Once in the house, she looked at the scrap of paper in her hand and realized that she'd fallen for the man who had given it to her.

Thirty-Five

Monday morning, Mira met Bill as he headed for the dining room. "I've been thinking."

"Oh?" He motioned for her to precede him into the dining room.

"Yeah." Nerves attacked, but she drew in a calming breath. No matter how anxious it made her, she had to make her request. "I'm sure you've noticed that this house is kind of far from anywhere."

"That's part of why we chose to build out here." Bill sat in his usual place at the head of the table. "The privacy is nice."

"I like it too, but getting anywhere is a bit of a problem." She took a seat to his left.

"Was there somewhere you wanted to go? I could have Lucas drive you."

"I'm meeting with that literacy tutor tomorrow, but I was hoping to drive myself. If you're willing to let me borrow a car, that is."

"You said something the other day about having a driver's license. I assume it's valid?"

"Of course." She clasped her hands in her lap and

waited for his decision.

"All right." Bill leaned back in his chair and studied her. Then he straightened again. "Here's what we'll do. After breakfast, you and I will go for a drive. If all goes well, I'll let you borrow the SUV until you can get your own vehicle."

"Thanks, Bill." Mira smiled as Charlotte arrived with breakfast.

"Don't thank me yet. You still have to prove you're as good a driver as I'm sure you will be."

"You know Harley wouldn't have had it any other way." She had fond memories of him taking her out on empty country roads and teaching her to drive his old truck. He'd been a patient teacher, as calm and steady with her as he was with a skittish horse.

After breakfast, they got the SUV out of the garage and headed into the city. Mira navigated the roads with no problem. Even when they ran into rush hour traffic, she proved she'd learned Harley's lessons well.

When they arrived back at the house, Bill refused to accept the keys from her. "You might as well keep them. You're going to need them."

"Thank you." She felt like flinging her arms around him in a hug worthy of Tabby, but she wasn't sure how he'd react. Besides, that wasn't really her way.

"You're welcome." He checked his watch. "I have to go. If you need more gas and I'm not here, talk to Della."

He strode over to a luxury sedan, climbed in, and drove away.

Mira slipped the keys into her pocket and headed for the stable. With the freedom to come and go as she pleased, she felt more independent than she had since arriving in Dayton. She hadn't realized how much the ability to drive herself places meant to her, but now she wished she would have asked Bill about borrowing a car a week ago.

She spotted Ben's truck parked at the other end of the stable. Lightness filled her heart. Even if she only got to see him for a few minutes, it would be enough. Seeing him each morning was one of the highlights of her days.

Lucas met her as soon as she stepped inside. "Hey, Mira. You here to work with Maggie?"

"If that's all right with you."

"You know it is. That horse has made so much progress with your help. There's no way I'd stop you from working with her."

She stopped by the tack room door. "In that case, is it okay if I go ahead and groom her to help her relax?"

"Sure. Just don't take her farther than the crossties before I'm there to keep an eye on things."

Mira hung her coat in the tack room and collected a bucket of grooming tools before heading down the aisle to her favorite horse's stall. The big gray head came over the stall door to greet her.

"Hey, pretty girl," Mira said in Hebrew. The horse consistently responded better to that language than English.

Maggie lowered her head for a forehead scratch. She seemed a little nervous, but she was nowhere near as skittish as she had been a few days ago.

Mira rubbed the horse's face a moment longer, pleased to see the animal relaxing. "Okay, Maggie, let's get you groomed."

She grabbed a lead rope hanging nearby and clipped it to Maggie's halter to walk her to the crossties. One she'd secured the horse, she picked up a curry-comb and got to work.

By the time the grooming session ended, Maggie had lowered her head and relaxed to the point of resting her weight on three legs. Mira returned the soft body brush to the bucket, pleased with the horse's mood. With her this relaxed, she would be much easier to work with.

The clip-clop of hooves on the concrete aisle caught Mira's attention, and she watched Ben put a bay in crossties.

"Hey," she said as she approached.

"Morning, Mira." Ben clipped the rope to the horse's halter and faced her with a smile. "I was wondering if I'd see you this morning."

Knowing Ben had been thinking about her made her want to dance. "Bill wanted me to prove I'm a good driver before I came down."

"How did it go?"

"He let me keep the keys, so I'd say it went well."

"Congratulations." He retrieved a currycomb from the grooming bucket by the wall. "Does this mean you don't need a ride to church anymore?"

"Yeah." Her own disappointment at the realization matched the expression on his face. "But I wouldn't mind if you still wanted to come get me sometimes."

"It's like I said the other day. I don't mind going out of my way for you." He tried to play it cool, but she could see how much happier he was.

Before she could respond, Lucas joined them. "Is Maggie ready to get to work?"

"She sure is." Mira wished could she spend the morning talking to Ben, but the horse needed her attention and he had work to do.

"All right." He turned to Ben. "I'll finish grooming this guy. You go help Mira with Maggie."

"Okay." He handed over the currycomb and walked beside Mira toward the gray waiting patiently. "Are you going to longe her or work her on a lead rope?"

"Longe her." She stopped by Maggie's head and faced him. "Actually, I need to go grab a longe line."

"I'll get it for you." He strode toward the tack room before she could protest.

While she waited for him to come back, she stroked Maggie's cheek and glanced toward Lucas. "What do you think, girl? Is he irritated that I come down here and talk to Ben every morning?"

The horse blew out a hay-scented breath and nudged her shoulder.

"I'll take that as a no," Mira said with a soft laugh.

Ben returned and handed her the longe line. Within moments, they were on their way to the indoor arena. Maggie danced a little, showing she was still the same nervous horse despite how calm she'd been in the crossties.

Even though Mira knew most people wouldn't understand it, she was relieved to see a little skittish behavior from the horse. Harley had told her to always be wary of a horse acting out of the ordinary. Experience with the abused horses they'd taken in had taught her that a sudden change from skittish to as calm as an old plow horse could be a precursor to the horse version of a hissy fit.

Ben took up a position inside the arena but out of the way while Mira worked with Maggie. The training session went fairly smoothly with only a little balking here and there. When Mira gathered up the longe line at the end and headed for the gate, Ben joined her with a smile.

"I'd say that was a success."

"So would I. If she continues to do this well consistently, I'm going to talk to Lucas and Bill about the possibility of working her with a saddle on her back in a week or two." Mira held up a hand to stop Ben's protest. "I'll still be on the ground for a while longer, but I think she's almost ready to practice moving while wearing a saddle."

"You could be right. I just want to make sure you don't rush trying to ride her." He touched her shoulder. "I don't want to see you get hurt again."

Her heart melted at his show of concern for her well-being. "Trust me, I don't want to get hurt again either. But I don't want to hold Maggie back out of fear. I plan to do what she needs me to do, when she needs it done. Assuming I can get permission, of course."

"I don't think you have anything to worry about there. Lucas and Mr. Montaigne are so impressed with the progress you've made with Maggie that they'll probably agree to anything you want to try."

"It's nice to hold all the power."

Ben chuckled. "Just don't let it go to your head. Power hungry isn't attractive."

"But not being power hungry is?" Mira asked as they

reached the crossties closest to Maggie's stall.

"When it's you, yeah." He winked and walked around to secure the horse's other side.

Had he just admitted he found her attractive? Her heart thumped as she considered the possibilities. Maybe Marnie had been right all those times she'd said someday Mira would find a man who liked her regardless of her ethnicity or the accent she spoke with.

She'd just started brushing Maggie when Lucas walked up with a cordless phone in his hand.

"You have a phone call."

She accepted the phone, unsure of who would call her so early in the morning. "Hello?"

"Hi, Mira. This is Pastor Jeff. Did I catch you at a bad time?"

"No, it's fine." She stepped away from the horse so the conversation wouldn't bother her. "What can I do for you?"

"Be the best fiddle instructor you can be."

Mira gasped. "I got the job?"

"Not yet. I just got off the phone with the Hank Moore, the director of the Mercer Center. He wants you to come in for an interview. Now, there's no guarantee you'll get the job, but Hank sounded excited about the possibility of having a fiddle instructor, especially one willing to donate her time."

"When does he want me to come in?"

"Next Tuesday at three o'clock." Pastor Jeff gave her a few more details, and then ended the call.

She returned the phone to Lucas and headed back to Maggie. Ben had taken over brushing the horse, who was getting restless.

"Guess what," Mira said as she rubbed the horse's forehead.

"So many possibilities come to mind, but most are probably far from accurate." Ben stopped brushing Maggie and faced her. "Why don't you tell me?"

"I have an interview with the Mercer Center next week. Assuming it goes as well as I hope it will, I'll be their new fiddle instructor."

"Hey, that's great!" His smile brightened the stable.

A scraping sound drew Mira's attention to the fidgety horse. Maggie pawed at the ground again.

"Easy now, pretty girl," Mira said in soft Hebrew. The horse's ears pricked up, but she remained nervous. "We haven't forgotten about you."

Ben put his brush back in the grooming bucket. "We better get her back in her stall before she starts acting up."

"Good idea," Mira said, switching to English.

Once Maggie was safely in her stall again, Mira walked beside Ben to the tack room. He put the grooming bucket on a shelf and checked his watch.

"I need to get going. I've got a class later, and I learned a long time ago that my classmates and instructors prefer it if I don't show up smelling like a barn."

Mira laughed and retrieved her coat from its hook. "I thought everyone loved the smell of hay and horses."

"So did I, until the day I was late getting out of here and didn't have time to clean up before class."

"Better not make them suffer again, although I'm convinced they don't know what they're missing."

"So am I, but they seem happy enough missing out."

They left the tack room and met Lucas coming out of a stall.

"Are both of you leaving?" he asked.

"I have a class," Ben said.

"I'll probably be back later to check up on Maggie." Mira often returned to the stable after lunch to spend time talking to Maggie and the other horses.

"You two have fun, then." He walked off down the aisle.

Mira and Ben parted ways at the stable entrance, and she headed up to the house. Even though the uncertainty of what she'd inherited still hung over her like a cloud, she felt as if her life was finally coming together. She would soon be financially independent. She had a vehicle she could drive whenever she wanted. And most importantly, she had a good friend who just happened to be a handsome stable boy.

Thirty-Six

Mira arrived back at the Montaigne estate in a great mood after her literacy appointment with Norma Burchard. The pastor's wife had been impressed by the speed with which Mira picked up on reading. She was convinced that in a few months Mira would be ready to enter their GED program to help her prepare for the high school equivalency test.

Lucas met her halfway between the garage and the house.

"Mr. Montaigne's waiting for you in his office. Richard Halliday is with him."

"Thanks, Lucas." Her upbeat mood dissolved in a flutter of nerves.

He headed back to the stable, and Mira took a deep breath before going inside. No matter how much it scared her, she needed to find out what Richard had learned. She almost hoped he had discovered that she was descended from another Potter family and still poor. Unfortunately, in her heart, she knew that wouldn't be the case.

The office door was open when she arrived, and

both men looked up at her.

"Mira, come in," Bill said with a smile. "Close the door and have a seat."

She did as he asked and perched on the edge of a chair to wait for Richard to speak. Thankfully, he didn't make her wait long.

"I have some good news for you. I was able to find out the details of your great-grandparents' wills and the trust fund your grandmother set up for you." He handed her a file folder.

She flipped though the papers inside and gasped. "These look like the papers I saw in Harley's desk!"

"They're copies of the wills and trust fund documents," Richard said. "Would you like me to give you a general idea of what they say?"

She nodded and laid the folder on her lap. "Please."

"First off, let me tell you that in a couple of weeks, you will be a very wealthy woman. Everything is being held in trust for you until your twenty-first birthday, at which time you will gain full control of your assets."

"Okay..." What did he mean by "very wealthy"?

"Your great-grandparents were extremely generous to you in their wills. Both the Potters and the Doyles left you controlling shares, among other things, in their respective companies. That means you essentially own Potter Porcelain and Doyle Manufacturing. Nothing can be done with those companies without your permission."

"I don't know how to run a company." Just the thought quickened her pulse.

Richard smiled. "You don't have to. Each of those companies has a whole team of people running them.

They just can't make any major changes or sell the companies without your approval. In other words, you own the companies, and they do all the work for you."

"Oh." Though relieved she wouldn't have to run the companies, she wasn't sure how to feel about having employees. She'd never seen herself as the managerial type.

"The Potters and Doyles also left you various stocks and bonds," Richard continued. "You inherited a large estate from the Potters and several items your mother apparently loved from the Doyles. The trust fund is pretty straightforward. You were allotted twenty-five hundred dollars a month for your personal use until you turn twenty-one, at which time you gain full control of the remainder of the fund. Your parents were named as the original administrators. After their deaths, that responsibility was passed on to Harley and Marnie Davis when they became your legal guardians."

"Who is the administrator now?"

"Your grandmother's lawyer." Richard studied her, his expression thoughtful. "I learned something interesting when I researched your trust fund."

"What's that?" Mira braced herself for bad news.

"No one ever took any money out of it for you. It has the amount your grandmother originally put into it, plus a lot of interest from nearly twenty-one years of sitting untouched."

No one had ever used the money? She tried to absorb what Richard was telling her, but it was difficult after a lifetime of feeling unwanted and unloved by the relatives who had never even wanted to meet her.

After a moment, he spoke again in a gentle tone. "I

know this is a lot to take in, but there's more you need to know about."

"There's more?" Wasn't everything he'd listed enough?

"Your mother had a trust fund of her own, and she put nearly everything she earned as a concert violinist into a savings account. Your father also had a few assets. You are their sole heir, so all of that is yours now."

She knew she should ask something, show at least a little interest in her inheritance, but she had to think for a minute to come up with anything. "What does all of this mean? I keep getting told I'm wealthy. What exactly does that mean?"

Richard exchanged a glance with Bill, and then refocused on her. "It means that depending on the stock market, you're worth around three billion dollars."

Mira couldn't breathe. Three *billion* dollars? Billion, with a *B*?

The amount was mind boggling. How could one person possibly own that much?

She stared at the file folder on her lap as she struggled to comprehend her newfound wealth. Even with her mind racing, she could feel Bill and Richard watching her. They had to be concerned about her, but she couldn't find anything to say that would assure them she was okay. She wasn't all that sure herself.

Finally, she looked up at them. "I need to think about this for a while."

"Okay." Understanding and sympathy filled Bill's face. "If you have any questions or just want to talk about it, we'll be here."

She nodded and left the room. Needing comfort and familiarity, she headed out to the stable and sat on the bleachers beside the arena. At first, all she could do was wonder if her life would ever be normal again. Then she realized she still carried the folder Richard had given her. Opening it, she scrutinized each document and tried to understand what they said, but she couldn't read English well enough yet. The few words she did recognize didn't tell her anything.

A couple of hours later, Mira wished she had someone to talk to, someone who might understand her turmoil. The folder now lay beside her, but its contents still weighed heavily on her mind.

The sound of approaching footsteps brought her gaze to the aisle leading to the stalls. Her heart skipped a beat when Ben came in. She tracked his path to her side, barely able to believe he was there as he sat down beside her.

"Hey, you okay?"

"Only sort of." Would she ever be okay again now that she was a billionaire? "How did you know I needed a friend?"

"Believe it or not, Mr. Montaigne called me. He told me that you found out what you inherited and could use a friend to help you sort everything out. Apparently, Lucas has told him how much we talk while I work."

"I hope I haven't gotten you in trouble."

"You haven't. Actually, Mr. Montaigne seemed pleased that we've become friends."

Mira managed a weak half smile. Her thoughts weighed her down too much for anything more.

Ben removed his coat and laid it beside hers on the

bench behind them. "You want to talk about it?"

"Do you remember in your uncle's barn when I told you I was scared of being rich?" Tears stung her eyes. "Well, now I have to face that fear."

"Is that such a bad thing?"

"I don't know, but I'm going to find out whether I want to or not."

"Or you could give away everything you inherit and be poor again," he said in an obvious attempt to cheer her up.

"Believe me, I considered it. But I feel like I'd be betraying the people who loved me enough to make their families mad even though they never saw me, let alone met me."

"I could sound cliché and tell you that you have the rest of your life to adjust. Or I could give you the only advice I can think of. Don't worry about it. Live your life however you're comfortable, and let society deal with it."

She considered what he said, and some of the dread lifted from her heart. Facing him, she offered a much stronger smile than the last. "Thanks, Ben. That advice is just what I needed to hear."

"Glad I could help."

"I guess I better go tell Bill and Richard I'm fine now. They looked pretty worried when I came out here."

"They might appreciate it."

Mira stood up to put on her coat, and Ben did the same. As they headed for the door, she glanced at him.

"You know, I think you're good for me."

His eyes widened. "Where did that come from?"

"I've been doing a lot of thinking this afternoon. I realized that you've never once judged me, and you let me talk all I want about anything I want. You always seem to know how to make me feel better. Somehow, you've managed to give me confidence in myself and made me feel like I'm okay just the way I am."

Ben's face reddened. "Okay, now you're embarrassing me."

She laughed softly as they stepped outside. "There's one more thing. Even though there are times you've got to be dying of curiosity, you have never once pressed me on anything."

"That's because I figure you'll tell me whenever you're ready."

"And I appreciate you letting me have that freedom."

When she opened the door to the house, Ben hung back. She gave him a questioning look.

"Aren't you coming?"

"I'm not sure Miss Della would like that too much."

"You need to take your own advice. Live however you want, and let society deal with it."

He chuckled. "Now, how did I know you were going to say that?"

"Because we're friends." Mira grabbed his hand and led him inside. "Come on. You said you'd come with me to talk to people, and I'm going to hold you to it."

"Me and my big mouth."

Thirty-Seven

Mira kept her hand in Ben's as they walked down the hall toward Bill's office. Although she felt better about her inheritance, she was still scared and the strength in his grasp was comforting. He gave her hand a gentle squeeze and smiled when she glanced at him.

"You're going to be fine."

"I know, but it's a big adjustment to get there." Knowing he supported her helped make the adjustment a little easier.

The door to Bill's office was open again. Mira stepped inside with Ben, and Bill and Richard looked up at them.

"I just wanted to let you know that I'm okay," she said before either man could speak.

"I'm glad to hear it." Bill sounded relieved. "I was concerned about you. This must have been quite a shock."

"It was." He had no idea how much of a shock.

"Richard," Bill said, "I don't believe you've ever met Ben Petros."

The lawyer turned to Ben. "Ah, so you're the young

man Bill called. I'm Richard Halliday, Mira's attorney for the moment."

"It's a pleasure to meet you, Mr. Halliday," Ben said.

Richard smiled and shifted his focus. "Mira, there are a few things we need to discuss."

"What kind of things?" Apprehension struck, and she held tighter to Ben's hand.

"Business related things," Richard said with a glance toward Ben.

"I should probably go." He pulled his hand from Mira's.

She grabbed his arm. "No, please stay."

He studied her. "Are you sure?"

She nodded.

He shrugged and resumed his position beside her. Richard turned toward Bill with a doubtful expression.

"Ben's a good man. Trustworthy," Bill said.

"I'll take your word for it." Richard still looked a bit unsure, but he didn't say any more about it. Instead, he focused on Mira and Ben again. "Why don't you remove your coats and take a seat?"

They did so, sitting beside each other in a pair of chairs in front of the desk.

"Mira," Richard continued, "do you happen to have a copy of your birth certificate?"

"No, I don't." As far as she knew, it had been in Harley's desk when his relatives cleaned it out.

"That's okay. I can get a copy for you. I just need to know your birth date and where you were born. I already have your parents' names."

"My birthday is December twelfth." When she gave him the name of the village she had grown up in, he raised an eyebrow.

"How do you spell that?"

"Uh..." Mira thought for a moment, but then shrugged. "I have no idea how to spell it in English. I could give you the Hebrew or Arabic spelling if you want."

"That's okay, I'll find the English spelling." Richard made a couple of notes. "Now, you're going to have to meet with a couple of lawyers before everything is transferred to you, but I'll go with you for that. You're probably also going to get a lot of media coverage for a while."

"Why?" Attention from the media held zero appeal.

"Ten years ago, there was a lot of speculation as to who inherited the majority of the Doyle and Potter estates. The people originally thought to be the heirs received a lot less than expected. Since you were a minor at the time of your great-grandparents' deaths, your name wasn't released to the press. Your grandmother's attorney has managed to keep it a secret since. Now that it's been leaked that you're the heiress, the media will jump all over the story."

"I've already had a request for an interview from that society reporter who was at the Mercer Center fundraiser."

"Did you agree to do it?" Richard asked, studying her.

"Only sort of. I told her I had to check my schedule. She wants me to call her as soon as possible."

"You did a good job of stalling gracefully. That's going to become a very useful talent. If you get any more requests for interviews, refer whoever is asking to me. Eventually, you'll have to do some interviews, but I'll help you prepare."

"Okay." How much preparing did one need to do an interview?

Richard went on to talk about inventories, trips to visit what he termed Mira's holdings, and various other details. Finally, he finished telling her everything he thought she needed to know right then and left after promising that they would talk again soon.

Ben checked his watch, and then looked at his employer. "Excuse me, Mr. Montaigne. May I borrow your phone? I need to call home real quick."

"Of course, Ben." Bill rose from his seat behind the desk. "You can use this phone. Mira and I will wait in the hall."

"Thank you."

Mira followed Bill into the hall. "Thanks for calling Ben for me."

"You're welcome. I figured you could use a friend when you left my office looking so overwhelmed."

"But how did you know to call Ben instead of someone else?"

"Lucas has told me how well you both get along. And you came home Sunday looking happier and more relaxed than I've seen you since I brought you here. I figured Ben would come since Lucas told me last week how worried he was after he heard about Maggie kicking you."

She smiled as the subject of their conversation stepped out of the office.

"Why don't you two go out to dinner?" Bill said. "It's getting late, and you've both had a long afternoon. Go out and have fun."

Mira glanced at Ben. His face mirrored her surprise. She shifted her attention back to Bill and found him holding out some money.

"Go on. It's on me." He placed the money in her hand.

She stared at it. He was paying for her dinner on the same day she learned she was a billionaire. The whole scenario begged for a laugh, but she looked at Ben instead. "Do you want to go?"

"Sure."

"Good!" Bill said cheerfully. "You kids have fun."

He walked off down the hall. Ben volunteered to drive, and as they headed out to his truck, he glanced at her with a puzzled expression.

"That was strange."

"I know, but he's right. It has been a long afternoon."

"True," he said as they climbed in the truck. "So, where do you want to go?"

"I've only been to one restaurant around here."

"Did they have good food?"

"Excellent food." Mira smiled at the memory of the day she'd met Zeina, Akram, and the others. "The people are nice, too."

"Why don't we go there?" Ben steered his truck down the drive.

"Okay." She gave him the name of Omar's restaurant. "Do you know where it is?"

"Sure. It's close to where Akram and Sa'id live. And you're right, they do have good food."

"Would you believe that's where I met Akram, Sa'id, Zeina, and Yasmina?" Mira said with a laugh.

"It doesn't surprise me. They're good friends with the owners, so they go there all the time. It's possible we'll run into them there tonight." He glanced at her. "Are you prepared for some teasing if they see us going to dinner together?"

"I've already dealt with some teasing. Besides, Ibrihim's *mujaddara* is worth the risk of putting up with more."

As soon as they stepped into the restaurant, Zeina waved to them.

"Mira, Ben, come join us!"

Akram pulled a couple of chairs over to the end of their table. Yasmina and Sa'id grinned as Mira and Ben sat down.

"Ben, man, this is what you call a hot date?" Sa'id shook his head. "You need to learn a thing or two about romance."

"It's not a date." Ben glanced at Mira with amusement shining in his eyes. "And she chose the restaurant."

"I can't resist Ibrahim's cooking," she said with a shrug.

"He is one of the best chefs in the city," Yasmina said, "but Ben still could have given you some flowers."

"How do you know I didn't?" He raised his eyebrows.

Akram returned to his seat. "Did you?"

"No, but I could have and you wouldn't know," Ben said to a chorus of laughter.

The lighthearted banter continued until Omar brought Mira and Ben their meals. Then the talk shifted to other things, including the excellent food. Toward the end of the meal, the members of Akram's band came in. Akram joined them, and soon invited Mira and Ben to their table as well.

They ordered a round of coffee and discussed Mira's fiddle playing. The conversation soon drifted to music in general, and before the coffee was gone, the men had invited Mira to audition for their band. From the way they talked, she sensed it was more of a formality than an actual audition, but she didn't mind. Any excuse to play was a good one.

Thirty-Eight

Hank Moore, the director of the Mercer Center, listened to Mira's fiddling for a few minutes and promised to call the next day to discuss a schedule. Spirit buoyed by the successful interview, Mira thanked him and drove across town to the block housing Omar's restaurant. Akram's band rehearsed two buildings away and across the street.

She parked at the curb and grabbed her violin case. It hadn't taken as long to get there as she'd expected, so she was a little early. With any luck, they wouldn't mind if she went on in. Waiting in the cold didn't appeal, but she'd do it if they were sticklers for scheduled times.

When she entered the building, she discovered it housed a handful of small shops as well as the room the band rehearsed in. She followed the instructions Akram had given her and headed for the room at the far end of the hall.

Akram stepped out and smiled. "Hey, Mira, you're early."

"Is that okay? I can come back in a little bit."

"No, it's fine. Go on in and get your fiddle tuned. I'll

be back in a minute."

Mira entered the room and was surprised to see Zeina there along with the band members. No one had mentioned a non-musician audience. She set her borrowed violin on one of the tables along the wall as Zeina jumped up from her seat and joined her.

"Hi, Mira! How did the interview at the Mercer Center go?"

"The director is going to call me tomorrow to discuss a schedule." She pulled the violin out of its case and checked the tuning.

"That's great news! Congratulations."

"Thanks." Mira paused to adjust a string. "So, what are you doing here? I thought this was just a band thing."

"It is." Zeina glanced toward the men and lowered her voice. "I'm kind of a chaperone. A couple of the guys decided you would be more comfortable with another woman here, but I think they're the ones uncomfortable with you being the only woman."

"Let me guess. You got volunteered for the job because you're Akram's sister."

"Actually, they thought about asking one of their wives, but I volunteered because I've never heard you play," Zeina said with a grin as her brother returned to the room with several sheets of paper in his hand.

Mira finished tuning the violin and set it on the table so she could rosin her bow. "You know, you could have just asked me to play."

"That's way too logical for me." Zeina laughed.

Akram joined them. "You ready?"

"Absolutely." Mira picked up the violin.

She followed him to the center of the room and waited until he was seated with the other band members. Then she launched into a popular Israeli folk song.

While she played, the band smiled and nodded. They held a whispered conference toward the end of the piece. When the last note faded away, Akram set a music stand in front of her and placed a piece of music on it.

"This is one of our songs. I'll turn the pages for you."

Mira glanced through the music so she could get an idea of what she was in for, and then nodded to Akram. "I'm ready."

She took a deep breath and began to play the unfamiliar piece. It was a beautiful piece, but she had no idea if she was playing it correctly since she'd never heard the song before. When she reached the end and lowered her bow and fiddle, Akram smiled.

"I'm going to ask you and Zeina to wait outside while we talk."

"All right." She set her violin in its case and followed Zeina into the hall.

Akram closed the door behind them, and Zeina faced Mira with an excited smile.

"You sounded great! I wish I would have asked to hear you play before. I had no idea what I was missing."

"Thanks." She glanced toward the closed door. "What do you think they'll decide?"

"I think they'd have to be insane to say anything but welcome to the band." Zeina's expression shifted to overly innocent. "How's Ben?"

"Busy." Mira ignored the teasing grin creeping across her friend's face. "He's finishing a couple of term papers and studying for his finals."

"So, no more dates until the semester's over?"

"I already told you, that wasn't a date. Bill practically shoved us out the door."

"I'm sure he won't have to shove you out the door again. I have a feeling you'll willingly go to dinner with Ben just as soon as he has time to take you."

Mira's face burned with the knowledge her friend was right, but she didn't want to admit it yet.

Akram opened the door, saving her from further teasing.

"You can come back in now."

They reentered the room, and Zeina closed the door. Mira stood in front of the band.

Akram took his place with the other men and smiled. "Welcome to the band, Mira."

"Thank you so much." Her heart soared. She'd finally found a place where she could share the music of her childhood with people who loved it as much as she did.

He handed her several pieces of sheet music. "This is what we're working on today. Listen, follow along, and try to get a feel for the music. A couple of them are traditional pieces, so feel free to join in if you know them."

The next week sped by for Mira. Between meetings with lawyers, teaching her first fiddle students, and learning the band's songs, she was almost as busy as

Ben. By the end of rehearsal Thursday evening, she was ready to go back to the Montaignes' house and relax.

Akram had other ideas.

He joined her as she picked up her violin case. "Come with me to my parents' house."

"Why?" As much as she liked his parents, they'd never invited her to their house before.

"It's a surprise, but you're going to love it."

"It's not related to my birthday, is it? Because you know how I feel about people making a big deal out of it." She'd already told everyone to skip giving her anything. With as much as she was inheriting, she didn't need anything else.

"Birthdays are a great excuse to celebrate, but this has nothing to do with your birthday."

"And I can't postpone this visit until a less busy week?"

"Nope. You have to come now." He was nothing if not tenacious.

"All right. Since you insist and you said I'm going to love it, I'll come."

"Great!" He grinned and guided her out of the rehearsal room.

She drove the few blocks to a quiet neighborhood and parked behind him in front of a large duplex. Akram met her on the sidewalk and grinned.

"There's someone here who wants to see you."

"See me?" Why would anyone who wanted to see her go to Akram's parents' house rather than showing up at the Montaignes' house? "Who is it?"

"You'll see." He led her up the front walk and inside.

"Mom, Dad, we're here!"

Kamila came into the living room. "Mira, welcome! Hello, Akram."

"Hi, Mom," he said.

"Hi, Kamila," Mira added with a smile.

"Everyone is in the back," Kamila said as she took their coats.

Mira stepped through a doorway and found herself in a dining room separated from from the large kitchen by only a counter. Several people filled the two rooms. Mira recognized most of them from Omar's restaurant and the church, but there were a few unfamiliar faces mixed in.

In the center of the group stood an older version of a very familiar face from her childhood.

Mira gasped. "Aisha?"

The woman, only a couple of years older than her, grinned as she rushed forward to give Mira a big hug. "You remember!"

"Of course, I remember!" She laughed and returned the hug. Joy overflowed her heart and filled her eyes. "How could I forget my best friend?"

"It's been a long time," Aisha said, taking a step back. "I want you to meet my husband and daughter."

Mira raised her eyebrows. "It has been a long time."

A handsome black-haired man guided a little girl forward. Aisha joined them with a smile. "Mira, this is my husband, Nasim, and our daughter, Marwa."

"It is so nice to meet you," she said.

"I am glad to finally meet you," Nasim said. "Aisha speaks all the time of her friend Mira."

Aisha laughed. "He always complains that I talk

about you too much."

Akram introduced Mira to the other people she didn't recognize, who turned out to be members of the Talhami family. Then she and Aisha sat in a corner of the dining room to talk while the others continued their conversations.

"It is so good to see you." Mira could barely believe she was sitting with her old friend. "But what are you doing here?"

"Visiting my family. My mother is Rashid's sister."

Mira thought back to a conversation she'd had a few minutes earlier. "Oh, yeah. I think Zeina told me that. How long are you going to be here?"

"Until the twenty-seventh. That way we'll have lots of time to visit with family." Aisha put her hand on Mira's arm. "And friends."

She smiled in return. "So, how is everybody back home?"

Aisha told her about all of the people in the village that Mira had known as a child. Hearing about them was bittersweet. For the most part, they were doing well. But she had missed so many birthdays, graduations, marriages, and births. She'd also missed a few deaths, which brought a different kind of sadness. Yet she didn't regret hearing about the people from her past. It laid to rest years of wondering what had happened after she emigrated.

Mira was telling Aisha about her life since leaving the village when Marwa walked up and tugged on her mother's arm.

"Mommy, when are you going to give Mira her present?" the four-year-old asked in Arabic.

"Right now, I suppose," Aisha said with a laugh and stood. "Why don't you talk to Mira while I go get it?"

"Okay." Marwa crawled into Mira's lap. "Hi. You're pretty."

"Thank you." Mira smiled and gave her a hug. "So are you."

"Great-Grandmother says you and Mommy used to play together."

"Yes, we did. I knew your mother when we were your age."

"Mommy was little like me?" Marwa's eyes widened, and Mira struggled not to laugh.

"She was at one time. And you look just like her."

Aisha came back carrying a box that was about half as wide as it was long, a letter-sized envelope, and a larger manila envelope. She set the box on the floor in front of Mira and handed her the smaller of the two envelopes.

"This is all from Grandmother," Aisha said. "She wants you to read this first."

"Okay." Mira's heart thumped, and she opened the envelope. What could Teta Nida have sent that needed an introduction?

As she read the letter written in Arabic, tears stung her eyes. Teta Nida had spoken to Mira's great-grandmother Hassan several times over the years. The woman felt terrible about her grandson being disowned just for falling in love.

Nida explained that Mira's great-grandmother had saved several things taken from Khalil's house while Mira was in the hospital. When she heard that Aisha planned to visit America and would be seeing Mira,

Great-Grandmother Hassan had given the items to Nida to send along.

After reading the personal greeting from Nida, Mira set the letter down and found everyone in the house watching her. When had they gathered around?

She turned to her old friend. "Do you know what's in the box?"

"Yes, I do." Aisha smiled and patted her arm. "I think you'll be pleased."

Curiosity took over, and Mira opened the box...and gasped. She pulled out a violin case covered in stickers from all over the world.

"I can't believe it," she whispered. She opened the case and ran her fingers over the smooth finish of the violin as tears coursed down her cheeks.

Aisha wrapped her in a hug. "I told you you'd be pleased."

"I thought it was gone forever."

"I know, but now it's where it belongs—with you."

Marwa peered into the case. "What is it?"

Mira took a deep breath and wiped the tears from her eyes. "It's my mother's violin."

"Do you know how to use it?" Marwa stared up at her with an awed expression.

"Yes, I do."

"She plays beautifully," Zeina said.

"Can I hear?" Marwa asked, her big brown eyes pleading. "Please?"

"You know, Marwa," Akram said, kneeling to his cousin's level, "Mira might be tired of playing from our rehearsal."

She looked up at Mira again. "Are you tired?"

"A little, but I don't mind playing this violin," she said, touching the instrument again. "I just need to get some rosin out of the truck."

"I'll get it for you," Akram said.

"Okay, it's in the case in the back seat." She pulled the keys out of her pocket. "Actually, do you mind just bringing the case in? The violin probably shouldn't sit out in the cold any longer than it already has."

"Sure, no problem." He took the keys.

"Thanks, Akram," she said as he left the room.

As she tuned her mother's violin, Nasim studied her.

"You're in Akram's band?"

"Yes, I am."

"I'm glad to know you still play," Aisha said.

Mira smiled as she adjusted a string. "I got lucky. My mother's cousins that took me in both loved music, and Harley was a fiddler. He taught me a lot of Appalachian folk songs."

"What do those sound like?" Aisha asked.

"I'll play one for you."

Akram returned with the borrowed violin and handed her the keys. "I locked the truck for you."

"Thanks."

Once she rosined the bow, she played a tune her mother had taught her on the violin she hadn't seen in nearly eight years. Marwa danced to the lively music while the others listened with impressed smiles.

When Mira finished the song, Aisha had misty eyes. "You play that piece just like your mother."

"Thank you." Tears pooled in Mira's eyes, evidence of how much the compliment meant to her. After taking a moment to calm her emotions, she lifted her bow with a smile. "Now for that Appalachian folk song I promised..."

Thirty-Nine

Mira awoke to whiskers brushing against her face. Opening her eyes, she found Frank the cat staring back. He let out a soft meow and purred as she ran her fingers over his silky gray fur.

"Good morning, Frank."

She turned her head and smiled as her gaze landed on the sticker-covered violin case lying on the desk. Receiving it had been one of the best gifts ever. The fact that Aisha had been the one to deliver it made it even more special.

Thoughts of special gifts brought her mind to the day's upcoming events. In a few hours, she would be a wealthy woman. A mind-bogglingly wealthy woman. She and Richard were scheduled to meet with her grandmother's lawyer later in the morning to sign some paperwork regarding her inheritance. By lunch, she would be worth around three billion dollars.

She shook her head and petted Frank again. Would she ever adjust to having such a vast amount of wealth? At the moment, the thought of having so much still terrified her. The one thing providing comfort was the knowledge that she had a group of friends who didn't care whether she was rich or poor.

With that thought in mind, she left the cat lying on the bed, took a quick shower, and dressed for comfort in a pair of jeans and a nice sweater. Today provided the perfect opportunity to find out if she could get away with wearing whatever she wanted without anyone saying anything because she was rich.

Downstairs, she walked into the kitchen and found Charlotte already working.

"Morning, Charlotte."

"Good morning, Mira." The cook gave her a big, warm smile. "Happy birthday."

"Thanks." She wasn't sure her birthday would ever be the same again. How could any future years compare to the momentous occasion this one brought?

"Why don't you go on into the family dining room?" Charlotte said. "Mr. Montaigne and Miss Della are already in there. Richard Halliday is with them."

"Okay."

When she entered the small dining room, everyone greeted her with smiles.

"Happy birthday, Mira," Bill said.

"Thank you." She sat down across from Richard.

"Are you excited about today?" Della asked.

"Yeah." Despite everything, she was hours away from the financial independence she craved. "I'm nervous, too."

"There's nothing to be nervous about," Richard said. "All you have to do is sign a few papers."

"That's not why I'm nervous. It's knowing how to handle everything I'm inheriting."

"We already took care of that, remember? You hired an accountant earlier this week, and I'll take care of any legal matters as long as you want me as your attorney."

"I know." Mira sighed. He clearly didn't understand her worry, and she didn't know how to convey it. "But it's different now that the responsibility is actually mine...or will be after I sign those papers."

"I'm sure it is, but just remember that you have as much help as you need to figure everything out."

If only she had someone who could help her feel like a rich woman instead of the poor immigrant farm girl she'd been for so long, she'd be less worried. After all the faux pas she'd committed since the Montainges' took her in, how could she feel confident in her ability to be one of the wealthiest people in America?

After breakfast, Bill took Mira and Richard to his office to go through the papers in the manila envelope she'd received the previous evening. There were several legal documents, some in English and some Mira had to translate for the men. In addition to her parents' wills, she found information on savings accounts she hadn't known about, a couple of deeds, and her mother's passport.

She pulled the last two papers out of the envelope and grinned when she saw the one on top.

"Oh, cool, my birth certificate!"

Richard reached for it. "We may be able to use that today." After glancing at the document written in Arabic, he handed it back. "Then again, maybe not."

Mira absently accepted it and laid it on the desk as she studied the last paper from the envelope. Tears blurred her vision, and she ran a fingertip over two of the signatures on it.

"Mira." Bill sounded concerned. "What is it?"

She blinked back the tears and managed a small smile. "My parents' marriage certificate. They were married on Valentine's Day before I was born."

"The perfect day for a wedding."

Richard gathered the papers spread out across the desk. "We've done all we can with these right now. I'll get the ones in Arabic and Hebrew translated next week and go through them again."

"Why?" Had her translation not been good enough for him?

"These prove that you are the rightful heir to your parents," Richard said. "They also detail exactly what you inherited."

"Oh." She traced her parents signatures one more time, and then relinquished the marriage certificate. "I'll get the original papers back, right?"

"Absolutely." He slipped the stack back into the envelope. "It will be several days, but I'll keep them safe for you."

"Okay." She hated letting them out of her sight, but she had to trust Richard. Otherwise, having him as her attorney would be a terrible mistake.

Richard checked his watch. "We'll need to leave in about half an hour or so."

"Is it okay if I go out to the stable for a few minutes?" She hoped Ben was still there. She needed some moral support to give her the courage to face the meeting with her grandmother's lawyer.

"Sure." Bill gave her a knowing smile. "Just don't take too long talking to Ben."

Mira's cheeks heated, and she left the room. Of course he would realize she wanted to see Ben, not the horses. Hadn't he called Ben when she needed a friend the most and sent them to dinner together?

After a quick stop to grab her coat, she hurried toward the stable. The back of the familiar brown pickup peeked out from behind the building, and a weight lifted from her. He hadn't left yet.

She was several feet from the door when Ben came out.

"Hi, Ben," she said.

"Hey, Mira." His smile brightened the already sunny day. "I didn't think I'd see you this morning. Happy birthday."

"Thanks," she said as they slowly walked toward his truck. "I have to leave in a little while to sign the paperwork I told you about."

"Are you nervous?" He stopped and faced her.

She looked into his warm brown eyes and sensed he already knew the answer. "Very."

"I figured you would be. I think things will get easier once the papers are signed and everything is yours, free and clear."

"I hope so, because right now it's terrifying." Her eyes burned with unshed tears, and she dropped her gaze. Why did talking about this stuff with him always make her cry?

Ben stepped close and wrapped his arms around her. "I know you're scared, but you'll be fine."

Mira breathed in the scents of hay and horses, and relaxed in the strength of his comforting embrace. "I'm so glad I got to see you this morning."

"I am, too." He stepped back, and she melted under the tenderness in his gaze. "You are such a wonderful person, so sweet and innocent in spite of everything you've been through."

Her pulse raced as he brushed a strand of hair off her face. "You're pretty wonderful yourself."

He searched her face, and then looked away.

"I need to get going before—" He stroked a finger down her cheek and smiled. "You're going to do great. I'll see you later."

"Bye, Ben."

As she walked back toward the house, her thoughts kept returning to the sentence he'd broken off. Had he been about to say, "before I kiss you"?

She hoped he had.

Mira added her signature beside the last little red flag on the page and laid the pen on the polished conference table. Her grandmother's lawyer, Harold Kleinfelder, picked up the sheaf of papers and glanced through them, and Mira glanced at Richard.

He'd been by her side since they left the Montaignes' house, and she could never thank him enough for his support. Having someone who knew where she came from, knew how poor she'd been a few weeks ago, helped her more than if she'd hired someone who only cared that she was now a billionaire.

"It's looks like you're good to go," Kleinfelder said. He handed the papers to his assistant. "Congratulations, Miss Hassan. You are now one very wealthy woman."

"Thank you."

She fought the urge to grab the papers back and tear them up. Her great-grandparents and her grandmother had gone out of their way to make sure she never had to worry about money again. They'd wanted her to have the privileges of the family she'd been born into, and she couldn't give that up out of fear.

"Now," Kleinfelder said, "if you'll accompany me downstairs, we've arranged a short press conference to reveal the identity of the mystery heiress of the Potter and Doyle families."

"Press conference?" She turned to Richard. No one had said a word about any press conference.

"It's expected in a situation like this," he said with a smile. "Don't worry. Mr. Kleinfelder and I will do all the talking. You'll just stand there and smile for the cameras."

Mira followed the men toward the elevator and tried to convince herself she could handle the publicity. Why hadn't she gotten Della's help in picking an outfit for the day? The jeans and sweater were some Della had bought for her, so they were appropriate for a rich person, but Mira had serious doubts about their appropriateness for a press conference.

Too late to worry about it now. A uniformed security guard met the elevator when it reached the ground floor, and it sank in just how much her life had changed by signing those papers. Anonymity was a thing of the past, and there would likely be some security issues she would have to figure out now that she was one of the richest people in the country. She'd have to talk to Richard about it after the press conference.

A man in a suit followed along as they headed for the lobby. Mira glanced back at him, and then leaned close to Richard.

"There's a guy following us." She didn't know if she should worry about him, but now that she'd considered the possibility that she might need security, she couldn't help it.

Richard glanced back, and then met her gaze with a smile. "He's part of your security detail."

"My what?" Maybe she didn't need to worry about her safety after all.

"We'll talk about it after the press conference. For now, smile and show the world how thrilled you are to be an heiress."

She doubted he would have added that last part if he knew "thrilled" wasn't one of the things she felt at the moment. Scared and overwhelmed topped that list.

They entered the lobby, and cameras started clicking. All the flashes reminded her of hyperactive lightning bugs. Kleinfelder led the way to a podium at the front of the crowd, and Mira fought a wave of anxiety. She had to stand in front of all those people, smile, and pretend she was ecstatic to be a billionaire. She wasn't sure she had that much acting ability.

As Kleinfelder spoke, Mira scanned the crowd hanging on his every word. Most appeared to be journalists holding out microphones, smartphones, and other recording devices. A few took notes on pads of paper or held cameras of varying kinds to take more photos and video footage.

Richard took his turn behind the podium, and in the back of the crowd, Mira spotted a group that turned her fake smile into a genuine one. Ben stood with the Montaignes, including Josh and Tabby. Behind them stood Zeina, Yasmina, Akram, and Sa'id. Aisha and Nasim were there as well, with Marwa in her father's arms.

The closest thing Mira had to family had come to witness one of the most important events of her life.

A weight lifted from her heart. No matter how terrifying it was to be so rich, she had an amazing group of people who had befriended her when she had nothing. She never had to worry that they were only interested in her because of her inheritance. They were her friends because of who she was, not what she had.

When the press conference ended, a uniformed security guard, the man in a suit, and another who could be his twin escorted her and Richard to an underground parking garage.

"What are we doing?" Mira asked Richard. He had parked his car in a lot behind the building when they arrived.

"Going to your car."

"My car? I don't have a car."

"You do now." He indicated the shiny black limousine ahead of them.

She stopped and stared as the uniformed chauffeur opened the back door. "That's mine? Where did it come from?"

"It's part of the estate you inherited from the Potters." Richard pressed his hand to her back to get her moving again. "For today, it's the best option for your transportation."

"You drove me here. What's wrong with me leaving in your car?"

"You're a billionaire now and very high profile for the moment. There haven't been any threats made against you, but there's no reason to take chances with your safety."

"And that's why I now have a limo with a chauffeur and a security detail?" Why hadn't anyone warned her how drastically her life would change when she signed those papers?

"Right. It's just a precaution, but it's one you'll need to keep for the next few months at least." Richard ushered her onto the leather seat in the back of the limo and sat beside her. "It wouldn't hurt to have some kind of security even longer."

"That's crazy." She waited until the chauffeur closed the door to continue. "So, not only do I now have more money and stuff than I know what to do with, I could be in danger because of it?"

"Yes, but the risk is quite low. As I said, there haven't been any threats."

"Are you expecting any?" She didn't want to think about anyone hating her that much for gaining control of an inheritance, but she had years of experience that told her people could hate anyone for anything. Being a Hassan from a Middle Eastern country was an extra strike against her.

"No, but people can be unpredictable and your relatives weren't happy with the change in the wills that made you the main heir."

"They've had years to get over it."

"True, but we are talking about a rather large sum."

"Don't remind me." Even without him mentioning it, she couldn't forget. She wasn't sure she'd ever fully adjust to her new station in life, but she could never go back. Not now. Not with everything she'd learned about herself and her family.

The limo pulled into the parking lot of an upscale restaurant and went around to the back. Mira glanced at Richard.

"What are we doing here?"

"Having lunch." He nodded toward the building. "And celebrating your birthday."

She looked at the building as the car stopped. Her friends waited beneath the dark green awning protecting the back entrance. Ben stepped away from the group and opened her door. She took the hand he offered and gracefully stepped out onto the pavement.

"Hi," he said, guiding her away from the car.

"Hi." She glanced toward the waiting group, and then met his gaze. "I didn't expect to see you here. Actually, I didn't expect to be here at all."

"Surprise." He chuckled as Richard joined them.

"Shall we go inside?" Richard lifted a hand toward the entrance.

Each of her friends greeted her with congratulations and birthday wishes. Tabby threw her arms around Mira.

"I'm so excited for you! This whole inheritance thing has to be the best birthday present ever."

"I don't know." She didn't want to disappoint her friend, but Tabby clearly had no idea how much she didn't want to be rich. "I think getting my mom's violin back was a better present."

"Hmm..." Tabby stepped back and studied her. "You could be right. But gaining control of your inheritance is still awesome."

"I can't argue with that." It didn't get much more awe-inspiring than going from impoverished and homeless to a billionaire in a matter of weeks.

The group went inside, and Bill led the way to a private dining room on the far side of the entryway. Mira spotted her two suited shadows taking up positions near the exit.

Ben grasped her hand, drawing her attention. "Can I talk to you for a minute?"

"Sure." Her heart thumped under his warm gaze.

Richard smiled as he passed them. "We'll see you inside."

Once they were alone in the entryway, except for the two security men who kept their backs turned, Ben stepped closer to Mira.

"You did great at the press conference. Seeing you up there, so beautiful and composed... You looked like the billionaire you are."

Her face heated, but her spirit soared. He always knew just what to say to boost her confidence and make her feel as if everything would be okay.

She took a deep breath and smiled. "You have no idea how glad I was to see you in that crowd."

"Actually, I do." He took both of her hands in his. "The way you lit up when you saw me and your other friends let me know how glad you were to see us."

"It's nice to know I'm easy to read," she said with a soft laugh.

"Well, maybe not easy." He tugged her closer. "But I'm willing to learn."

Her pulse raced as he lifted a hand and traced a finger along her jaw.

"Happy birthday, Mira." He pressed his lips to hers in a tender kiss that melted her.

When he straightened, she smiled. "Thanks, Ben."

He kept a gentle grasp on her hand as they walked to the private dining room where their friends waited.

After being alone for so long, unloved and unwanted by so many, she'd finally found the place she belonged. The home and family she'd dreamed of since leaving Palestine. And with Ben by her side, the future and her newfound wealth didn't seem quite so scary.

Author's Note

Dear Reader,

So often we hear about immigrants as a group of nameless, faceless people who left their homes for any number of reasons. Sometimes they're fleeing violence. Sometimes they're hoping for a better life. Sometimes they immigrate for work.

Whatever the reason for coming, all immigrants have one thing in common—they must adjust to life in a new country. For some that means learning a new language. Others may have to adjust to a vastly different culture. But all have to adapt to their new home in some way.

As someone who was born and raised and still lives in the United States, I can never fully understand the difficulties faced by immigrants. But as an author, I can help bring awareness to some of their struggles and the prejudice they face simply because of where they came from.

While Mira Hassan and her story are products of my imagination, I've done my best to make her experience as an immigrant as realistic as possible. That said, even the most thorough research can never replace the knowledge brought by actual experience. If I inadvertently included any errors in Mira's experience, I apologize.

It's my hope that Mira's story has shown that rather than letting the differences divide us, it's the similarities that can bring people together. Kindness and compassion are universal concepts. Even if two people speak different languages, showing a little kindness can open the door to friendship.

Thank you for reading *Out of Her Element*. I hope you enjoyed the story as much as I do.

Happy reading!

E.A. West

About the Author

Award-winning author E.A. West is a lifelong lover of books and storytelling. In high school, she picked up her pen in a creative writing class and hasn't laid it down yet.

For more information visit: https://eawestauthor.com

E.A. West loves to connect with readers!

Hearing from readers is one of the highlights of being an author. To stay up-to-date with E.A. West's latest news, chat, and more, connect with her on social media.

Follow her Facebook page
https://www.facebook.com/EAWestAuthor

Follow her on Twitter
http://twitter.com/eawestauthor

Sign up for her newsletter to receive inside information and more
https://eawestauthor.com/newsletter